★

The world went crazy. The bartender called over that she was dialing 911. In a moment we were laying my friend flat on the floor and other hands were covering her with coats. Somehow, suddenly, people had gathered around us. One woman—the keyboardist?—raised Bunny's feet, pushing more coats under them, and my friend's eyes flickered. By the time the EMT team showed up, she was coming around, trying to talk and shaking her head, as if she was trying to push through whatever had gotten her. But when one EMT started in with his questions— "Ma'am. Do you know where you are? Can you tell us your name?"—she just mumbled.

"Her name's Bunny Milligan. Barbara, that is. I'm her friend, Theda. We were just—"

"What did she take?" His question threw me, and I paused. The EMTs hoisted Bunny onto the stretcher and began fixing straps around her. "Club drugs? Ecstasy? What?"

"Nothing! We had dinner, that's all." He and his partner exchanged a look.

"Drink? Smoke?"

"Nothing, nothing. She only drank soda. She's pregnant."

I didn't know what was happening, but I knew how much my friend wanted this baby. They had to know, too.

★

Previously published Worldwide Mystery titles by
CLEA SIMON

CATTERY ROW
MEW IS FOR MURDER

Clea Simon

CRIES AND WHISKERS

W✦RLDWIDE®

TORONTO • NEW YORK • LONDON
AMSTERDAM • PARIS • SYDNEY • HAMBURG
STOCKHOLM • ATHENS • TOKYO • MILAN
MADRID • WARSAW • BUDAPEST • AUCKLAND

Recycling programs
for this product may
not exist in your area.

CRIES AND WHISKERS

A Worldwide Mystery/September 2009

First published by Poisoned Pen Press.

ISBN-13: 978-0-373-26684-5

Printed in U.S.A.

For Jon

PROLOGUE

SHE FELT SICK. Sick as a dog. Hot and feverish despite the icy rain, the thought made her laugh. She was here for the cats, after all. But the laugh had her doubling over in pain, her head bowed so that the whipping wind chilled the sweat on the back of her neck. She had to get home, get back to bed. This was no night to be out, and the cramps were getting worse. No more laughing, she told herself. No more distractions. Tonight, it was all about the cats. She shone her flashlight under a pile of windblown trash. Hadn't she seen a pair of yellow eyes here earlier? Nothing looked back at her now and she stumbled forward in pain. Where were the cats? She'd been sure the tabby would be back, and the orange spotted one, too, still searching for their lost kittens. A tremor shook her and she dropped the flashlight, tripping over the broken edge of the pavement as she tried to force her numb fingers around the cold metal. There! What was that? The flashlight had rolled and as she crawled forward to get it, she saw the two bright spots spark toward her. She knelt, unable to rise, and stared as they grew brighter. Another cramp, sudden and fierce, doubled her over and sent the flashlight into the gutter. No matter, she was unaware of the darkness now, lying in the road as the two lights glowed brighter still.

From the cover of a nearby holly, two yellow eyes watched as the lights bore down. Blinking once, they turned and disappeared into the night.

ONE

DAY HAD BROKEN, cold and gray. Exceedingly cold and gray, and I burrowed further into the snow for warmth. Sleep was the enemy, it meant death in this frozen world, but the desire to succumb was seductive. If I just let go, soon the cold would be gone, or at least I would no longer feel it. There would be stillness, a quiet drifting off. Peace.

But just then something damp touched my face, and I struggled to open my eyes. Round green eyes were close, too close, waiting for me to relax. To give in. Hypothermia had a gentle embrace, but I feared the fangs that went with those unblinking eyes. I opened my mouth to breathe, to call for help, and felt the touch of fur. The green eyes leaned in.

"Kitty!" My Jack London dream burst. I wasn't on the Yukon trail, buried in a snowdrift with my sled dogs. I was in bed, with—I sputtered—cat hair on my lip. "Musetta!" I spit and reached out from under the covers to wipe who-knew-what from my mouth. The kitty in question—my black and white Musetta—drew back, but only to the edge of the fluffy white duvet we shared. The room was freezing, and those round eyes were indeed staring, full of accusation. She was furious, but I couldn't help smiling. Puffed up against the cold, that offending paw now tucked beneath her white tuxedo front, my pet appeared even rounder than usual. Only the off-center white spot on her nose disrupted the symmetry, making her look ever so slightly cross-eyed and so adorable. But no less pissed. Those eyes were ruthless: I was the boss of our little pride, so such inclement weather was my fault, endangering us both. She'd been within her rights to wake me, with nose and paw or any means necessary. She was waiting.

"Hang on." Dreading the shock of the bare wood floor, I swung my legs around her, out of bed, and pranced gingerly toward the window, slamming it shut as another blast of icy wind and, yes, some snow, blew into the room. At thirty-three, I still lived like a student, a result of budget as much as preference. But this one wasn't my fault. I remembered opening that window, hours before. I'd come back from a show, the band's bassist a friend of a friend, and while the music had been unremarkable, a lousy sound mix swamping whatever hooks there were in the mud of distortion, something had inspired me to take notes. And while I'd been trying to write, pecking away at my computer keyboard, the heat had kicked in full blast, turning my one-bedroom apartment into a sweat box. Musetta had been thrilled when I'd cracked the window then, jumping up on the sill to sniff at the night air.

But that had been hours ago. The radiator was cold now and silent, without the clanking that preceded the flood of steam into its antique pipes. Maybe the super had actually re-set a thermostat somewhere in this big ugly box of a building? Or could something have gone wrong? The giant furnace in the basement had a reputation as a temperamental monster, a creaking remnant from decades past, and it also had an entire brick apartment building to heat, six floors of renters. The whole place was falling apart, bit by bit, just out of neglect. Someday the management would kick us out, would sell the building for condos. A nasty thought crept into my sleepy mind.

"They wouldn't let us go without heat in January, would they?" That illegal, but effective, move had been tried before elsewhere. "Think they'll try to freeze us out, Musetta?" I always talk to cats. Who knows how much they understand? Besides, I wanted some sympathy in our mutual plight. But all I saw was her sleek black back. Although one ear shifted slightly, she didn't deign to answer.

I peeked around the blind. Outside my Cambridge apartment, the streetlights were still on. In their glow, I could see the snow turning slick, shifting into the kind of freezing rain that would glaze the city I loved with a deadly beauty. Already, the tree out front sparkled with a coating of ice, and the road below glistened. New England in January: pretty, but treacherous for any poor creature stuck in the storm. And too cold for me. I grabbed the cat—who gave a small protesting "meh!"—and snuggled back under the comforter, trying to find the warmth I'd left. That was one of the pleasures of city living. Someone else in the building would deal with the heat, or the super if that was necessary. With any luck, by the time I was ready to get up, the radiator would be hot again, steaming my worries away. I curled around Musetta and she gave up a purr, grudging, maybe, but steady. I stroked her smooth head and nestled closer, my dark red hair falling over her black bulk. Her nose, still cold and wet, settled against my arm as her head dipped down and we slept.

THE PHONE WOKE ME what seemed like moments later. The phone, and Musetta kicking free in reaction. I followed her bouncing jodhpurs into the living room, rubbing my eyes. Yes, the room was warm. Time must have passed. My own dry mouth confirmed the functioning of the radiator.

"Nyah?" I needed coffee.

"Theda, you awake?" It was Violet. "Stupid question, sorry. It's not even eight. But Theda, if you can wake up, I need you."

Violet knew my hours—and my caffeine addiction—as well as anyone. She's a musician, but we'd met when she'd been working as a barrista at my local coffee house, the Mug Shot, and I had just started freelancing. Now I write about music and by choice I write at night, Vi's band gigs regularly, and we both share a social life that centers around the Boston-Cambridge club scene. This was way too early, and she knew it.

"Hang on." I leaned into the tiny alcove the landlord called a kitchenette and filled a glass at the sink. Two gulps later and my tongue worked. "Okay." I could hear Violet humming to herself, one of her own songs probably. "Okay, I'm awake now. What's up?"

"Cats."

"Huh?" Since leaving the Mug Shot, Violet ran a small local shelter for her day job. Usually her charges kept the same hours she did.

"I'm not sure, but I think we've got a cat-trapping emergency. Caro's working out in Amherst all week, and of course my drummer's got our van. Can you help?"

I looked over at Musetta, who had settled onto my old sofa. With her feet tucked under and her eyes already starting to close again, she was the picture of a contented feline. But she'd been a shelter cat once, and, before that, a homeless kitten. I thought of last night's storm.

"Give me twenty minutes to get dressed and pick up some coffee?"

"Thanks, Theda. I wouldn't turn down a large French roast, and maybe a lemon poppyseed muffin if they've got 'em."

WHEN I PULLED UP at the old Victorian that housed both my friend and the Lillian Helmhold House for Wayward Cats a half hour later, bag of muffins propped between two travel mugs, Violet was waiting out front. Caro—Violet's partner and a jill-of-all-trades carpenter-contractor—had reinforced the old house's sagging gutters and replaced its missing shutters. She'd even painted the three-story building, home to Caro and Vi and more than two dozen felines, in a lively palette of greens and golds. But although it glowed in comparison to the brick block next door, the grand old dame was no match for the diminutive purple-haired punk on the sidewalk. In deference to the icy cold, Violet had a bright red ear-warmer wrapped around her head, one that made her spiked locks stand up straighter. In a day-glo orange parka she looked like an elf gone bad.

"Damn, I hate winter." As she clambered into my old Toyota, I could see that her nose matched the ear-wrap. She grabbed a mug and took a swig. "Ah, thanks." Popping a piece of muffin between chattering teeth, she looked back out at the street. "This is brutal."

"Slick, too. I fishtailed when I turned onto Putnam. At least the sleet has stopped. Where to?"

"Down by the river. You know where the old bottling plant is?" I nodded. Punctuating our neighborhood of triple deckers and the occasional red brick box, the towering "Industrial Space To Let" sign was a local landmark, the last bit of working-class Cambridgeport as drivers crossed over to Boston. "Good, this might be nothing, but when it's this cold out, I've got to check."

"Check on what?" Violet was cupping her hands over the heating vent, hoping for warmth I knew wouldn't start up for another ten minutes. I broke off a chunk of muffin, sour cream and poppy with a fresh, lemony tang, and pulled out, watching for the slick spots that indicated black ice.

"I got a call from Eva. You know, Luisa's mother?" I nodded, chewing. I didn't have a clear picture of the mother, but I remembered the shy, dark-haired girl who had adopted a huge, mellow tabby months before. "She's a nurse in the E.R. at Cambridge City and she was working the lobster shift when they brought in our old buddy, Gail Womynfriend."

I rolled my eyes. Gail was an animal rights activist, a cause I believed in—in principle. But Gail was so far out on the edge that she considered Violet's shelter work to be collusion with the enemy, those who would keep free animals enslaved. "Psychotic break?" I reached for more muffin while Violet held the bag.

"No, she'd been hit by a car. Hurt pretty badly, Eva said."

"Ticked-off breeder?" I was half serious. Gail didn't believe in propagating domestic animals, and wasn't averse to protesting. Loudly. "Someone at the university?" I remembered when the short, wiry-haired woman had "liberated" thirty lab rats and chained herself to their cages instead.

"Could be," Violet's voice turned quiet. At least her teeth were no longer chattering. "It was hit and run."

Just then I came up to the traffic circle under the BU bridge. We'd caught the tail end of the commuter rush, and I had to wait before accelerating into the shaded roundabout. The pavement had a suspicious sheen, and I could feel my rear wheels spin a moment before catching.

"The weather was pretty foul last night." My own near-skid reminded me. "It was probably an accident."

"Yeah, but to drive away? That's low."

"Maybe whoever it was didn't know they'd hit someone?" Violet looked over at me. I didn't believe it either. "No, you're right. That's horrible. But what's it got to do with cats?"

"Pull up here." We were getting close to a long, low industrial building, a dozen of its windows knocked out and covered in plywood, backed up against the riverside Memorial Drive. Mostly brick, with a base of granite blocks the size of my work desk, it was an impressive landmark. It used to be more. When I'd first come to Cambridge as a college freshman, fifteen years ago, this had been a thriving bottling plant, employing dozens of my neighbors. Last I'd heard, maybe a quarter of the big brick factory was occupied—small-scale software outfits and the like—and I had my pick of parking along the side street that led to the main entrance. We got out and I cupped my gloved hands around my insulated mug, following Violet up a cracked cement walkway.

"You know they're going to build condos here?" I didn't, but considering how fast my little city was changing I wasn't surprised. Cambridge, Boston's "left bank," was a realtor's wet dream. "One of Sally's friends was looking into renting the basement, turning it into practice spaces, when she got the word: no more rentals. So some of us started asking why. Gail was taking care of a colony of feral cats that live somewhere around here, and I think someone must have passed the news on. Last I heard, Gail was going to try to relocate them."

"I didn't realize she'd get that involved." Gail was a member of Animals Now, which as far as I could tell focused on making human lives hell in retribution for all our sins. "I mean, wouldn't she rather have killed the developer?"

"I wouldn't put it past her, if she had access to an ecologically sound weapon. But really, she wasn't that bad." Violet caught my look and shrugged. "I mean, we're basically on the same side, trying to save the animals and all." I bit back my response, taking a long swig of my swiftly cooling latté instead. Violet took in strays and often got them adopted as pets. She worked hard at teaching our Cambridgeport neighborhood about the need to spay and neuter. I'd heard Gail speak: She didn't believe in pets, and only supported neutering because we'd "corrupted" cats by domesticating them and she wanted the species to die out. Given her druthers, the intense little activist would have euthanized half the human population for revenge, and turned Cambridge into a sanctuary for the native possums, pigeons, and woodchucks.

Some of this must have shown on my face, despite the soft wool cap I'd pulled down over my eyebrows. "Whatever you think of her, she was doing good work," said Violet, leading up a wide set of stairs. We reached a set of metal doors, secured with a chain and heavy padlock, and after tugging on the door, Violet started back down. "There was a big colony living here and she'd asked me for some help."

I followed, draining the last of my coffee. "You? What about her coven?"

"I'm telling Bunny." Our friend Bunny's a Wiccan, but too softhearted for anyone outside of liberal-lefty Cambridge to call a witch. Violet walked along the building's brick and granite front, stopping occasionally to peek under the sad yews that passed for foundation shrubbery. "Anyway, I think Gail had a falling out with the Animals Now guys. She called me to ask about humane trapping. I thought she wanted to do TNR. You know, trap, neuter, return? But she said something about moving the cats. I thought she meant fostering them, trying to turn them into pets, and I made some suggestions. She just lost it. Said I was trying to pervert nature. Screamed about letting them be. Then, when I heard about the condo plan, I realized she must have meant getting them out of here before the bulldozers come."

Tagging along after, I wondered how long that would be. The sprawling factory complex took up almost an acre along the river. With that view and so close to the universities and Boston right across the Charles, condos here could go for a million easy.

"I can't believe this old place has lasted so long."

"Development rights. And some of us in the neighborhood have been lobbying for a park." She smiled, and I wondered just how active that "lobbying" had been. Our Cambridgeport neighborhood, nestled into a bend of the river, served as a microcosm of the city: Students and professors shared blocks, and often buildings, with new immigrants from Asia and Africa, while older communities of Cape Verdeans and Haitians added their traditions to the mix. Usually, we all found some way to get along. With a population this tightly packed, we'd better. But these days the uniting factor tended to be resentment toward developers, the speculators and big-money investors who wanted to turn our little city by the Charles into the next Gold Coast.

Not that any realtors were going to stroll by on a subzero morning like this. I stamped my feet on the concrete; my toes were going numb. Whatever their prospects for the future, the old building's remaining windows were blank today. My hopes of a hot caffeine refill faded.

"So, what are we looking for?" Violet was on her knees peering under a hedge.

"Oh yeah. Sorry. Cats. Cats and traps. Eva said she didn't have a chance to breathe until her shift ended, but she called as soon as she could. Gail was in pretty bad shape when they brought her in, but I guess she recognized Eva. I don't know, from the shelter, or just from around. Maybe she was delirious. Anyway, she reached up and grabbed Eva when they were taking her into surgery. 'Cats,' she said. 'Get the cats out.' Eva couldn't get anything else out of her, not in the few seconds she had. Probably Gail was just out of it, but Eva called and asked if there was something going on that I should be aware of, something with the shelter. And that's when I thought about the trapping. If Gail had been out here, maybe trying to move the cats before the storm, maybe she set some traps. Any cats out in this weather wouldn't last another night. I mean, they can deal with a lot of cold, but not if their fur gets wet. So I told her we'd have a look around, see if we could find any traps and free any animals that might be inside. It's a long shot, but even with a fur coat, this is no weather for any living creature."

I COULDN'T MUSTER UP a ton of sympathy for Gail, accident or no, but if she'd been hit trying to save cats I figured I could at least help finish her work. Besides, the idea of terrified animals, freezing after a sleet storm was too much for me. For the next half hour, Violet and I poked around the old building's front yard, looking under bushes and into every broken window big enough for the petite Gail to have crawled through. Violet was a few years younger than me, shorter and more lithe, but I did my best to keep up, peering under anything that looked like a possible hiding space.

Nobody would see my blue-jeaned butt up in the air anyway. The place was deserted, the empty grounds isolating the building from the neighborhood that began only a block away. It was Monday, well past nine, but any tenants who'd sublet space here either didn't keep banker's hours or had long ago given up the ghost. Even if they'd been evicted, there was no sign of any development. No flagged stakes squared off the frosted gray earth. Someone at some point had driven some heavy equipment here. Treads like the mark of giant claws dug into what had once been lawn. But these were frozen hard, the tracks of dinosaurs made back when the earth was moist and young. Beyond those marks and a few sad hedges, the grounds were as bare and hard as a moonscape.

The front covered, we walked around a silent corner. The plant, which had seemed liked a stone-and-brick monolith from the street, actually had two small courtyards on its river side, making a shape like a giant letter "E" that had fallen forward onto its face along Memorial Drive. The design hinted at better days, and I could imagine a time when owners valued fresh air and windows for their workers. But as we walked into the first courtyard everything looked lifeless, old chips bags the only color beside the faded brick.

"So I should be looking for cats?" I called over to Violet.

"Traps, actually. Big, boxy wire cages, like big Hav-A-Hearts," she yelled back, already on her hands and knees, peering under a sickly yew. "Gail might have tried to camouflage them under branches or a blanket."

Along the far wall, a gray tangle of twigs reaching to the windows suggested some variety in the long-dead landscaping. Rags and bleached newspaper plastered over the branches like postindustrial papier-mâché. Perfect place for a trap, but as I crossed the bare courtyard the dirt crumbled under my boots, brittle and dry from repeated freezes. No person had walked here, not recently, and true enough the dead shrub held nothing except ice and more garbage.

"It doesn't look like anyone has been here since the first freeze." Or the last Ice Age. "You sure the developers are coming here?"

"Yup." Violet's voice was muffled as she examined a pile of fallen branches. I picked one up and poked a hillock of leaves. I didn't ask how she knew. Violet and I overlapped in a lot of areas, but not all of them.

We moved onto the next courtyard. Set back from the entrance, separated from Memorial Drive by a few sad-looking trees, stood a wooden outbuilding. Maybe it had once held gardening tools. At some point, it had been painted a cheery blue. Now the dominant color was gray, and it looked like a good wind would do for it. But I could see a heavy chain and bolted metal catch on the warped door. The tiny structure might seem abandoned, but somebody had once cared.

"No way there's a trap in there." Violet walked up to it anyway, rattled the door. I turned back toward the courtyard, kicking at leaves until a movement made me freeze.

There, underneath an evergreen bush, a flash of orange. Then another. I caught a brief glimpse of a long, lean shape, orange striped with white. I reached back to motion Violet, but she was already beside me. We craned toward the bush at the opening of the courtyard, but that small movement had been enough, and the cat backed into the dark olive leaves. What could have been a rustle was covered by the sound of the wind.

We inched forward, into the shelter of the courtyard, and crouched low, waiting. My hair blew into my mouth and I realized I was holding my breath.

"There!" My whisper was louder than I'd meant it to be, but the wind took it. I saw a head peek out, then an entire body, skinny to the point of scrawniness.

"She's watching us." We both fell silent. The marmalade head dipped to a half-frozen puddle and began lapping furiously. Beside me, Violet shifted. We'd been crouching for several minutes by then. The cat started—and ducked into the bushes.

"I'm surprised she's even showing herself." Violet knew more about feline behavior than I ever would. "She should be hiding from us."

The cat peeked out again, her mouth opening in a silent mew. "What's wrong with her? Do you think she's hurt?"

Violet inched forward, but it was enough. The cat took off, this time for good. "Well, she's healthy enough to run. Something was bothering her, though." We both stood and stretched.

Violet kicked the dirt with a frustration I shared, and we went to work on the second courtyard.

Once again, we split up, Violet tackling a low brambly-looking shrub against the far wall, while I found myself examining the evergreen that had sheltered the marmalade cat. The bush was half dead, broken brown branches hung off the glossier green ones. It looked like a good hiding place to me. An almost cozy home, but she was nowhere to be seen, even when I crawled along the low-hanging bush. I couldn't find any signs of a trap, either, but the end of the long low bush revealed a basement bulkhead, partially caved in. More fallen branches, blown from the courtyard's one surviving elm, almost covered the shattered wood of the doors.

I knelt and peered into the gloom of the bulkhead. Even in the frozen air, a whiff of ammonia came through. Eau de lit-terbox, descending into deep shadow. "Violet?" I wasn't sure how a cornered feral would react.

"Theda! I got 'em! Over here!" Getting stiffly to my feet I trotted over to the other side of the courtyard, where Violet's orange parka was visible through the brambles. Crawling in behind her, I saw what had caught her attention: two traps, one sprung. Huddled in the back of one orange-crate-sized wire cage was a yellow-eyed tabby, hissing at us weakly. A bit of greasy bacon was still caught in a clothespin clipped to the side. That must have been the bait, but she'd been too freaked out to claim her prize. "Stand back." Violet waved me away. I moved to the side, watching for thorns, and Violet lifted the door. No movement. She reached gingerly for the trap's handle, expecting a swipe of claws, and gently shook the wire cage. Nothing—the cat was too scared, too cold, or too ill. She just huddled in the corner, dingy fur fluffed. Another weak hiss seemed to take all she had, and then she hung her head.

"Poor girl, she's wiped out. I guess we're taking her to the shelter." Violet let the door back down, and the tabby roused enough for another round of hissing and spit. "At least she's got some fight left in her."

"Yeah, but she sure looks like she could use a meal, not to mention a dry, warm bed."

Violet sighed. Her shelter, which didn't euthanize, was nearly always full, and on principle she focused on strays and abandoned pets. Those already socialized animals not only got along with each other, they had the best chance of being placed—which meant, in turn, that Violet could take in the next litter or lost animal the neighborhood kids brought around. "Okay, kitty, you like us so much, you're going to love a car ride."

I used a stick to spring the other trap shut and pulled it from its covering of brush. We'd began the long walk back to the car when it hit me. "Violet, there was a bulkhead over by where we saw the other cat. It smelled like there might be some cat activity there."

She looked at the terrified feline. Despite the movement of the cage, the cat remained pressed to the back corner. "We've got to get this little girl out of the cold."

I handed her my car keys. "Here, go warm yourselves up. I'll just be a minute."

"Wait." Putting the cage down, Violet rummaged in the pockets of her oversize parka, coming up with a small flashlight. "If it's the feral, she'll probably bolt. Let her. If there's a cage…"

"I know, I'll watch my fingers." I took the flashlight and ran back to the bulkhead. Darkness. Through the broken door, I couldn't see anything but splintered stairs and dead leaves. There didn't even seem to be much snow or ice collected in the dark hollow. Taking a deep breath, I grabbed the broken door and pulled. It came open more easily than I'd expected, and I jumped back as it fell to the ground with a thud. Nothing moved, and I listened for a hiss. The wooden stairs before me didn't look any sturdier with sunlight on them. But Violet knew where I was going. If I didn't return…

This was silliness. I stepped in and caught my breath at the stench. Down three stairs, I felt a spider web on my cheek.

Could this get any more gross? Thanking my foresight for
wearing a hat, I brushed the offending web from my face and
continued down to the concrete floor. Flicking on Violet's
flashlight, I peered under the stairs. No eyes reflected back, and
I turned to open the bottom doors, also made of wooden planks.
They gave ever so slightly, but then held firm. I shook them,
hoping to free them from whatever ice or debris held them fast.
Nothing. With the flashlight, I examined the bottom of the
doors, kicking away the dead leaves gathered there to expose
solid wood, no holes or broken boards. Then up the gap
between the doors—all the way to the shiny new lock. Well,
good. Either a renter or the property's owner had the foresight
to secure the basement. I thought of Violet's contact and
wondered if some band had been taking advantage of an open,
empty building. No musician would want to leave equipment
here, but before the latest deep freeze it might have been a good
space for a party.

At any rate, I was off the hook. Even if a cat might still have
found a way in, a cat trapper couldn't. Ducking to avoid the
remnants of the spider's weavings, I trotted back to the light
and lifted the rotten outer door back into place. Maybe that little
entranceway would be shelter for some poor beast, stuck in the
bitter cold of a New England winter. I gave the courtyard one
last look. The marmalade cat was nowhere to be seen.

WE WERE LOADING the cages into the backseat when I heard a
rush of notes, the five-beat bass line to "Police and Thieves."

"The Clash?"

"I know. Old school!" Violet reached into her parka as the
reggae-punk riff repeated and opened a tiny purple cell phone.

"Chic!" She smiled, and then listened.

"Wow. Okay, okay. We'll be at the shelter soon. And Eva?
Thanks." She snapped it shut.

"What was that?" I tucked a blanket around the trapped
cat's cage and got hissed at for my troubles.

"Eva just had a visit from the cops. It seems someone saw Gail talking to her in the emergency room, and they're asking questions."

"Because it was a hit and run?" We pulled away, and my old car responded with a blast of almost warm air. "Can't Gail tell them anything yet?"

"Gail's dead, Theda. And the cops seem to think that the hit-and-run wasn't an accident."

TWO

"NO, BEFORE YOU ASK, I'm not taking in a wild cat." The tea kettle had begun whistling, but I could still hear Bill from the living room. "And Womynfriend? What kind of name is that? I mean, she wasn't born with that was she?"

"Hang on," I yelled back to my beau. Laid up by a busted kneecap, he had no choice but to holler from the sofa. But I didn't want to shout a conversation, not this conversation anyway. I took my time with the tea, pouring the boiling water over the loose leaves in the strainer, then adding two mugs to the tray. I needed a moment. Driving away from the old bottling plant, Violet and I had passed the intersection where Gail had been hit and, now we knew, killed. A blue-striped Cambridge cruiser still stood guard by the yellow crime-scene tape. We'd slowed, with traffic, and I'd tried not to look too closely at what the uniforms were studying on the ground. Still, I couldn't help glancing over, and had spied a strange patch of darkness on the slate-gray pavement. My imagination did the rest. Violet had told me about Gail's injuries, a crushed rib cage, internal bleeding…. Eva said she'd died on the operating table. I took a breath and tried to push the images from my mind.

"Here we go." Focusing instead on the task at hand, I nudged a pile of magazines out of the way to make room for the tray and looked over at Bill. It was his leg that was cast in plaster, from his size-12 sneaker up all the long way to his basketball player's thigh after two bouts of surgery. But as that leg progressed into recovery he seemed to be losing control of his other limbs as well. "Bill?"

"What? Oh, sorry." Tossing the television remote, he moved two books and a yellow legal pad to the floor, then piled up a dissembled newspaper to make room for his mug. I reached for a crusty cereal bowl, the spoon stuck to its side. His place was a mess.

"Your place is a mess." I took the bowl into the kitchen and ran hot water into it.

"I know." My prone beau had the decency to look embarrassed, biting down ever so slightly on his own broad grin. "I'd have cleaned up a bit, but I didn't expect you so early."

"You're lucky I come by at all." I smiled to show I was joking. I had to stop thinking about the road, about that long, dark slick. "I could leave you to starve!"

It had been nearly three weeks since Bill's accident, and although his mishap certainly didn't compare to Gail's, it had lasting consequences. Two days into the new year, and my fit and healthy boyfriend—a homicide detective with the Cambridge police—had finally been taken down. Not by a murder suspect, or even a fleeing witness, but by the ice. One wrong step from his Jeep onto the black ice of his building's parking lot, and he'd slipped. His long legs, one of his more attractive features, had been his undoing as he'd come down, hard, on one kneecap—the other leg splayed out. If he hadn't been right near busy Inman Square, he could have laid there all night. At least, that's what he'd told me when he'd called from the hospital several hours later. At the time, I'd thought he was making a play for sympathy. Bragging about his injury, no matter how he got it. But when I saw the X-ray—his leg was bandaged by then—I couldn't help gasping. Stark white against the black film, his kneecap looked dented, like someone had tried to turn it inside out. Even without the torn ligament, which I couldn't see, there was clearly no way he was walking away from this one.

Two surgeries later, Bill's leg was on the mend, but the rest of him was close to fracturing. He hadn't played serious team sports since high school, but the man I'd been seeing since last spring was essentially athletic. An extrovert, albeit a smart one, if he couldn't walk around while he thought problems through, he couldn't function. Televised sports, which seemed to be on 24/7 on Bill's oversize flat-screen, were not an alternative, and his temper showed the strain.

Mine was following suit, though heaven knew I'd been trying. Since the hospital had let him come home, I'd been coming by almost daily bringing food, newspapers, and as much good cheer as I could muster. Bill didn't need any actual nursing. Following the second surgery he could just about hobble around with the help of crutches. But he did need distractions, needed the noise of voices and human activity around him. Live action, the kind that demanded his brain function, and not just the kind provided by the giant TV, a Christmas gift to himself. Even more, he needed some kind of physical outlet—or at least to be able to leave his apartment. And that wouldn't come for a while.

My regular visits were a poor substitute, and I knew my cheer sounded forced. Not that we didn't make a good couple, in our own way. But I'm a writer, freelance since I quit my last job at the *Morning Mail*. It's easy for me to go days without human contact. In fact, I preferred solitude, and would have rather kept Bill as a night time companion with the occasional daylight outing limited to brunch. Mornings in particular I was best left alone. Then I could rouse myself slowly and enjoy a couple of cups of coffee with just the cat and the computer. I'm not a nursey type. But I loved Bill, and for a tall, rangy guy laid up in a city apartment, he was being as good as he could be.

So this morning I'd brought him my latest adventure, much like Musetta's predecessor, James, used to bring me voles. Only I'd tried to spin it like an adventure story. I'd told Bill about the feral colony at the old plant, about the marmalade cat and her odd behavior. From there, I'd worked backward to the call from the hospital that had gotten me and Violet out in the cold so early. And at that he'd changed. Instead of listening like my boyfriend, he'd homed in like a cop. Before I knew what was happening, he was asking about the victim, the evidence, and the accident scene, and I was realizing that I knew next to nothing. In fact, I had more questions for him than answers.

"How can they tell if it wasn't an accident?" Violet and I had chewed that one over.

"Skid marks, for one. Or the lack of them. But Vi might have it wrong, Theda. If someone tried to stop, there'd be marks where they tried to brake. But if there's no indication of braking it could mean a lot of things. That the driver didn't see her. Or, yeah, they might be looking for a drunk driver. What they'll be doing next is analyzing the data." As he wound into an explanation of measurements and glass samples, I found myself withdrawing, recognizing too late that this wasn't just a tale to tell. I didn't like Gail much, but I still didn't want all this clinical detail. To Bill it was an intellectual puzzle: statistics, evidence, facts. To me, it was too much—physical traces that made me picture Gail's final moments. A screech, a scream. That horrible, horrible slick. When Bill started asking me about the little I had been able to see, who was at the scene, and how large an area had been cordoned off, I'd retreated into the kitchen, queasy. That's when his questions had begun to get bratty.

Make tea, not war. I poured myself a mug and settled into the worn green chair across from the sofa. The hot liquid settled my stomach, and looking over at Bill's thick salt-and-pepper hair, my mood eased, too. A little too long over the collar, the way I liked it—and he didn't—his shaggy mop begged to be tousled. He was such a reasonable man, really. Being stuck indoors, even in frigid January, would be tough for anyone.

"Okay, second things first. Womynfriend. I'm guessing that's one of those self-renamings. You know, dumping the old 'slave name' for something gender neutral?" My beau was being dense. "And the cat is feral, Bill. Feral, not wild.

Domestic cats can't go 'wild,' Bill." We'd been together for the better part of a year now, long enough for him to pick up at least some of my vocabulary. My tea tasted bitter. I'd let it steep too long. "Probably on the street since birth and terrified of people. I don't know if she'll ever make a house pet."

"Besides, I'm a one-woman, one-cat man." I reached for the honey and saw him grinning at me. The morning had wound me up so much I'd missed his teasing tone. "And what would Musetta say?"

"'Neh,' probably." I gave him my best impersonation of my voluble pet, along with a smile, a real one this time. "Or 'eh-eh-eh.'"

"I thought that's her 'I see a squirrel' chatter?"

"You're good."

"Hey, I've been working on listening to the women in my life. But come here." Shifting his leg on the sofa, he sat up, patting the cushion beside him. I moved over and snuggled in. It had been a rough morning.

"Sorry if I was grilling you." He wrapped an arm around me, nearly spilling my tea. I didn't mind. "I didn't realize I'd gone into work mode until you got up. Did you know this woman well?"

I shook my head. "Actually, I couldn't stand her." Saying it out loud was a relief. "She was one of those holier-than-thou types. Whatever she was doing was right, and anything else was contrary to all of nature."

"An animal rights extremist?"

"Just about. I couldn't believe she was working with ferals. A lot of those Animals Now people see domestic animals as trash and want nothing to do with them."

"So there was some good in her. And now she's dead." He pulled me near. I closed my eyes and felt the tension begin to ebb away. Five more minutes….

"Until what?" I hadn't realized I'd spoken my thoughts.

"Until I've got to get to work. I've got 'Clubland' to write up." January is slow for freelance, but that didn't mean I could slack off. I had my one ongoing assignment, the column I wrote each week for the *Morning Mail*. But although that was regular, it was freelance, too. No contract, no security. If I messed it up, I'd be worrying about bills again, hitting up every bridal and home decor magazine in town with story ideas for spring nuptials and manicured gardens.

Not that "Clubland," my column, was perfect. For starters, the two-hundred buck fee I'd been happy to get three months ago didn't seem like quite enough anymore. Maybe I wouldn't have minded the short cash, but my one other perk—the freedom to choose my subjects—was going by the wayside, too. I was the one out in the clubs. The one who heard the bands, who got all the demos and downloads. But increasingly, my editor Tim was sticking his hand in, suggesting who was in, who was out, and who I should be writing about. Still, even if it was neither enough or perfect, "Clubland" was my gig, my best gig, for now.

"You could work here." Bill brought me back to the present, and I caught a pleading note in his voice. "Go get your laptop?" I turned away. "Theda?" The pleading was undercut by concern.

"It's Musetta. I don't like leaving her." God, it felt silly to say that, but it was the truth. Because I had a pet and he didn't, we used to spend more nights at my place. Since Bill's accident that hadn't been an option, and I'd done my best to accommodate my injured beau. But each morning as I headed home after a night away, I knew Musetta would come rushing down the hall to greet me, chirping her litany of all the adventures that I'd missed. She'd butt into me with her smooth black head and purr like a tiny bellows. For hours—or until I left the house again—she'd keep me in sight, twining around my legs or curling up on top of the filing cabinet to watch me while I typed. I was her world, and I couldn't explain my absences to her. Besides, I missed her, too.

"You could bring her over here."

"She hates the car."

"That's because she associates it with the vet. Bring her here a few times. She'd love my windowsills." He knew how to get to me. Besides, he was right. Bill's condo—a former factory space turned into loft apartments—sported huge windows on two sides. Even better, they had wide sills where a cat could sleep for hours. "And you could bring her cave, too." Musetta had finally taken to the plush covered cat bed I'd fallen for months before, and Bill had listened to me coo over her new nap site, white nose just visible when she curled up inside.

"Maybe." Would moving my cat here mean I was moving in, too? Or would we both end up commuting?

"I can't believe I'm jealous of a cat." Some of his grumbling was in jest, I thought. Not all.

"Yeah, but what a cat." Best thing I could think of was to play along. Just then, I heard the "brrring-brrring" of an old-style telephone, and I roused myself to get my cell from my coat pocket.

"Violet?"

"I didn't wake you again, did I?" She was outside. I could hear traffic and wind.

"No, I'm at Bill's. But I was just heading home to do some work. What's up?"

"You couldn't come with me to the bottling plant again, could you? It seems we've missed a trap. One of the women Gail worked with told me she had three of them. And if the condition of that tabby we brought in this morning is any indication, any other animal that's been caught and left out here doesn't have much time."

SO MUCH FOR getting down to work. I met Violet at what had been Gail's headquarters, the official base of Animals Now New England. The Central Square storefront was wedged between a ninety-nine cents place ("Nothing Over a Dollar!") and a package store that advertised Portuguese *vinho verde*. A couple of empties out front showed they sold the harder stuff, too. Looking up from the numbers on the door, I could still read a faded paint advertisement for shoe repairs. But the room I entered looked more like an office, even if it was plastered over with posters of trapped animals and meat processing plants. Violet was waiting inside, sitting on top of a metal desk covered with fliers for a protest in Providence.

"Wanna grab a burger later?" I meant it as a joke, but Violet shot me a look.

"Theda, have you met Ruth? Ruth, Theda is helping me with the rescues."

I thought my voice had been pretty quiet, but the short, stout brunette who stepped out from behind a row of filing cabinets glared at me anyway. I smiled in apology. This was Cambridge, the People's Republic, after all.

"Hey, Ruth. Good to meet you." Saying anything else would just dig me in deeper. "And, well, I'm sorry for your loss." No response. Maybe she was the kind who hid her deepest emotions. "Violet tells me that Gail had more traps set out?"

Ruth grunted, dropping a handful of files onto the gunmetal gray desk, and rubbed one hand over her close-cropped hair. I took the grunt as an acknowledgment. "Gail, man," she seemed to be talking more to herself than to us. "Taking all the traps again. I can't believe the energy and resources she wasted on those animals."

"The feral cat colony?" So much for collegial grief. At least Ruth's mood didn't seem aimed at me.

"Yeah. Those cats." She waved us over, still looking down at the papers on her desk. "Let me see what I can find here." Settling into the one chair and putting her vintage army boots up on an opened drawer, she dragged a pile of files onto her ample lap and began leafing through them. "I pulled these for Violet when she said she was bringing our cages back. Those cages are communal property."

I looked at Violet, who just raised her eyebrows. She didn't know what was up, either.

"Here we go." Ruth pulled out a bunch of papers that had been clipped together. I could see "River Street Colony" written in marker across the top. "She kept tabs of everything that was going on with those animals. Of course, she didn't write up how many of the native species they killed. Birds, moles, voles, you name it. Just another one of humanity's mistakes. So-called civilization." She handed the package to Violet. "Check the last page."

Violet did. "This is dated from last week. Two traps, it says."

Ruth shrugged her big shoulders. I wouldn't have thought Gail was worth the effort. "She came by on Sunday for the last one. Just took it. Maybe she wanted to set it someplace else. But that was the colony she was working with, trying to get them out of there."

"You have any idea where she would have set the other trap?" I'd figured I wasn't going to be her favorite person, but I had to ask. We'd been all over the old factory's grounds that morning. Another shrug. "You sure she used it?"

"It's not here. Maybe something happened with the first two. Who knows? Gail didn't ask, just grabbed our last trap. I guess some of the cats kept trying to go back."

I didn't understand. Ruth looked at the clock like the time meant something to her. Time for us to go, probably, but, with a sigh, she relented. "Gail was trying to move the colony." She talked deliberately, like we were stupid. Maybe we were missing something. "She kept saying that the pressure was on. Like she had to get them out, and get them out soon. But I don't know why. I mean, she also said that the cats had abandoned the actual building down there, left it for the yards. She said they were acting like they were looking for a new shelter, 'cause a bunch of the kittens were close to freezing from exposure."

"Kittens?" I'd straightened up in concern, but Violet slammed the packet of papers closed and leaned in on Ruth, her voice rising. "Gail was trapping nursing mothers with kittens? This early in the season?"

"Yeah, they started early. Another great side effect of global warming. Gail got some of them, took 'em over to Fresh Pond. But I guess some of the kittens were missing, and you know how the mothers get." Ruth looked annoyed rather than sympathetic. "Gail was hoping to find them. Personally, I think the fishers probably got 'em."

"Come on, Theda." Violet grabbed my parka sleeve before I could ask another question. "You'll get your trap back." She practically yelled over her shoulder as she marched me out the door.

"That marmalade cat!" I trotted to keep up with Violet. "She must have been looking for a kitten." Violet turned and nodded. "Poor thing. But what was up with Ruth? Sounds like she missed the third trap more than she missed Gail."

"Some of those Animal Nowers…" Violet flapped her arms in frustration. "I mean, Ruth is okay, but don't get her started on cats. She gets nutty." I couldn't help but agree and I took the opportunity to turn her onto the next side street where I'd parked. "God, those people drive me over the edge."

"But you liked Gail?" I was playing devil's advocate, but I was also confused. "And…we're still going back to the bottling plant, right?"

"Yeah, that okay?" I started the engine in response. I'd noticed she still had Gail's notes.

"Of course. I'm not letting kittens die of exposure. But you have to explain."

"Well, Gail was an Animals Nower, all right." Violet settled into my Toyota's bucket seat and twisted toward me. "But she'd gotten into feral rescue."

"Yeah, you said: TNR. But walk me through it?" Something wasn't making sense.

"Well, it's just what it sounds like. You trap ferals, neuter them, and give them their rabies shot. Maybe distemper. You know, whatever you can afford. Then you bring them back to where they were living."

I must have made a puzzled noise. "It's not like most of them can be turned into pets, Theda. Most ferals, if they're born in the wild, can't get over their fear of people. Unless they're handled as kittens, they might as well be bobcats."

I'd heard one or two stories of ferals tamed, but this didn't seem the time to bring that up. Besides, that wasn't what had been bothering me. "So why was Gail trying to move them? Isn't that against the whole idea? It sounds like they were settled in, as much as they could be. They had shelter, a family system. Would she be trying to relocate an entire colony just because of some rumors about development?"

"I guess so. Maybe she thought she could move them before the spring kitten season really kicked in?" Violet sounded as puzzled as I was. "But, no, Ruth said that the cats themselves were moving. Like, they wanted out, and Gail just wanted them someplace safe. Maybe there were too many cats there, or some predator had moved in?"

"Maybe." It didn't quite make sense. "She said something about fishers?"

"Yeah, they're these nasty weaselly things. But I think she's full of it. Word among the rescue people is that they're showing up in the suburbs. Supposedly they've really taken a toll on feral colonies out on the Cape. But they're not here, not yet. We'll probably get coyotes first."

Great, I thought, and turned on the radio as we swung left on Putnam toward the plant. Maybe we'd find our answers there.

TWO HOURS LATER, I was thinking like a coyote. Famished and freezing, I'd given up on my fingers—numb was better than painful—and was wondering about my toes.

"Violet?" My voice sounded whinier than I'd intended. "I don't think we're going to find it. I don't think it's here." My face was going numb, too. "If some of the cats were moving, she could have put the trap wherever that was, wherever they were moving to."

"Yeah, I know." We'd worked our way around the building,

front and back including both courtyards, patting down every
pile of leaves and dirt to make sure no cage had been buried
there. We'd even poked around the bottom of the old shed,
looking for holes or loose boards. Now we sat on the frosted
ground, leaning back against the rough granite base of the main
building.

"Vi." I stopped myself. If this cold was so painful to me, I
could imagine what it would be like for an animal, trapped,
scared, possibly wet and starving. But I'd run out of ideas. I
pulled a blue splinter out from the loose wool of my glove.
"Let's go back to the car. We can warm up, get some food, and
look through Gail's notes. Maybe we'll find a clue." Violet
sighed her assent, and we both creaked to our feet.

"Soup's On?" I tried not to sound like I was pleading. "We
can read while we warm up."

Violet nodded, her purple locks bouncing around her bright
red ears. "Worth a shot."

Half an hour later, I was a renewed woman. Split pea with
ham, a large peppermint tea, and a seat pulled right up to
Soup's On's huge, hissing radiator made sure of that, and with
all the steam in the little café some curl had even woken up in
my flattened hat hair. But even though we'd split the file
between us, each of us reading half before handing it over, we
could find no hints of anywhere else Gail might have laid that
third trap.

The notes did give me a little more sense of the woman who
had written them. Gail was practical; she'd kept track of what
had and had not worked as bait. (Bacon and Kentucky Fried
Chicken strips had been the most successful.) And methodical.
Through her chicken-scratch handwriting, I felt I was getting
to know the cats she'd observed, particularly the two females
she'd seen lurking about. One seemed to be the tabby we'd
picked up, the other was definitely the marmalade. As I read,
I could picture the distraught cat, darting from her hidden den
to search for a lost kitten. It gave me a sense of Gail, too,

and I could imagine the tiny woman crouching in the cold to watch and take notes. I'd thought of her as purely political, but she was more.

"What's concaveation?" At the very least, Gail knew something about animal behavior.

"What?" Violet looked up from the chart she was reading. "Oh, that's when a neutered female will start nursing a kitten."

I must have still looked puzzled, because she broke off a piece of bread and reached for the page I held. "Were the other females helping out? I missed that. It's pretty common in social animals. Rats, too. Helps the colony survive. I read a study on that last semester."

Getting Violet to talk about cat behavior was better than thinking about Gail, or about any cat or kitten we might have missed. Wherever that third trap was, we weren't going to find it.

"You looking forward to classes starting again?" After years away from formal education, Violet was once again tackling college with the goal of veterinary school. She'd begun with gusto, and aced organic chemistry in the fall, so I thought she'd make it. But instead of the eager smile I expected, she turned away to stare out the café's window.

"Vi? You're just on break now, right?" She drew a circle in the window's fog and breathed on it, filling it again with condensation.

"Yeah, and I'm registered for spring semester. Caro saw to that." She turned to face me again. "But the thing of it is, Theda, I don't know if I need it anymore." She leaned over the table. "I mean, I've got the shelter, and I know I'm helping animals there. Plus, the shelter endowment means the gig pays okay. More than okay, and I love it. Love living there. Besides," she moved closer, "if the band is going to go anywhere, we really should go back into the studio. Soon, and that takes time and money. And with Caro…"

"Now, don't tell me Caro doesn't want you to get your degree." Violet's partner was life smart, rather than book smart.

But she'd painted houses for years to finance her apprentice-ship to a master carpenter, determined to get the education that mattered to her. She now taught for the crafts school that had hooked her up with her apprenticeship. And, unlike a lot of con-tractors, she had very strong feelings about leaving a project—any project—unfinished.

"No, no, she does. And I'm going to finish. Get the bachelor's, do the whole cap and gown thing, too. But beyond that? I just don't know. Life is very full right now, and I just don't know where I want to put my energy."

What could I say? I'd been writing about local bands long enough to know how they functioned. Most musicians put out tons more than they got back, in terms of money, hours, dedi-cation—at least for bands at the club level. This morning, my diminutive friend had showed me how devoted she was to saving animals. If she wanted to put half that much back into her punk-pop trio, the Violet Haze Experience, how could I fault her? I had a hard time getting my own work done.

"Which reminds me," I pushed back from the table, "I really should to get to work at some point. But, it's up to you, Vi. Do you want to go back to the bottling plant?"

She shook her head. "There's no point."

Our failure weighed on both of us, and as we began donning our various layers, I looked for a way to lighten the mood. "You do know that if you release a CD—or even a download—I'll sneak it into the column." She smiled at me. We both knew that, having written up her band that fall, I shouldn't put in more than a mention for at least a couple of months.

"Yeah, I know. And believe me, I'm grateful. How's the boy?" Filling her in on Bill as we walked to my car made my day look smaller still. I should head back there later, maybe with some books or a movie. But for a few hours at least, I could go home and write. Live my own life, with the company of my computer and my cat. Right now, that sounded like heaven.

THREE

"KITTY! I'M HOME!" No eager squeaking feline greeted me, but as I pushed the door of my apartment open, I did see an offering. The belt to my terrycloth robe was stretched down the hall, laid out as if it had been dragged from my bedroom. "Kitty?"

Then she came, bouncing and chirping, and I scooped her soft bulk up in my arms. "Hello, kitty. Thank you for sharing your 'kill.'" She purred as I nuzzled her head, and for a moment I remembered Gail and all her careful notes. "Or was that your kitten?" Musetta wasn't talking, so I made sure to rub the base of her ears before releasing her. As I unwrapped my scarf and began to shed layers, she began to groom, twisting sideways to lick the base of her tail.

"Sorry, Musetta. You bring me a nice present and I mess up your fur." No response. That tail was going to be clean. "Well, I'm going to be in my office if you need me."

As soon as I sat down at my computer, Musetta's silent treatment ended. "Meh?" She reached her front paws up to gently claw at my thigh. "Meh?" I drew her onto my lap and felt her settle into a nap as I logged onto email.

"Theda: Nix the Dragon Breath piece. Call me."

Only my editor, Tim, would use a word like "Nix." I blamed his Lou Grant fetish. But I couldn't blame his TV fixation for stealing my column topic for the week. Was he giving the band, a sensitive foursome with a ferocious name, to a staff writer? Or had Dragon Breath, a rising "emo" quintet, done something to alienate the *Morning Mail?*

The next new message was no better. "Tess canceled! I'm so bummed." Bunny, who still worked at the *Mail,* had planned on meeting me at Amphibian Tuesday night to hear our mutual friend play. A singer-songwriter, but far better than the fake-folk phonies who usually perform under that label, Tess wrote songs that sounded like they'd been around for ages and sang them in a voice that conjured up bourbon and honey and long, hot nights. I'd been psyched to hear more of the rootsy song cycle she had been working on. Tess was good, and not just because I liked her. But being on the Tuesday night level of the folk-club circuit wasn't a living. Tess had a day job, too, punching numbers at one of the university labs. And I'd gathered from her absence on the club scene—and from the infrequent times I could get her on the phone—that work had been hairy. Not all of the Boston colleges were closed for winter break, not behind the scenes anyway.

"Bummerama," I typed back. I was making light—I missed Tess, her smart sometimes snarky humor. Her direct take on everything. But that intensity was one of the reasons she got so caught up in work, and to love Tess meant to live with the fact that she sometimes disappeared for weeks on end. "Dinner anyway?" Someone in the *Mail's* library must have needed Bunny's prestigious research skills just then, or she'd gone for a late lunch, 'cause I got no reply. Our plans would have to remain on hold. Just as well. With Tim pulling my story, I'd have to scramble for a subject. Unless I could talk him out of it.

There was nothing for it but to call. Although I hated dislodging Musetta—"eh!"—I left my desk and rang up the Arts extension.

"Tim? It's Theda. I just got your email."

"Krakow, good! Yeah, Dragon Breath is out. Turns out Jackie's got plans to shoot them for a Styles spread." Jackie Quan was our fashion writer, and how a bunch of scrawny musicians would fit into her weekly two-page pictorial was beyond me.

"Dragon Breath? You got the right guys?" The band I was thinking of played melodramatic "emo-core" rock and sang about how sensitive they were. "Whiney kids from Quincy?"

"Yeah. Jackie's putting them in the lobby of the Ritz with some girl models. They'll all be wearing those funny old T-shirts from the '80s. Those cute gas station jackets, too. Jackie says emo is all very retro, very street."

I rolled my eyes. Fashion has never been my strong point: clean jeans and a nice top is about as fancy as I get. But I'd learned by now not to argue with style's arbiters—or with the editor who signed off on my checks.

"Okay, no Dragon Breath." I reached for my pad, which had a list of upcoming gigs, record releases, and the like. "Buckner's Knee is going into the studio—*are* going into the studio? Anyway, that might be fun. Czechlist has come back from tour, and there's a buzz going about the new Wake Up Screaming on the *Zine* blog." I flipped a page. "Then there's a new trio, all women. They play Led Zeppelin covers on cello and viola…"

"Cello? Oh, no. And forget those other small fry, Krakow. I've got a story for you. Swann's Way."

"Huh?" Somehow, I didn't see portly, bluff Tim as a Proust fan.

"Swann's Way." He chuckled. "You're not getting too old for this gig, are you? Didn't think my cutting-edge club reporter would've missed the biggest thing to come out of Peabody."

Nothing big ever comes out of Peabody, though I'm sure it's a fine suburb to grow up in. Still, I had a reputation to maintain, and the dig about my age hurt. "Swann's Way…" I thought fast. "I've seen some very glossy posters for them recently. Some big gig. But they didn't come up through the local clubs. I know I've never seen them before."

"That's just it!" Tim sounded positively gleeful. "They're starting out huge. An overnight sensation, they're *that good!*"

"You've heard them?" Tim's office often emanated Jackson Browne. "And you liked them?"

"Yeah, really melodic. Melody's coming back, you know."

I never thought it left, but I couldn't count on Tim to hear what I did. What was important was keeping the gig. "Sure, Tim. Swann's Way." I wrote down the name. "I'll call photo to set something up." Much as I doubted Swann's Way would be the next big thing, I would check them out. I wasn't promising to like them. Speaking of which: "Hey, Tim, I've got a question." I was rewarded with a grunt. "Have you heard anything from the news side about a hit-and-run? About an animal rights person named Gail Womynfriend?"

He guffawed in response. "Is that a joke, Krakow? One of your Cambridge things?" I bit back my response. The day before, I'd felt close to the same way. Call waiting saved me from having to explain, and I made my apologies, switching over to hear Bunny, talking fast.

"Theda, You're there? Thank the goddess I reached you."

"What's up?" Her voice worried me. Since her handfasting—what her mom had called a wedding—with Cal last fall, my sweet, plump friend had become more settled than ever.

"It's Tess. She's been in an accident."

I thought of the black ice, and of Gail. "Is she okay?"

"I don't know. I mean, I think so but I called to find out why she'd canceled, and the lab told me she was at home. You know her, Theda. Tess never misses work. Anyway, I got her at home and she says she's fine, but she *sounds* really messed up."

So much for my afternoon. But without friends, the city would be too cold to bear. "I'll call, check on her, see if I can bring her anything."

"Thanks, Theda. I'm stuck here till late, and I probably shouldn't plan on dinner tomorrow either. Seems like everyone is calling in sick, and they're pre-printing the weekend sections again."

"Arts, too?" My editor hadn't said anything about early deadlines.

"I think so." Damn Tim, did this mean he was planning on

holding my column? Usually, I figured he wanted my Thursday column on Tuesdays not because he needed it then, but because it gave him a feeling of security. I knew for a fact that he hardly ever read it before 3:00 p.m. on Wednesday, 'cause that's the earliest I ever got his questions.

"So, is this going to be every week for Arts?" Would anyone besides my buddy have told me?

"Let me poke around. I'll find out, Theda."

"Thanks, Bunny. And I'll call you as soon as I've checked in with Tess."

Musetta was lolling on her back as I took my coat off the radiator. Her front paws tucked up and her white booties crossed, she looked too adorable to leave, and I reached down to rub her fluffy white belly fur. She wriggled with pleasure, and I was struck for a moment by the thought of those missing feral kittens, out there somewhere in the cold. "I've done what I could." She tilted her head quizzically, so that one fang showed. "I know, kitty. It's not enough. But for now, Tess takes priority." I chucked her under her chin. "Sorry, kitty. I've got to run."

Despite what I'd said to Bunny, I knew Tess would brush me off if I called. She never did take to coddling, so just stopping by seemed the best bet. I'd hit the convenience store first: orange juice and chocolate always seemed more comforting to me than flowers. With luck, I'd be back in an hour.

Pulling the door shut behind me, I heard footsteps and started. Usually my building is empty in the middle of a Monday, and my morning must have gotten to me. But the figure who smiled down at me from the next landing was far from threatening. Was quite pleasant looking actually. Mocha brown skin. Dark, thick lashes over darker eyes. Gold earrings revealed under long dreads looped casually back.

"Hey, neighbor." His voice had a vaguely familiar lilt. Not quite Southern.

"Hi there. You're the new guy?" I vaguely recalled Carol, the potter on the third floor, finally packing up. The building was a wreck, she'd said, and the city was going downhill fast. She was moving in with her daughter in Vermont.

"Three C. Lucullus Reddington." He switched an instrument case from his right hand to his left and reached out in greeting. "But my friends call me Reed."

We shook, his hand was warm, and I looked down at the instrument case, recognizing the soft diagonal shape of a saxophone. "Yeah, it's a bad joke." There was a laugh in his voice. "But once I got to MuzeArts, it stuck."

"You're studying there?" Reed looked about my age, elegantly decked out in a long wool coat and plaid muffler. But Cambridge was friendly to lifelong scholars. Besides, MuzeArts—or the Massachusetts College of Musical Arts—was open enrollment. A lot of working musicians circulated in and out.

"I was, years ago. Now I'm teaching. They had pity on me."

I finally recognized the accent. My new neighbor had the rounded, courtly tones of Allen Toussaint. "Are you from…." I hesitated.

"New Orleans." He closed his eyes, his smile softening to something more wistful. "Originally. I've been moving around a bit recently. So when MuzeArts called…"

"Well, welcome to Cambridge. Or welcome back, I should say."

"Thank you." He bowed slightly, then pantomimed a shudder. "But I must say, I don't remember the winters being quite this inhospitable."

"On behalf of Massachusetts, I apologize." His courtly manners were catching. Besides, he was cute. I couldn't believe I hadn't noticed him earlier. "When did you move in?"

"January first." We walked down the stairs and he held the door open for me. "New city for a new year."

That meant he probably hadn't seen me with Bill. Not that this meant I wasn't attached to a fully committed relationship. "Well, I hope it's a good one."

We parted at the sidewalk, as he turned left toward Central.

My car was right across the street, but for a moment I stood there, watching Reed walk away. I loved living in this city, freezing cold or not.

FOUR

I SAW TESS'S CAR before I saw her. Pulled up in front of the triple-decker my friend called home, her baby blue Volvo caught my eye among its more prosaic neighbors. No longer new, by any standard, Vera had her share of dings and rust, but when I walked in front I saw what had to have laid Tess up. The shine of metal, where the paint was freshly scraped, marked the car's front left corner, outlining a concavity that looked like it had been punched. The headlight in that corner was shattered, too. I didn't know how Tess looked yet, but her car had a shiner.

My friend's face would have matched, were it not for some heavy foundation that matched her light brown skin, and the thick moussed bang arranged to fall over her left eye. But I didn't get the chance to look for long. By the time I'd climbed the stairs to her second-floor apartment, care package in hand, Tess was on her way out.

"Hey, should you have a doctor look at that?"

"Thanks, Mom!" She greeted me with a kiss and a quick hug, bending over me as if I were a child. "It looks worse than it feels." Standing back, Tess smiled and then winced, as her broad grin pulled at sensitive tissue.

"You sure?" She nodded, more carefully than vigorously as she reached for her coat. "Are my keys behind you?" I turned to look at the bowl sitting on her bookshelf, but Tess was already snatching up the heavy ring. She must have the keys to half Harvard there.

"What happened, anyway?" I've had my share of head

injuries. If Tess seemed unclear, I'd throw myself at her ankles to stop her.

"Checking for a concussion?" This time the smile was genuine, although I could see the last bit hurt her. She shrugged her long quilted parka onto her slim shoulders and stood still, looking at me. "Theda, I was stupid and the road was icy. I'm sore today, but it's just bruises and I'm basically okay."

"I saw your car." Standing in front of my taller friend, I leaned back against her door.

"Another ding, I know. And Vera's such a beaut." Tess's car was too old for airbags, and I was grateful for the vintage Volvo's heavy, all-metal construction. "But she's a solid old girl."

"Looked like you lost a headlight." Tess made a face. I gathered she hadn't noticed.

"God, I hope not. I don't want to lose my car to the shop, not in this weather."

"You don't think you should have it looked at anyway?"

"What? Vera? She's solid steel, Theda. I just don't want to get a ticket."

"What did you hit, anyway?"

"Just one of those concrete thingies. You know, to keep you from driving up on the construction?" She grabbed a pile of papers and folded them into her bag. "Nothing that's going to complain."

"And your head?"

"I missed this morning, already. Woke with a splitting headache, called in, went back to bed. But Lucy woke me about twenty minutes ago, and they need me."

"So, you're fine to go into work, but you canceled tomorrow night's gig?"

"It's deadline, Theda. You understand deadlines." She reached behind me to open the door and herded me down and out to the stoop. "We've got to get these results collated if we're going to make the grant deadline next week." I knew little of Tess's work except that it was nearby and had to do with how nerves functioned. That the Spinal Cord Foundation was one of their few reliable sources of funding, and despite their university backing, everything else seemed to be constantly up for renewal. "If we don't get it, it's my job and no job definitely means no new headlight for Vera."

"You're working too hard, you know that." I followed Tess to the curb, hustling to keep up with her long strides. She took one look at Vera and turned back onto the sidewalk, toward the university.

"I'm working hard, Theda. But I love it." In the sunlight, I could see where her skin was purpling under the creamy brown makeup. She looked drawn. "I know I'm only the data processor, one person on the team, but I feel like we're close to something. Everyone's so excited. If this round of tests works out like we think it will, there may be real-world payoffs. Real breakthroughs. People may walk again."

She was outpacing me now. I gave up, winded, and she spun around to wave gaily. "I'm fine, Theda. Don't worry so much!"

I smiled and waved back. Not until she turned the corner, did I realize that I hadn't even given her the orange juice.

THE CHOCOLATE I didn't mind keeping, and I managed to unwrap it and break off a corner as I drove home. By some prophetic instinct, I'd chosen my own favorite: dark, with almonds. The bright sun had melted most of the night's ice, and I relaxed with the candy and the music on the radio. Maybe I would get some work done, after all.

A black SUV cutting me off brought me back to earth, almost literally. The melt hadn't gone all the way to the pavement, and as I slammed on my brakes I felt my little Toyota start to skid. A parked Verizon van loomed. My car headed straight for it—and then stopped, sputtering out with a cough. Leaning my forehead on the steering wheel, I took a deep breath. The SUV was nowhere to be seen. Perhaps it hadn't even noticed me in my subcompact. Someone behind me had, and honked in impatience. Well, I was blocking a one-way, one of those small Cambridge streets that make the neighborhoods so cozy, and the driving so frustrating. Waving a chocolate-smeared hand, I restarted my little car and drove slowly away.

First Gail, and now Tess. I could almost add myself to the casualty list. This wasn't a good season to be on Cambridge roads, and I found myself thinking again about Gail's death. I hadn't wanted to listen, hadn't wanted to picture what had happened, but some of Bill's explanation must have sunk in. Violet had said that her death wasn't an accident. But according to Bill, nothing would be that straightforward. Most likely, he'd said, there was no sign that the car that had hit her had tried to stop. But there were a million other factors at play. The cops would have checked with the weather service, he had told me. They'd have figured out if the rain had been heavy enough to obscure visibility or if the reflection of a street light could have blinded a driver. There were a lot of reasons for an apparent lack of skidmarks, even beyond the sheer insanity of city drivers. Okay, maybe whoever had hit Gail hadn't braked. But just because the driver had not tried to stop didn't mean that someone had wanted Gail dead. Did it?

"WOW!" I HADN'T BEEN at my computer for more than ten minutes when the wailing started. "Woooo-wow!"

"Musetta! What is it?" I knocked my chair back to run toward the unearthly sound, convinced my cat had gotten her paw caught in a door hinge. Somewhere, she was hanging, trapped, in pain.

"Mrrroow!"

Then I saw her, coming down the hall. In her mouth she held the belt to my robe, the bulk of it trailing behind her. Somehow, with a mouth full of terrycloth, she still managed to howl, although in my presence the volume fell off greatly. "Wow?"

She dropped the belt and sat, looking up at me. "Meh?"

Waiting. I reached for her, and she stood on her hind legs to meet me, rubbing her head against my upraised hand. I scooped her up.

"What was that about Musetta? Did you kill this 'python' for me?" But her eyes were half closed with satisfaction and the only answer she gave was a deep, rumbling purr.

"IT'S THE ODDEST THING," I found myself telling Bill about Musetta's new trick a few hours later, when she had settled in for a long nap on the sofa. "I don't know if she thinks it's her kitten, if she wants me to play, or reward her for her kill or what."

"The cat killed a what?" I could hear the TV in the background. Sounded like more football.

"The belt to my terrycloth robe. She must have 'hunted' it and brought it to me." I didn't think I could explain Gail's feline behavior notes over the phone, especially with the Patriots as competition. How many times could they replay the playoffs?

"Maybe it's just a stage she's going through? Oh!" A recorded cheer went up. Goal? Touchdown?

"Maybe. But I'm wondering if it's because I'm spending so much time away from her these days. I mean, with the column and all…"

"And with coming over to take care of me, is that what you're saying?" I had all his attention now.

"Well, we used to spend most nights at my place, Bill. She's used to having me around."

He sighed, and the television sound disappeared. "Theda, if you don't want to come over as often as you do, I understand it. I know you've got your own life. But it's not like this is forever. I mean, a few more weeks and I'll at least be in a smaller cast. And if I can go to physical therapy, I can go to your place, too."

"I know." I flashed briefly on my new neighbor, and immediately felt like a heel. Better to focus on the cat, who had woken up and was staring at me with knowing eyes. "It's just that I wish I could make her understand, too."

"Well, you know you could bring her over here."

"I know." We were back on familiar turf, and that was somehow comforting. I reached over to pet Musetta and got nipped for my troubles. She knew guilt pets when she got them. "So what are you up to tonight, big boy?"

He laughed, and I heard the television come back on again. "Pre Superbowl analysis. They're replaying some of the old games and comparing defenses and offenses." I tried to make an interested noise, but he laughed again. "Okay, more my thing than yours. But I'd be willing to trade one hour for a 'Law and Order' re-run if you wanted to come by. I could have that new Vietnamese place deliver."

The offer was tempting. But part of being a rock critic is staying in touch. For every gig you write about, you have to see a dozen more. Otherwise, how do you know what's good or even new? Now that I was coupled, the pressure to go out almost every night presented more of a downside than I'd figured. But this gig was as close to my dream job as I was likely to get, barring the sudden retirement of the *Mail's* full-time staff critic. Work didn't necessarily come first in my life— that was a call I wouldn't make for the world, not yet, anyway—but I did have to give it precedence over cuddling, at least some nights.

"Gotta work tonight. There's a music thing happening at the Shamrock." Silence. I liked the idea that he was disappointed, rather than just watching the game. "But, tell you what. I'll come by after. It shouldn't be too late."

"I'll get an extra order of spring rolls and save them for you. And, Theda?" I waited. "If Musetta feels like stepping out, we can always make room for her, too." I was smiling as we hung up. Sometimes the status quo is just fine.

THREE HOURS LATER, I was back in the cold. The mercury had plummeted with the sun, and I regretted every bare inch of face that met the night. At least I'd spared myself the six-block walk from my building to the Shamrock. Cambridge is a quintessentially walkable city, even in winter. But I'd need the car to get to Bill's later, and knew myself well enough to avoid the temptation of a stop at home first.

"Hey, Theda." I pushed the heavy wooden door open into a world of warmth. The bright blue Michelin man who'd walked in right behind me stopped as his glasses steamed up, but even under the layers of down I recognized Mitch.

"Hey, Mitch." I pulled the scarf from over my mouth. "Cold enough for you?" He snorted and wiped his glasses. "I thought you'd have been here hours ago."

"Car wouldn't start. I was waiting for the Number 1 bus for hours. Days. At least twenty minutes anyway. I think my nose is about to fall off." He unzipped his heavy parka, waving to the bartender, who handed him a large canvas duffle bag from behind the oak bar. "So let's see what we've got here tonight."

Mitch didn't work for the Shamrock, per se. The corner bar, dominated by the portraits of Irish patriots, had no real music program and no stage. But it did have a cabaret license, meaning live entertainment was legal. And though most weekends the little pub would be packed with serious drinkers and college students who aspired to that status, early in the week was a different story. And in that gap, Mitch had seen an opportunity. Ingratiating himself with management, he'd made himself the organizer of its Monday night festivities. In return for a small cover—two or three bucks that he'd split between the musicians—he'd created another live music venue. The bar was happy. Anything that brought in drinkers on a Monday was good.

Mitch himself, a sweet, chubby guy with curly brown hair that defied style, served as the MC. A jovial host, his humor carried over into his songs, and his surprisingly deep voice could be heard even in a crowd. He always played, too, and that brought in some regulars, old friends like me and even some curious college types.

All of which made the night a good bet for the musicians

who came to play, and for me as a writer. For some musicians, this might be a first gig. For others, a chance to try something new, a different style or another instrument. The room might not look like much. The remains of some Christmas tinsel still hung from the broken trombone someone had jammed up into the acoustic tile ceiling. But Mitch's "Mixed Mondays" were getting a rep. That meant people were dropping by, and those that did were hearing new things.

But not just yet. The chubby guitarist was in his impresario role—producer, promoter, and soundman, all in one—as he quickly worked to turn the bar into a music club. He unzipped the canvas bag, packed with mic stands and cables. I tucked my own oversize messenger bag behind the bar as he handed me a mess of black piping, which I automatically started unfolding, extending the mic stand's metal base and angling the arm just right.

"Here." A coil of cords followed. "We're running late."

"Hey, I'm the critic, remember? Isn't this conflict of interest or something?"

Mitch looked at me over the black rim of his heavy glasses. He was trying for stern, but with his bright red cheeks the result was peeved gnome. I laughed, and he relented.

"Okay, okay. Let's get the first act on and I'll buy you a beer."

"That's definitely graft! I want a Jameson."

We got set up and Mitch bustled about. Turned out six of the dozen or so people in the long, narrow room were musicians scheduled to play that night. Mitch got the first trio, two guitars and a singer with a tambourine, set up and we retired to the bar.

"So, who are they?" The whiskey felt warm going down, and I was finally willing to shed my coat.

"These guys? They're brothers, at least the two guitarists are. They sent me a tape that had a hardcore Americana vibe, sort of urban 'No Depression,' real roots."

The song they'd just finished could have been a sea shanty, long wailing harmonies with some kind of Old World tang in the rising harmony. But the next, launched with one loud unison chord, had a definite rock edge. With the whiskey freeing my fancy, I heard the sound of a factory, of the long-gone industries that built the city in its throb and volume. Boston's rock roots from before the college kids discovered, and diluted, them. College kid that I had been, I longed for that tougher sound, and after the first chorus I found myself humming along.

"You'll go on next?" I saw Mitch look at his watch as the song ended, plaintive, unresolved. I nodded to the bartender, who refilled my glass.

"No, no." Mitch waved his hands, the master plan visible to him in the space before the stage. "Just keeping things moving. Louella Grub is next."

My face must have registered surprise. "You'll see. I have no idea if the name is real or not, but her sound is great. Sort of crazy country, but smart. Funny, too. I'll play after that, and then bring the Dan Rathers on."

By then, I knew from past experience, either the little pub would be full to bursting as other night workers, musicians and bartenders, free early on their "off" night came by—or completely empty. Given the weather, I'd bet on the latter, but that was fine. The musicians now here would stay to listen to each other, and so would I. Someone from this group would probably bring a guitar up to join the closers, and Mitch would have everyone jamming by the time the bartender announced last call. The take—if there was anything—would be minimal. On a good night, the bartender would look around and add to the pot, maybe giving Mitch as much as a hundred bucks to split, but nobody expected more. This kind of gig epitomized what I loved about clubland, the loose network of musicians and fans and venues. As much as Bill scoffed at my naïveté, I knew that at its heart were nights like this. No money, no fame. Just the joy of sharing music with friendly ears.

FIVE

"HELLO, NEIGHBOR!" I was fumbling with my finicky lock again as Reed bounced down the stairs.

"Good morning." Managing a smile for the handsome musician, I leaned into the door, and fought the urge to smooth my sleep-mussed curls. Of necessity, with his cast, Bill slept on his back. And that meant a night interrupted by snoring.

"You're out and about early." He turned as he passed, with a high-wattage smile that did more than the coffee I'd grabbed on my way home.

I smiled in return. Why not enjoy the illusion? But someone else had already heard my voice.

"Mrrrrup?" I could hear her outstretched claws reaching for the doorknob. "Rrow?"

"She's a slave driver." I earned one more of Reed's hundred-watt grins and reentered my real life. "Hey, little girl. What's shaking?" Her purrs answered me as I pushed open the door to find a catnip toy that I'd have sworn I last saw in the bedroom. "Want to play? Okay, fetch!" Even before losing my coat and hat, I tossed the small stuffed butterfly and she went running. This was a game we had developed from our earliest days together. Rarely did she actually bring the toy back to me when I threw it. But she sure loved chasing after it, and I loved watching her bouncing butt canter down my hall.

Fifteen minutes later, and we were both exhausted. But while she could recline for a brief bath and longer nap, I had to get to work. Swann's Way, in particular beckoned. How could my editor know more about a band than I did? Despite all the emphasis on "new media," I secretly doubted Tim was all that web savvy. But someone must have printed out the Swann's Way site for him, giving him a primer on the band. I googled their site and found pretty much what I'd expected: a quartet, all male, all white, with a fashionably scruffy look undercut by the smart production of their site.

Clicking through to their MySpace page revealed that, despite Tim's assurance, they were relative newcomers, not the next big thing yet, at least not if you counted web "friends." I downloaded a song, "What Madeleine Means," and listened while I read through their brief bio: Paul Berman, who seemed to be the main songwriter, had indeed come from the suburbs to attend MuzeArts. No word on whether he'd graduated, but here in the big city, he'd hooked up with a singer—another Paul, Paul Wexner—as a writing partner. The song reached its keyboard heavy conclusion, and I realized I hadn't been listening.

I hit "play" again, and tried to concentrate. Two repetitive riffs in, I found myself focusing on the bios, rather than the song. Reading between the lines, Paul Berman, who I started thinking of as "Paul One," seemed to have written what looked like a manifesto. He was probably the brains behind the operation, while Paul Two, Wexner, was taller, with better hair and the kind of round boyish face that would look good even when he hit fifty. He must be the chick magnet. The other two, Nate and Dave, sounded like support staff. They'd actually been in bands that had played out, at least in the 'burbs, but were only featured in group shots. The song had ended. One more time, I hit "play" but I knew what my ears were telling me. Nothing in this tune merited the attention. Still, if I had to write about them, I might as well get it over with. I began to take notes, and poked about their site, wondering when I could finally see these geniuses in action. There, under a tag about photography by the band—what a multitasking bunch!—was a listing for gigs.

"MuzeArts?" Behind me, on her chair, Musetta grunted and yawned. I'd woken her. "Musetta, they're playing the MuzeArts Hall in two weeks." Musetta might not be impressed, but I was. The college concert hall was a serious music venue: Visiting jazz performers and major-label acts performed there. Tickets ran twenty bucks or more. This was not your usual baby-band gig.

I needed more info. "Violet?" She answered on the first ring. "Have you heard of a band called Swann's Way?"

She snorted. In the background I heard a crash. "Hang on! Gustav, no!"

While she went after the tough-guy tabby, I read further. Sure enough, the band had only formed a few months before. But in a bio that was coy with the details, they hinted that some self-produced samples were generating heat. Supposedly enough major label interest existed to merit what they were calling their "true debut" at MuzeArts.

"Sorry, I'm back. Potted plant accident." Violet sounded breathless.

"Everything okay?"

"Yeah, just the usual around here." Last I'd counted, Violet and Caro had close to thirty cats underfoot. "Lizzy, the eight-year-old from the corner house, brought a rat in here." I shuddered, and Violet must have heard me. "No, a domestic one. It had gotten its foot caught in something. Its paw? Anyway, once I got the other critters settled in, I was able to do a simple dressing. It'll be fine. And that rescue tabby looks better, too. Ate like a little horse, washed up, and went to sleep. She's not in great shape. I don't know if it's worms or just something I couldn't catch, but Rachel will be by to check her out tomorrow." Until Rachel, who worked full-time as the city shelter's main feline vet, came by, I knew Violet would be keeping the feral isolated. "What's up?"

I told her about Swann's Way, about Tim's insistence that I write them up, and how stymied I was by their apparent early success.

"I mean, the first sample on their site was no great shakes. I don't get it."

"You're not listening for the right sounds, baby. They're hot if you listen right."

Violet's tastes ran to raucous, emotional punk. This wasn't making sense. "Vi?"

"The marvelous music of cash changing hands." She paused. I wasn't getting it. "They're rich kids, Theda. I bet they rented MuzeArts. I mean, why not? It's gotta be pricey, ten grand at least, but if you've got the cheese…. Political groups do it all the time." I knew she was right; I'd attended my share of community gatherings there.

"So, make a big splash and people will think you're a big deal?" This pissed me off. The club scene might not be perfect, but it had a system, a meritocracy of sorts, and I resented anyone buying their way out of it. "Do they really think people will think they're hot because of a fancy showcase?"

"That's my guess. I mean, it's already sort of working. Nobody heard of them before last month. But now…"

"You've heard of them?"

"Theda, girl, everyone has now. They've been all over the chat boards. Their fliers are everywhere. And their posters? Glossy, four color jobs! And, hey, something's getting them in the *Mail*, right?"

I had to agree. So much for keeping my ear to the ground. Maybe I *was* too old for this gig. But I wasn't going without a fight. Firing off an email to the band's press contact—whoever heard of a band at this level having a press contact?—I made myself listen to the site's three other downloads. By the time I heard the "ping" of my own email, I knew as much about Swann's Way as there was to know.

"Dear Ms. Krakow. The band would love to talk to you for a preview of their MuzeArts performance. Please call me to arrange a session."

A session? No matter, I called and found myself talking to

a young woman named Heather. She threw around phrases like "press access" and "understanding their mission," but her voice was high and tentative. Someone's girlfriend, I figured, but when she promised to call me back with an interview time, I gave her a pass on the pomposity. So many boy bands were managed by a long-suffering girlfriend, I couldn't blame her if she grasped at a professional veneer. Still, I didn't expect my phone to ring again as fast as it did.

"Theda?" We were on a first name basis then. "Can you meet me tonight? I can give you some materials. And, well, there are certain issues I'd like to get straight before we proceed with getting you access."

I didn't like the sound of that. I wasn't about to let the subject control the story; that way madness—or at least, celebrity journalism—lay. When you talk to a journalist who has identified herself as a journalist, then everything you say is on the record, and, no, you don't get to see it before it goes to press. But the woman—Heather—was undoubtedly new to management, or press, or whatever her title was, and she'd learn. I'd teach her if I had to. Tess's gig had been canceled anyway, so I agreed to meet her at the Casbah at nine.

This week's column took up the rest of my morning. I'd interviewed a band called Ambulette a few days earlier, and had dutifully transcribed the tape while I could still make out some of the less coherent ramblings. But even though I'd spent a cheery time with the four members, I was no longer thrilled about the piece. Yes, they'd gotten to work with their dream producer, a big name in Memphis soul, on their upcoming rootsy rock release, and they all had plenty to say about his quirky studio habits. Yes, the radio airplay that the first track was getting across the Midwest had been encouraging. But I just couldn't get worked up writing about them. Not anymore. After Mitch's Monday night, Ambulette just seemed too polished, too audience ready. How did the singer get his voice to crack the same way every time? In retrospect, even the interview seemed staged: were the drummer's jokes a little stale, like he had rehearsed them to use on interviews? I bounced around the room, making myself dance to the Ambulette album, but a slight bopping was all I could manage, and I regretted committing to them.

It wasn't that the music at Mitch's gig had been any better. The country singer, Louella, in particular had been troublesome. She had a good voice, true and clear, and her choice of material had been interesting. Old-school country, with all the heartbreak and none of the Nashville glitz. But she didn't seem to know if she wanted to satirize the done-me-wrong country sound or play it straight, taking a Tammy Wynette persona into the new millennium. The result had been confusing, with swallowed notes that should have soared and exaggerated emphasis on the more maudlin lyrics.

That's when it hit me, so elementary I could've slapped myself. Louella didn't lack conviction. She was still experimenting, trying out different approaches to a musical style that obviously held some attraction, but also harbored some truly awful clichés. If she could try something new out in public, well, so could I. I had my obligations: Ambulette had given me time, and—even more important—the *Mail* had sent a photographer. But backtracking and erasing, I cut their interview short and typed the code for a three-star break, a change in subject. Ambulette would be my lead, but the remainder of the column would focus on Mitch's Mondays, and the spirit of freedom they engendered.

Writing about that Monday, in particular Louella, gave me something to chew on, the kind of writing I like best. Critics who just give a "thumbs up" or "thumbs down" don't really offer much to the reader. A judgment, sure, but no information, no argument, no room for thought. But by explaining what Louella had sounded like, how she'd changed from song to song, and what I thought she was trying to do, I found my hook. Mitch's Mondays weren't about perfection, or even semi-polished performance. They were about trying things out, about process, and I threw myself into describing just such experimentation, and how the interplay with a live audience, no matter how small, helped a performer find her voice. That story put my lead, on Ambulette, in perspective. And much as it bothered me to admit, the trims improved what had been a humdrum interview. Satisfied with my morning's work, I backed the file up to re-read before sending, and began to think seriously about lunch.

"THEDA?" I'D PICKED UP the phone with my mouth full of turkey-and-chutney sandwich and gulped the half-chewed glob painfully, regretting the error of my ways.

"Bunny? Sorry, I was just having lunch." I reached for my OJ.

"You never called me back about Tess." I winced. She was right.

"I'm sorry. She seemed fine when I saw her and I guess it just slipped my mind." As if in illustration, some chutney leaked from my sandwich. I wiped it up with two fingers and ate the evidence.

"That's okay. I figured if it was anything bad, I'd have heard. But tell me now. She's okay, right?"

"Yeah. She's got a nasty shiner, but that's about it. She was actually on her way to the lab when I went by."

I heard a sigh. Then a crunch. Bunny must be taking her lunch at her desk, too. "That girl." I grunted in agreement. At least Tess's haste had resulted in my having fresh juice in the house. "I'm glad it was a truck."

I swallowed. "A what?"

"A truck. She said that she'd skidded and rear-ended some big construction truck, parked by the river. It always ices over there first."

This didn't sound right. I put down my glass. "I don't remember her saying anything about a truck, Bunny. I thought she hit a concrete girder or something."

"No, I'm pretty sure, because that's why she didn't worry about damage. It was something big that had to do with construction. A cement mixer or something else that didn't even dent."

"Well, she told me it happened around the construction. But a concrete girder. One of those road block things. Not a truck, I'm almost positive." Had one of us misheard her? How hard had she hit her head? "Bunny, are you sure she said 'truck' and not 'trunk,' or something like that? 'Cause I'll ask her about it."

"Maybe you should. I would swear she said 'truck.' Maybe she hit her head harder than we know." Bunny always was slightly psychic. "Or maybe she told us different things. But, Theda? Don't accuse her. You'll just scare her off, the way she is these days. Who knows? Maybe I didn't hear her right. I mean, she said 'car accident' and I went into panic mode. If she hit another vehicle, she wouldn't have just driven off, no matter how big it was, would she?"

I DIDN'T EVEN WAIT to finish my sandwich before calling Tess, but all my haste got me was her answering machine. When the phone rang again, as I was spreading chutney for one more go round, I jumped for it. The message I'd left for our friend had been vague. There was probably a good reason for the confusion, and Tess would end up laughing with me about it, so there was no reason to piss her off. Maybe Bunny had gotten it wrong. Maybe I had. Just the same, I wanted to clear this up.

"Theda? You live in Cambridge. What do you know about new riverside condos?"

It wasn't Tess, but the lack of a greeting was the giveaway. I knew that voice—and how to respond.

"Which ones?" Mina, editor of the *Mail's* glossy supplement, *"House"* supplement, expected her stringers to be up on everything house and garden. I wasn't, but I'd been freelancing long enough to fake it. "The new development by River Street or the conversion of the bottling plant?"

"That's going through? Been long enough."

Everyone knew about this but me, apparently. Still, I didn't want to paint myself into a corner. "It's just what I've heard around. Nothing's confirmed yet. But I can look into it!"

"That would be good." I could hear Mina typing. After two decades at the *Mail*, she still hunted and pecked. I waited. Her typing might be execrable, and her conversational style telegraphic but she was a good editor, with sound instincts. If she was booking the story into her schedule, then that conversion was more than a rumor. "I was thinking 'water views' for spring. Julie in Hull is doing the Cape and South Shore."

"I'd be happy to drive up to Gloucester…" Maybe I could even get Bill out of his apartment.

"No. I need urban. Southie. East Boston. Cambridgeport. Tell you what. Make some calls. Let me know. If there's anything, I'll take a thousand words by February tenth."

A thousand words at a dollar a word: I'd create a development if there wasn't one. Not that real estate in my beloved city was ever static. I'd find something, and as difficult as it might be to envision spring right now, I was enough of a pro to make the story work. As soon as we rang off, I called Patti, Violet's neighbor. A realtor, and a woman who wore pink without irony, Patti was also, at heart, a mensch. She'd adopted two of Violet's cats, and not just because they made a matched set. She'd know what was up, and if I could return the favor by mentioning her in the paper as a source, I would. We working girls had to stick together.

Of course, with Patti, it sometimes took a while to get to the point.

"Hi Theda, how are you doing, dear? How's that lovely man of yours?"

She knew about his knee. What she meant was how was our romance progressing. "We're fine, Patti. I mean, he's spending way too much time in front of the TV, but…"

"Now don't go trying to change him, Theda. Not now, anyway."

I rolled my eyes and bit back the comment. She'd been through a bad divorce, so I cut her some slack. "Patti, Patti, this is a business call." Silence at last. "I've been asked to write about new riverfront development and I thought you might know what's going on. If I can, I'll credit you."

"Oh, well. Of course." I could hear the disappointment, but she rallied quickly. "Now, let me see. There are some lofts being converted in the Fort Point area. You know, the arts district?" Most of the artists I knew had been priced out of the former industrial area long ago, but I grunted an acknowledgment. "I could get you the specs on that."

"What about Cambridge, all that heavy equipment and the road girders by the river?"

"I think that's municipal. Road work, you know, 'dig we must'?"

"And the old bottling plant?"

She paused, a rarity. "I'm not sure I'd want to steer any clients in that direction, dear."

I waited. Patti didn't take hints well. "But Patti, this is for a story. I'm not looking to buy—or even to sell to anyone. What's up?"

"There have been some issues with that." I remembered what Violet had told me about community action. Patti, a realtor but also a Cambridgeport resident, had a foot in both camps when it came to local development conflicts.

"Zoning issues? Neighborhood protests? C'mon, Patti, we're off the record. Spill."

"It's nothing I feel comfortable talking about, Theda. I've been told some things in confidence. Suffice it to say, I wouldn't put money down on those properties. Not anything using the existing structure, anyway."

"Patti? Come on, Patti."

"Now, I'll look into those Fort Point lofts and see what else I can find you." Her fake-cheery tone let me know she'd moved on. "Will tomorrow be soon enough? I've got a host of viewings today. Actually, Theda, one of them might be just perfect for you. Right in the area, with the cutest porch…."

"Patti, I'm a freelancer." Her doggedness made me laugh. "I'm lucky to make the rent."

"Yes, but your handsome man has a good job. Maybe he'd be interested in investing in a little love nest?"

"Goodbye, Patti. Call me when you have anything." I hoped she heard the affection in my voice. At any rate, I hung up. And, fighting the urge to leave yet another message on Tess's voice mail, focused instead on work.

I needed to send out more queries. The column was a good base, a steady check that showed up regularly in the box. But Mina's call had served as a wake up. Regular it may be, but "Clubland" didn't pay quite enough to cover all my expenses, not unless I wanted to be sharing those cans with Musetta. Even more important, I didn't want to completely rely on it—or on the *Mail*. I made sure I fulfilled the freelancer's number one key to survival: presenting clean copy, on time, each column one less problem for my editor to deal with. But being free-lance meant no security. Sure, I was free to sleep late or travel. The flip side was that anything—a drop in ads, the sudden appearance of someone's J-school dropout nephew—could cause Tim to drop me. Common sense prompted me to keep a few other irons warming up, and Mina's call reminded me that, in magazine land, winter had already given way to spring. Trying to summon vernal images, I grabbed Musetta, who squealed, but settled in with me on the couch, kneading my lap as I brainstormed. Warmth, fresh produce, shorts, deck chairs… I'd have to start writing these down.

I woke with a start that caused Musetta to jump to the floor. Something about the cold, or nights spent with a snoring partner, were getting to me. Tonight, I'd get in early, and sleep in my own bed. Until then, I could fire off a few queries: Fruit soups to the food editor of *Mass Bay Monthly*. Easy, nontoxic spring cleaning tips for *Cozy Life*. And the latest in porch and yard furnishings to *Yard and Sofa.* Did I know which trends would be hot in May, or even what besides vinegar made a good nontoxic cleanser? No, but I'd been in this game long enough to fake it, and if I got any nibbles, my research skills would take care of the rest.

SIX

I GOT TO THE CLUB a few minutes late. I never could just walk away when Musetta wanted to play. A smile to the bouncer on duty and I was downstairs, in the music room, where a small crowd had gathered for the first band. I nodded at some familiar faces. Ralph, staff critic for the *Mail,* was there, bellying up to the bar. For a moment, I had a flash of anxiety—was he on my story?—but no. The Casbah was his local watering hole, and he seemed more intent on getting the bartender's attention than on anything else. When he didn't return my wave, I figured I'd done my bit and looked around, picking out the Swann's Way manager immediately.

"Heather?" The slim brunette who turned toward me looked strangely out of place. It wasn't that her makeup was perfect. Lots of women put in the time, though hers had a little too much foundation for a face that couldn't have been more than twenty-five. Nor was it the shoes, pointy toed enough to hurt just looking at them. Or the fitted vest that came to the hips of her neatly pressed jeans. Even in the poor light, I could see the gold embossing on the portfolio she held; Swann's Way turned into a shiny logo. Very slick, the whole package, but not very rock and roll.

"Theda? I'm so pleased to meet you." She grabbed my hand a little too hard. "Thank you for meeting with me here, and on a Tuesday."

"I'm out most nights." That came out more as a brag than I'd intended, but something about her polish made me feel raggedy and defensive. I tried to cover with a smile as she handed me the portfolio. Her nails were flawless, dark maroon. "I mean, it's no problem. Are you here to see the first band?"

"Yes. We're thinking of working with them. Of bringing them into the Swann's Way family." Her eyes lit up. I nodded for her to continue as I leafed through the multi-page package. No press, as yet. That was a relief. But a lot of prose, photos, and a DVD. "You see, Swann's Way has been conceived as more than simply a band. The way we're positioning ourselves, as an organization—"

A wild shriek interrupted whatever Heather had been going to say and we both turned toward its source. Up front, where the band was setting up, a group of young women were horsing around. One in particular was laughing so loud she sounded nearly hysterical, her head thrown back to let her long blond hair cascade over her shoulders. It was her yelp that had interrupted us.

"Party starting early, I guess." Heather turned back to me, but I kept looking at the slim blonde. Her laughter had quieted, but kept on, like hiccups, and she reached for one of her friends for support. From the bar, Ralph looked over. The blonde was pretty, and pretty out of control. This was clubland; with a twinge of guilt, I turned away. "Someone's having fun."

"I suppose." Heather looked uncomfortable and glanced back over her shoulder. For all her poise, she now seemed uncertain of how to proceed. Her presentation had veered off script, and my heart went out to her.

"The dangers of doing business in a club." Taking her by the arm, I steered her away from the stage and the boisterous revelers. If the girl had looked a little younger, I'd have run interference. As it was, I breathed easier when Ralph turned back toward the bar. "Now, what were you telling me?"

She went back into her spiel, a little less certain this time through. But she gained confidence as she went on, telling me how the band, Swann's Way, was really just the first part of the business, Swann's Way. "There's no point in putting all this effort for just one project. With what we're putting together, we can handle marketing, distribution, and tour support." Five minutes in, she had hit her stride, her eyes wide with a novice's complete conviction. I held my tongue. Maybe there was a bigger story here than just one mediocre band. "We're looking into doing a co-op deal with a string of book and music stores. You know, set up Swann's Way displays and showcases throughout the …"

As soon as she stopped for air, I was going to ask her about the financing for such extensive ventures, Violet's words about "rich kids" echoing in my head. But before I had a chance, Heather's master plan was interrupted by a shove that sent the young believer flying into me. I'm tall enough, so that instead of us both stumbling to the sticky floor, I was able to grab and right her, and we both turned in response. Behind her, we could see the laughing blonde. She must have been heading toward the bathroom when she'd stumbled into Heather. Still not quite at the toilet's black-painted door, she turned and waved, the loose gesture almost throwing her off balance again.

"Sorry! Sorry, Heather!" She was hiccuping for real now, her face red and sweaty. She brushed back the hair that had fallen over her face and made a last lurch into the bathroom.

"Friend of yours?" No wonder Heather had looked uncomfortable.

"Amber? I just know her from around." Heather was blushing as crimson as the blonde. I handed her her bag, a smart leather satchel, which I'd caught when she fell into me, and gave her a minute to regain her composure. She started to take a compact out, realized where she was and put it back. "I'm sorry you had to see that." She gushed, and then laughed a little, nervous. "That girl, I mean." It was nothing, I was going to say. Not for clubland. Nor was it any big deal to me if she wanted to dab on some powder or check her lipstick. This was rock and roll. She could go wilder than that. But just as I was picking the right words to reassure her, another woman came running out of the bathroom, short, round, and out of breath.

"Somebody call an ambulance!" She ran up to the bartender who stared in surprise. "Call an ambulance!" She slapped both hands down on the bar. "Are you listening? There's a woman in there who's having convulsions. I think she's stopped breathing!"

A HALF HOUR LATER, Heather and I were seated at the diner next door, and I was her new best friend. The EMTs had come and gone, carrying out the blonde, still and silent on a stretcher. The young businesswoman's starch had gone with them.

"Theda, that was just horrible. The way she lay there." I'd bullied her into ordering soup, wanting to get something hot into her. But she just stared into the bowl in front of her. "Horrible. Do you think she'll be okay?"

"I don't know." I sipped my own coffee and watched her droop further. My honesty wasn't helping. "She's young," I offered. "She looks like she was otherwise healthy, fit, together. That's got to help." I was losing her. "I mean, you tell me, did she do this kind of thing often?"

The question seemed to rouse her more than my lukewarm optimism. "No, I mean, I didn't know Amber that well. But, I don't think so."

"Have some of that soup while it's still warm." She picked up the spoon and dragged it through the broth. "Where do you know her from?" If she wasn't going to eat, I wanted to keep her talking.

"Just around. The clubs. You know, since I've started working for Swann's Way. She's been seeing someone I know and, well, I thought we had things in common."

I reached out to her. "Heather, you're not her. I mean, she'll probably be fine. Probably has a massive hangover right about now." I tried to laugh. "But she's not you. Look, you're out meeting with the press. Setting things up. Making things happen."

"Thanks." She looked up at me and tried a smile. "I'm sorry about all that, how I reacted in there. I mean, I know I'm not her. I'm new at this. But I do take my management responsibilities seriously."

I had to smile back. How many other women—girlfriends, friends of the band?—had said exactly those words? But, hey, it would be a learning experience. Maybe she'd end up in business school. For now, she was getting her poise back, and I had a column to write.

"Of course you do, and they need you. When are you going to get me together with Swann's Way? You're their manager. Make it happen."

"WHAT'S UP, BABE?" It was close to eleven by the time I got home, and I was glad Bill was still awake.

"Just a lot of weirdness." I'd played it calm for Heather, but the night had unnerved me, too. That girl had seemed so full of life. Silly, maybe, but vibrant. Too full of energy to be as still as she had been, when they'd taken her out. As I told Bill about it, I found myself puzzling even more.

"I mean, she was high as a kite. But on a Tuesday? The music hadn't even started yet."

"Addicts don't need an excuse."

"No, Bill. You're not hearing me. She was a young girl, she looked clean and put together." It was the disparity, the lack of sense about the whole thing. But as I tried to gather my impressions into some kind of coherent thought, I realized Bill was no longer on the line. Through dead air, I heard a door close, and he picked up again. "Do you have someone over?"

"A couple of the guys. Don't worry, I'm in the bedroom. I just wanted to be able to think about this." I envisioned his cop buddies, several pizzas, beer. Was there a sports broadcast every night of the week? "Okay, that's better." I heard a few loud thuds and imagined him hopping over to his bed. "Theda, you know, I've been hesitant to say anything to you. I know how you feel about your 'scene,' and I don't want you to get bent out of shape. But we have been seeing a rise in drug-related incidents recently."

"In homicide?" That was his beat.

"No, honey, but in the city and in Boston. There've been a few reports and we've had some medical people in to talk with us. Ecstasy, GBH, even some new hybrids that haven't been named yet. Anyone with basic chemistry and a basement with decent ventilation can start experimenting, if they've got people fool enough to try their creations. They're out there, and young people are taking them. This could be what we're talking about here."

It didn't make sense to me. "Bill, those are disco drugs. That's for, like, all-night loft parties. Raves, if anyone does those anymore. That's a whole different scene. Rock's always been more about pot and beer."

"And speed and heroin, Theda." He must have heard my inhalation of breath. "And don't say it. I know your scene is important to you. I know it's a 'creative community.'" I didn't like the way he said that. "But there are bad apples in any community, Theda."

"She just didn't seem the type, Bill." I couldn't explain it any better. "I mean, maybe she was the type to pop a pill at a party. But there was no party going on."

"Maybe someone was planning one. Those new pharmaceuticals can all be used as date rape drugs, Theda." I thought back to the laughing girl. Her inhibitions certainly seemed low. Still, something didn't ring true. "She was with a bunch of her girlfriends!"

"Baby, I don't know. Maybe someone slipped it to her earlier? Maybe one of her friends has some issues? People are weird."

I settled down into the sofa to mull that one over. My old orange juice glass was still sitting on the coffee table. I guess I wasn't much better at housekeeping than Bill, though it did make me think.

"Bill, when the cops look into an accident, they gather paint chips, stuff like that, right?" I wasn't going to dime Tess, but I didn't like not knowing what had happened that night.

"When they can, Theda. But it's not like on your TV shows. Massachusetts doesn't even subscribe to the big paint databases. It costs too much for the little info they can get. We're usually better off looking at skidmarks. Rubber on the pavement tends to last. But if there's been rain or snow, a lot of other evidence gets washed away. Usually, we're stuck canvassing for witnesses or waiting for auto-body shops to call in about suspicious damage."

I wondered if Tess had gotten her headlight fixed yet.

"What's up, Theda? Are you thinking of that animal rescue woman?"

"Well, sort of." Tess's accident had been in the same part of town, the same night. But it had been a bad night. And the friend I knew and loved wouldn't have driven away from that kind of an accident. Would she? Bill was still talking. "Physical evidence can be elusive at a busy intersection. There's just too much debris. But I'm sure our people are on it."

"You couldn't just ask them about any paint chips, could you?" Gail had been killed the night of the ice storm, and plenty of freezing rain had followed the snow and sleet. But Tess's car had such a distinctive color that even a little bit of paint might show up. I both wanted and didn't want to know.

Bill sighed. He hated when I pushed my way into his work. "Well, Collins would kill me if he knew why, but I'll give him a call tomorrow. See what they've found." Sometimes I think he hated his work.

"I thought you said you had the guys over?" I could hear my voice rising. We'd been together too long for me not to trust Bill, but I'm human.

"Different guys. These are some folks from the New England Jazz Club. They heard I was laid up. Bob brought over the new Fats Waller reissue."

"I didn't know you were in a jazz club." Often, when I came by, some kind of instrumental music was playing. But Bill usually took it off as soon as I showed up.

"Yeah, we're basically only online buddies. I don't get to many shows, as you know." Was that a dig? "But we trade recordings—even CDRs sometimes, now that we're eking into the new century."

The idea of Bill burning a CD made me laugh.

"You sound better, honey. Are you okay now?"

"Yeah." I'd wanted to come home, spend a night in my own place, with my own cat. But hearing Bill say that made me wish for his warm bulk. "Tonight just freaked me out." I paused. "I miss you, sweetie."

"I miss you, too. You could come over, you know. The guys won't stay all night."

"No, I'm fine. I just needed to hear your voice."

"Sweet dreams, honey."

SEVEN

"THEDA, WAKE UP!"

I'd grabbed the phone out of instinct, as Musetta had kicked free from under my chin.

"I'm awake."

"No, you're not." Violet knew me too well. "Sit up." I did. "Theda, you're not going to guess who just came by here."

"Elvis?" I'd slept like a log and didn't take the early morning call lightly.

"Almost. The cops. They had a bunch of questions for me."

"Questions? About what?" Now I was awake. Although she made an exception for my guy, Violet didn't like cops much. Still, if she'd needed bail, she'd have gotten to the point faster, wouldn't she?

"About Gail's accident. Death. Something's definitely up." She had shaken the last bit of drowsiness from me now. "They know I was in touch with her and they wanted to find out what was going on with her. To be honest, I think they also wanted to see if I had a car, see if I could have killed her."

"They know you have the van?"

"Yeah, though I told them I didn't have it Sunday night. Sue had picked it up earlier so she could move her drums. They still checked it out, though."

Tire tracks. Bill had said the investigating officers would be looking for those. But if there weren't any skidmarks, what else were they asking about? Did Violet's van have any suspicious dents? "You think you're a suspect?"

"I don't know. I didn't get that vibe, though. I mean, they

asked me to come in for some questions, but when I said, 'No way,' they were cool with it. We sat here for a while instead. Sibley even came in and he's a good judge of situations."

I didn't quite trust the cow-spotted cat's instincts. He had too good a heart. But Violet sounded calm. "So what did they want to know? And what do you think the cops are after?"

"Well, you're going to have to ask Bill for the details. He can get the dirt. But the cops were definitely acting like the whole thing was hinky—asking, like, what was Gail into? Who were her enemies?"

This was more than an accident, more even than some stupefied drunk driver. "They think someone was gunning for her." Violet didn't answer, but I knew we were on the same track. "But why Gail?" I thought of my own dislike for her. "I mean, what was she working on recently?" Gail did have a history of making enemies.

"Just the feral rescue, as far as I know. It had become her new crusade, her big thing. She wasn't even that into the Animals Now stuff, anymore."

"No more blood tossing? No more sit-ins?"

"Seriously, Theda. She hadn't quit Animals Now or anything, but the cats were her main thing. That's why Ruth— you know, the big girl you met?—was so pissed at her. Gail had kind of dropped out of the whole Animals Now scene."

"Plus, she took their cages." A stray thought poked into my sleepy brain. "You don't think her dropping the Animals Now folks could've gotten her killed, do you?" It didn't make much sense, but murder seldom did. "You know, like she'd become a turncoat or something?"

"You know, I was wondering about that, too. I mean, those guys can be flat-out weird. But I can't see it. First, Gail wasn't a traitor. She'd never turn those guys in, no matter what they were planning." That made my ears prick up. "And more important, what she was doing wasn't that out of line. Animals Now has always been into the whole indie thing. You know,

DIY. Do it yourself. I think it fits into the whole 'cell' concept: Communal anarchy. Independent evolution." And little chance of an outsider learning about the entire organization, I kept the end of that thought to myself.

"Besides, bottom line, none of those guys drives." Violet was still talking. "Licenses are just the government's way of keeping track of us, fossil fuels destroy the environment, and all that."

"They have a point there." I couldn't resist. Violet snorted. "But that's a little simple. Are you sure there's nobody in the group with a car?"

"Oh yeah. I cannot tell you the times I've been called for a ride." She sounded honestly exasperated. "Nobody drives, nobody can spell you on the driving. But nobody wants to take the bus to Springfield or New York when there's an action planned."

"Hell, I didn't realize you were so close to them. Still, if the cops are going to talk to anyone…"

"They already did. At least, that's what I can figure. In fact, I think Ruth gave them my name. She's still sore about the third trap. But I'm pissed at her, too. I mean, we both saw Gail's notes. There were kittens missing! Though by now…"

"Vi, we looked everywhere." I hated being the voice of reason, but she didn't argue. I tried to think of everything else on my plate. "Hey, Violet. You talk to Tess at all?"

"No. I mean, she's okay and all, but she's more your friend. I used to see her around a lot, though. She hasn't been playing out much, has she?"

"She's deep into work these days. The project she's working on is up for a big grant." Suddenly, I didn't want to bring up my suspicions. Violet and Tess weren't close. If Tess was hiding something about her own car accident, Bunny and I would winkle the truth out of her. And just because she worked in a lab didn't mean that she and the Animals Now crowd were at odds. That she'd have a grudge against Gail, did it? Knowing Violet's own inclinations, that wasn't something I wanted to get into over the phone, but there was one question I could ask: "You never saw Tess with Gail, did you? Or with the Animals Now crowd? At a protest or anything?"

"Tess?" Violet was laughing. "She's way too uptown for that crowd. They'd bomb the university before they worked there. And, to be honest? Her music would fly right over their heads, too. Way too subtle, all that finger-picking and the metaphorical imagery. Very witty, very cool. I like it, though. She should get back to it."

"I'll mention it to her." If I could ever get her on the phone. Our recent history didn't bode well. But Violet wasn't part of that. "She respects you a lot."

I could hear the smile in Violet's voice. "Really? Wow. That's cool. That's really cool." My punk rock friend never ceased to surprise me.

I WAS MAKING COFFEE when the phone rang again and I leaned in to hear the machine. If it were Bill I'd pick up. Before we'd hung up, I'd promised Vi that I'd try to get her questions answered and, besides, I missed waking up with him. And if it were Tess, I'd grab it, too. That girl owed me some answers. But just in case, I waited. Editors are like young animals. The best way to train them is to ignore them. Any response at all— certainly, any response before ten a.m.—just encourages them to repeat the behavior.

"Theda? Theda, darling?" It was Patti, Violet's realtor neighbor. I reached for the phone.

"Morning, Patti. I was just making coffee."

"You freelancers! I bet you were out late last night." I smiled and, rather than disabuse her of her romantic notions, asked what was up.

"The early bird, and all that." God, she was chirpy. "I took the sweetest young couple around to a few two-bedrooms up on Avon Hill this morning. They wanted to see them in morning light, before they went off to work. I think they're going to make an offer on an adorable little place right on Raymond. But if they don't, Theda, it's extremely reasonable…"

"Thanks, Patti. Believe me, when Bill and I are ready to buy, we'll let you know."

"Oh, she's saying 'when' now!" I laughed; she'd caught me. "But, Theda, that's not why I'm calling. You asked about waterfront property?"

"Great." I grabbed a yellow legal pad and ballpoint. "What've you got?" A lot apparently. Although the spring selling season was still months away, the hot-and-heavy Greater Boston real estate market never really hibernated. With Patti's inside knowledge, I soon had notes on two commercial properties that were going condo and a new construction project, all in either South or East Boston.

"Artist-style loft living has become increasingly desirable…." Patti couldn't help slipping into sales mode. Musetta, meanwhile, was eyeing my pen. Her quick jabs didn't improve my handwriting any, but I was ready for them and managed to get the facts down. Patti's superlatives left plenty of time for play. "And the new development in Maverick Square will feature breathtaking panoramas."

"Yeah, if you don't mind looking at the airport." She gasped slightly and I realized I'd voiced my thought aloud. "I mean thank you, Patti. This is great." I wrestled the pen back from my cat. "Now what's up with our area? I can't imagine Cambridge waterfront is lagging behind Boston. You hear anything more about the old bottling plant?"

"That's a complicated situation, Theda."

"I can imagine." Cambridge, even if it is the People's Republic, probably has more rules and regulations than most cities. "Let me guess, a neighborhood group is filing for a variance, or something?"

"Do you even know what a variance is, darling? But no, it's more complicated than that."

I waited, trying to distract Musetta with the catnip butterfly. Patti, meanwhile, said nothing, which in itself was unusual. "Come on, Patti. Spill. Are there problems with the tenants who've been subletting? Is there something toxic in that old heap that's going to leak into the Charles?"

"Don't even joke about that, Theda Krakow. Everybody doing new construction by the water worries themselves sick about that. It's the bane of the industry." Not to mention the wild fowl and our water table. "But no, no problems of that sort. Not that I've heard anyway."

"So what have you heard?" Silence. "Just for me, off the record?" For a friend, I'd bend the rules.

"This has to be private, Theda. I mean, lives could be at stake." I started to laugh, but Patti didn't. "You're serious, aren't you?"

"As the grave, Theda."

"Okay, then. I promise. Just for me, and that's it. What's up?"

"Well, nobody knows for sure what exactly is going on. But one of the developers got a threatening phone call, and someone else who was checking out the grounds came back to his car to find his tires slashed. Two of them, so he couldn't even change to a spare."

"Someone's threatening developers? But that's criminal. We should—"

Patti cut me off. "Now, Theda, you promised. Yes, obviously such actions are illegal. And believe me, Peter Wilson of Wilson and Crave is not a man to be intimidated. He's had his lawyer talk to the chief of police. But it's very sensitive. It's right on the edge of an established neighborhood." Yeah, I thought. Ours. "Plus, Peter doesn't yet have all the permits in place, and there may be some neighborhood feelings about his plans for luxury high-rises."

I could imagine what those feelings were. Most of our neighbors were the peaceful sort. I'd expect to see petitions or maybe some kind of demonstration at the site, with people making speeches. We'd stopped development before, without anyone getting hurt. Of course, we had to know what was happening first.

"So, has any of the paperwork been filed yet?" I knew several community watch groups that kept their eyes out for new construction and demolition applications.

"No, Theda. And you can't, you just can't say anything." I bit my lip. I had promised. But I could make a few calls, let some people know that they should be on the lookout. The bigger question was, who knew already? And who would resort to violence?

"I promise, Patti, I won't say anything. But someone's already onto Peter, what was his name? Wilson. You think he's got a rival?"

Patti gave a little huff. "Not in this town."

"Well, someone doesn't like him, or doesn't like his plans." I tried to think of who would get physical, especially this early on when everything was just rumor and surveyors, and realized I had a good idea. If Ruth and the other Animals Now folks took offense at feral cats, what would they think of big shot developers?

"You think it might be an environmental group, like the Animals Now people?" Not that I wasn't sympathetic. But I was essentially nonviolent, and this wasn't my fight. Not yet.

"Are they the ones who freed all those lab rats?" She shuddered when I confirmed what had been one of their less well thought-out "rescues." More proof that the group wouldn't necessarily wait to work through legal channels. "Five dozen of those animals, wasn't it? Yuck!"

"Actually, they're very smart and very clean, Patti. Almost like cats." I was teasing, and she took the bait. Musetta, who had settled down for a nap by this point, gave me a look.

"Don't you say that about my beloved pussums! You're being evil."

"You're right. I'm sorry."

"That's okay, darling. Ick. But anyway, no, I don't know the details, but I don't think the threats came from that group. I mean, I'll mention it. Always good to have something to suggest to Peter Wilson. But I seem to recall that he had them checked out after the first call."

"Checked out?" Somehow that sounded scarier than any Animals Now threat, and I thought again of Gail. Had she been threatening to get in the way of the bulldozers? "What do you mean—and would he do anything illegal?"

"Why would he? He's got more than sufficient legal resources for any situation, Theda. Big lawyers, all on payroll." She chuckled, but I didn't see the humor. "What he does stands up in court, they make sure of that. I'm not worried about Peter Wilson. But, as I tried to tell you, and, please Theda, it would be worth my livelihood if this went further, I still wouldn't recommend anybody investing in that property just yet."

SHE'D GIVEN ME a lot to think about. Who would threaten a developer? And what would any of those people do to strike back? But as much as I didn't like real estate speculation, particularly on my home turf, I also saw the sense in what Patti had said about money and lawyers. Why would a wheeler-dealer like this guy Wilson resort to violence when he could buy the results he wanted? Patti had also, goddess bless her, given me a good start on my real estate story. So coffee in hand, I typed up my notes while I could still decipher them and checked my email. Nothing from Heather. She had been badly shaken up, but I had a piece to write. With a sigh, I reached for the phone.

"Hi, Heather. This is Theda. I hope you're feeling okay today. I'm calling to see if we can schedule an interview with Swann's Way. We do want to get this piece in before their MuzeArts debut." I figured pitching the story as a feature to the band's advantage couldn't hurt, might even spur her burgeoning professional pride. But while I waited for the young businesswoman to set up an actual face-to-face with the giants who were Swann's Way, I had some more basic investigating to do. The glossy package that Heather had handed to me was thick with photos and filler, creative folderol about how the band members saw themselves, and their artistic "mission." But in terms of real info there was nothing. Who were these guys? Those few songs I'd heard sounded extremely mediocre, and if they were plotting world—or at least Boston—domination, I needed to know more.

Back to the computer, although this time I skipped the band's site for a more general search. Typing in "MuzeArts Ensemble," brought up an announcement of a performance from four years back that confirmed that the two Pauls had attended the music school. Were the other two members real partners, or just hired help? Their names came up with some other bands, nothing big, and that left the question open. Clicking back to the music college, I opened a page called "Alumni Updates." Neither had posted anything. Didn't mean they hadn't graduated, though they seemed like the kind of self-promoters who would be bragging about their new band if they had. I typed in "Peabody" with their names and found what looked like a live link to a fan's page. When I clicked through, however, all I got was a "Thank you, your message has been sent." That was frustrating; I hadn't typed anything in.

I love the Internet, but at times like this it's maddening. Time to go old school: They say a good journalist can find out anything with three phone calls. As a freelancer, I prided myself that sometimes it didn't even take that many. For good measure, I tried Heather's cell again, and again got her voice mail. Directory assistance wasn't much more useful, though I did unearth a number for the drummer. A group rental didn't seem likely for this pampered crew, but it was a start. The voice on the machine sounded sullen, or half asleep, but I left a message and thought about where to make that magic third call.

"College of Musical Arts, office of public relations. May I help you?"

"Hi, Josie. It's Theda." As annoying as publicists can be, there are times when a freelancer needs the official mouthpiece.

"Hey, Theda. What's up? Did you get my latest mailing about the spring concert series?"

"Indeed I did." Now wasn't the time to tell her that I'd tossed it. A cappella swing and student clarinet recitals were not my thing. "But actually I'm wondering if you can help me with a different matter. There's a concert coming up in the MuzeArts Hall?" I gave her the date and the band's name. Sure enough, she didn't have it on the school's official roster of events.

"It could be that an outside group or promoter is presenting it or that a student group or department has rented it for a private event, Theda. Would either of those be a possibility?"

"Definitely could be." At least I'd gotten confirmation of one thing. Swann's Way weren't playing the big hall as a school-sponsored concert. Either they had rented it, or they had a big backer. A very big backer: Josie knocked a few thousand off of Violet's estimate, but it still sounded like renting the hall would cost at least six grand, once all expenses were paid. Could there be a sugar daddy involved? From what Heather had told me, it seemed likely that the big backer for Swann's Way, the band, was Swann's Way, the fledgling music industry-to-be. But since I had Josie on the phone...

"One thing, though. The band went to MuzeArts, at least the two principals did. I don't know if they graduated. Would there be any way to get some info on them—even just when they studied there—from alumni affairs?"

"I can put you through to them."

I sighed. Alumni affairs always gave me the run around. In all fairness, the alumni office's job was to help the college's grads, not to provide information to journalists. "Josie, you don't think you could put the request through for me, do you? It is related to a concert on campus, after all, and it just would all go a lot more quickly that way."

She hesitated, but only for a moment. "Of course, Theda. I'll call over there as soon as we get off the phone. I'll give them your contact info, but maybe if it comes from me, they'll be a little more forthcoming." She'd read between the lines, and I waited for her to call in the favor. "And while I have you here, may I tell you about our guest lecture series for spring?"

BY THE TIME I'd dutifully listened, and even made some notes, on the upcoming events, it was getting close to eleven. Musetta had gone off about her business and I was feeling a little stir crazy. January does that to me, at the best of times. And since this was my first winter as a freelancer, I was learning that it was worth the effort to go outside no matter what the weather. Even a brief outing could shake off cabin fever.

But when I looked out my front window, I was in for a surprise. The sunshine beating down was reflected not on ice but on what definitely looked like puddles. Yes, a car drove by, splashing up one such reflective surface and, as if on cue, a large drip splashed on my sill. It might only be thirty-five degrees or so, but the bright sunshine lit up my spirits. In a few months, this would seem like nothing. Right now, a January thaw was a gift to be enjoyed.

I rummaged in the closet for my oldest sneakers, the sidewalks would probably be a slushy mess, and layered an old turtleneck over my T-shirt and under my sweatshirt. In less than ten minutes, I was on my front stoop, breathing in air that not only wasn't frigid but was actually moist and almost fragrant. After a month of chapped lips and flyaway hair, this felt like heaven. I hit Play on my iPod and launched myself on the world.

And nearly on my butt: Frozen patches still alternated with dampness, and catching myself just in time I realized I'd have to be careful. No matter, it had been weeks since I'd had a proper run. A bit of restraint wasn't a bad idea.

Three blocks in, and I was flying. "Everything on the hog, everything on the hog is good!" It's an illusion, but I like to think that when I sing with headphones on, I sound like the singer on the record. The accordion probably drowned me out anyway. "Everything…" The shock on Reed's face as I turned a corner and into him disabused me of this notion. But, c'mon! He was from New Orleans, he must have at least a passing knowledge of zydeco.

"Morning!" I yelled, the music still loud in my earbuds.

"Same to you," I believe he said, smiling, before moving on. Then it hit me.

"Reed?" I chased the few feet after him and turned off the head set. "You're at MuzeArts you said, right?" A nod confirmed that he was.

"Well, I'm wondering. I'm writing a piece about a band that I think is renting the hall." He waited and I realized I was panting. Those few weeks had taken their toll. I leaned forward, hanging my head down and took two deep breaths before trying again. "Sorry." I was undoubtedly red-faced, but at least I could talk. "What I'm wondering, is there any way to find out if a show was programmed by a class or student group, some kind of booking that wouldn't show up on the official roster of events?"

"Maybe." He looked puzzled. "It might help me if I understood what you were getting at."

He had a point. "There's a band in town, they call themselves Swann's Way." His eyebrows lifted. "Exactly. Pretentious and not very good. But they seem to have a show at MuzeArts. Now, the public affairs office has no record of this, which makes me think it isn't a MuzeArts production. But that doesn't mean that some department or alumni group isn't sponsoring it. Now, what I suspect is that Swann's Way are a bunch of rich kids with more money than talent, and that they've rented the hall. If that's the case, I'd like to call them on that. But I'd like to know before I speak with them. That way, I can present it as a fait accompli, you see?"

"I do see, and my hat is off to you, Mademoiselle Journaliste." He didn't actually doff his cap, a smart black wool beret, though he did tip his head. "I knew you wrote about music, but I didn't realize you were in the habit of exposing artistic fraud."

He was smiling, but there was a serious note in what he said. "I wish," I smiled back. "I do my share of boosterism, I'll confess. But in a case like this, where it seems like someone is making a splash with cash, it gets to me, you know?"

"I do indeed. What's the date?" I told him and he promised to get back to me. I clicked my music back on and, dodging through the puddles, commenced singing once more.

BY THE TIME I got home, my machine was flashing. With any luck, Heather was one of the new messages. I could write quickly, but I hated not knowing when or how I was going to get an interview. The first message was from her, but not exactly what I'd bargained for.

"Theda? This is Heather, returning your call. I've spoken with Swann's Way, and they'd like to know what you intend to ask—"

I grabbed the phone and dialed her number before even listening to the rest.

"Theda? I just left a message for you."

"Yes, I know, Heather." There was no point in getting angry at the messenger. "I heard it. What I need to know is if Swann's Way want to be profiled in my column in the *Boston Morning Mail*. Because, if they do, we need to set up an interview, pronto."

"Yes, that's what I told them and they want you to make a list—"

This was too much. "Look, Heather. I'm not going to submit my questions to them in advance. I don't work that way—no real journalist does. We get together, we talk. If they don't want to tell me something, that's their prerogative. But that's how interviews are conducted in the real world."

"They just want to—"

"Control the media, I know." I was working up a head of

steam. "But Heather, that's not how it's done. Tell them that if they want an interview, they have to agree to a time, and soon. In fact, if they don't I can just do the story without them."

"Without talking to the band?"

"Sure. I've got my sources." I was stretching a bit, using a technique I'd picked up from doing straight news. You call someone and tell them you're writing a story. They can tell you their side, or not. You're just giving them the option—a courtesy call, almost. Most of the time, if they're involved, they'll end up agreeing to talk. The trick didn't quite translate to arts coverage. Who would want to read a profile of a band, when the band hasn't been interviewed? But if I had to, I could always report on them as a phenomenon, such as it was, and critique their music. And besides, I had a feeling these guys would want to be heard.

"I'm sure they… I'm sure that Swann's Way will agree to an interview." Her breathless response reassured me my bluff had worked. "They just wanted to be prepared. I'll talk to them and get back to you right away."

"Great, thank you Heather." I felt a twinge of guilt for bullying her. It went away. "I may be out this afternoon, but just leave me a message and we'll set something up."

While I was in the phone zone, I called information for Wilson and Crave. Yes, I'd promised Patti not to butt in. But I had a legitimate story to research, didn't I? The call got me nowhere, however. Voice mail to the receptionist and then forwarded to "press relations." I left my contact info, dropping the name of the *Mail* twice to lend some legitimacy to my home number. Phone tag was three quarters of the job, and now a Mel Baker was it.

Happy that things were finally moving, I put more zydeco on the stereo and blasted it loud enough to hear as I showered. "She's a hot tamale baby!" The Louisiana dance music got my blood moving. Maybe I'd been too immersed in rock recently, I thought as I grabbed the loofah. Maybe the more complicated rhythms of accordion and washboard were what I'd settle into as I aged out of the rock scene. Or just maybe, in the dead of winter, I needed something Southern to warm me up.

I felt the pounding on the door more than heard it, and grabbed my robe before turning the stereo down.

"Miss Krakow? Miss Krakow?" It was Julian, the super. I opened the door a crack.

"Sorry. Was my music too loud?"

"Well, I figured you were home. But no, nobody's complained." Even though I have a cat, which is expressly against the rules on my lease, Julian seemed to like me. I work at home, and that meant I could take in everyone's packages, let in repair people, and the like. But at times, I suspected his fondness went further. And that he'd heard my shower running. I pulled my robe closer. "It's about the heat."

A moment of worry grabbed me. "What about the heat?"

"Well, this old building—the radiators aren't working as they should be. Management is considering some upgrades."

Great, there went my affordable rent. "Mine work fine. Sometimes too well in fact."

"Yeah, that's what a lot of the other tenants have been saying. Strange." He looked at me. I tried to keep a straight face. "Anyway, he's going to have someone check 'em out. Bleed the air out of them and see if they can be retrofitted for some easier control dials."

"Control dials?"

"Yeah, so you can turn the heat down when you go out. Save some money, not have to open the windows in the middle of the night. Anyway, we'll be sending some guys by, so I wanted you to know."

"Okay. I'll keep an eye out for them." How did he know I opened my windows at night? I pulled my robe closer still. "Thanks."

I made sure every shade in the apartment was fully drawn before I got dressed. But I was still blasting the Zydeco Cha-

Cha's when the phone rang. I turned down my volume in time
to hear Violet, but there was something playing behind her, too:
fast, loud, with a rhythmic bass marking as much melody as
time. It had a pulse, a living beat.

"Okay, I still like rock."

"What?" Violet shouted over the phone.

"Never mind!" I shouted back. "What's up?"

"You like it?" I did, though I was grateful when she turned
it down.

"Yeah, what was it?"

"Guess."

The smile in her voice gave it away. "The Violet Haze Experience? Sounds great. That must be new, right?"

"Yeah, we've been recording some of our new songs. We're
thinking of going into the studio for real, working with one of
those producers who did the Cat's Eye album?"

I knew it. I'd written about it, and remembered the full-
bodied sound. If any producers could capture that live sound—
all immediacy and excitement—they could. "They're good.
They'll get it right."

"Yeah, I hope so. but that's where going back to school
plays in."

I bit my lip and nodded. Monday's simple solution now had
more wrinkles in it.

"So, what did Bill say?"

I winced. "Sorry, Violet. The morning just got away from
me. I'll ask him later.

"That's cool. Hey, are you coming on Sunday?"

She'd told me about the gig weeks ago, and I'd forgotten
that, as well. Too many shows for work, not enough for fun.
But a Violet Haze Experience gig was an event. "Casbah, right?
Middle set?"

"Uh-huh. Give us a chance to work out some of that new
material. I'll put you on the list, if you think you can make it."

"Yeah, I'll try. Maybe I can drag Bunny out, too."

"Bill's still laid up?"

I nodded. "A few more weeks. But I think he's more into jazz these days, anyway."

"My condolences." My punk-rock friend sounded like she was laughing. But I couldn't see her getting into anything with saxophones, either.

EIGHT

TIME TO BUILD SOME bridges. As a freelancer in this wired age, I don't really ever have to show my face at the *Mail*'s newsroom. It's important to get out and listen to music, to meet and interview bands in person, but I file everything electronically. Still, I figure it can't hurt to show up once in a while, and the paper was only a few blocks from the South End T stop. Besides, I was starving. The *Mail*'s cafeteria could be surprisingly good, and Bunny tended to take her lunch late.

"Meet me in the caf, Theda." I called her as I climbed up from the subway. The weak January sunshine made the walk almost pleasant, but there was something of a winter chill in Bunny's voice. "Don't go through Arts until we talk." She was almost whispering.

With that teaser as an appetizer, I only wolfed down half my tuna roll-up before my friend showed, ferrying a tray of lettuce.

"Diet?"

"Yeah, I've just been putting too much on." She sighed heavily, adjusting the cats-eye glasses that threatened to slide off her face into the mound of green. It was true that since moving in with Cal, and particularly since their hand-fasting commitment ceremony last fall, she'd become rounder than usual. "Besides, I've got to start thinking in terms of health."

I swallowed a slice of pickle and raised my eyebrows in question. Bunny's been zaftig, if not pleasingly plump, as long as I've known her. Cal didn't seem to mind. But she's always been healthy, indulging in everything from booze to junk food in moderation. It's not her fault that everything goes straight to her waist. "Oh?" I managed between bites. The cafeteria ladies remembered me, and had layered the inside of the tomato-basil tortilla with more sliced pickles.

"Yeah." She looked up from her plate of greens and beamed, the rhinestones on her glasses sparkling. "I'm pregnant!"

Just then a stray shred of lettuce found its way into my windpipe. Maybe it was my gasp of surprise, but I only coughed for a minute. Once I'd wiped the tears from my face and swallowed the water Bunny handed me, I was able to congratulate her. It seemed to be what she wanted.

"You and Cal! You're going to be parents." I hadn't ever heard my friend speak of baby lust or any interest in starting a family. "That's great, right?"

"Yeah. We've been trying for a while." She poured a healthy serving of creamy ranch on her greens. "That's why we got handfasted really."

"I didn't know." What an understatement. In my experience, pregnancy was something to be avoided. "But, well, congratulations! So, why the dieting?"

"My doctor." Bunny paused from shoveling in the cream-drenched lettuce. "She says that with my weight, I shouldn't gain more than about fifteen pounds. And I think I've done that already."

I looked down at what remained on my own plate. The sandwich was almost gone anyway. "You'll be fine." I popped the remaining wet fold of tortilla and pickle into my mouth, and pushed the plate, with its tempting pile of potato chips, away. "So, is that what you wanted to tell me?"

"Oh no, I forgot." Bunny reached for the chips, and I felt a minor stab of guilt—and jealousy. "It's Tim. He's in trouble. In fact, he may be on his way out."

"Tim?" My blowhard editor wasn't a genius, but he'd paid his dues, working his way up through the *Mail*'s ranks, from overnights on the copy desk to his current exalted position. He was as much a part of the paper as the grimy gray carpeting.

"He's an institution. Part of this institution anyway." I grabbed a few of the chips back.

"That might be the problem." We were both picking at crumbs now, and Bunny wet her fingertip to get the last bits of salt. "He's not hep to the cool trends." I looked up: she was joking. "No, seriously. The scuttlebutt is they're going to kick him upstairs, or maybe just sideways. Management is looking at arts as a showpiece, and I gather there is serious doubt among the top folks as to whether Tim can cut the cutting edge."

"Can you tell me who—"

"No." Bunny cut me off. I knew that she overheard a lot of gossip in the library. It was quiet down there, a marked contrast from the newsroom, and visitors tended to forget the librarians hidden away in their carrels. But I also suspected that Bunny's friendship with the women who ran the message center had been cultivated, at least in part, as a source of information. And, like any good journalist, Bunny protected her sources.

"Wow. Well, he did respond to the focus groups." The paper had paid big bucks to a marketing firm who'd told us what we should have already known: All our gardening and childcare features had attracted a largely suburban, middle-aged readership. My column was part of the attempt to win the elusive younger reader back.

"Yeah, but that's getting mixed reviews upstairs. They want more graphics. You know, readers love big pictures, and all that."

"Readers love good stories. It's the advertisers they're trying to please." I was getting cranky now. I'd eaten too many of those chips, and besides, what Bunny was telling me could threaten my beloved "Clubland."

"I know, Theda. And I think your column is great. I just wanted to give you a head's up before you next talked to Tim. He's feeling the heat to make his pages more fashion conscious—and that means your column, too."

"Great." I thought back to the emo band I'd had stolen out

from under me, and to Tim's insistence that I write about Swann's Way. Not how I would cover the local scene if I had my way, but I could weather it. "This, too, shall pass. Speaking of…when are you due?"

"Early June. Definitely before the solstice, so maybe a Gemini.

"Maybe you'll have twins."

She made a face and for a moment I saw my own reaction mirrored back. "Ugh. I don't know if I could deal."

A stab of guilt washed over me. We weren't on the same path, but she was my dear friend. "It would be an instant family, though! And you'll know soon enough. Right?" My knowledge of childbearing was limited, to say the least. She nodded. "You'll be a great mom, and Cal was born to be a father."

She looked a little better after that. "Yeah, it's just a big step, you know? So much for my misspent youth."

"You've got a few months yet. Speaking of which, any interest in going to hear Violet at the Casbah Sunday? We can have dinner upstairs first, and it'll be an early show, too. She's playing the middle set, working out some new material before going into the studio."

"Yeah, sure. I'll tell Cal it's his night to babysit the cats! Hey," she leaned forward and her voice dropped to a whisper. "Wanna share a frozen yogurt?"

"Only if you put sprinkles on it."

"Jimmies, Theda, you've lived in this town long enough." She was right, and so I volunteered to do the honors, returning with a strawberry-chocolate swirl piled high enough for two.

By the time I headed down to the newsroom, I was full and happy, and only a little nervous. Newspaper editors could be like schools of small fish, darting and turning on a moment's notice to hurry up toward something sparkly or flee an ominous shadow. I'd witnessed the way trends passed through the departments during my years as a copy editor here, when I'd come in five afternoons a week to hear that another redesign was in the works or that we were no longer using the serial comma. As a freelancer, I'd already weathered more than one storm. Last year, the so-called "youth initiative" had first given my column to someone else and then promoted that same twentysomething into management. That impulse had passed, as had so many others. More reason for me to be grateful for my freelance status. This was a very small pond, after all.

"Hey, Tim." I knocked on the open door of my editor's glassed-in office, and his balding head popped up with a start. "Got a minute?"

"Sure, come in, Krakow, come in." He jumped up from behind his seat and began picking papers off the guest chair, piling the glossy press folders on top of an already overloaded desk. Such courtesy was unusual. "What's up? You're on Swann's Way, right? We're thinking of them for the cover for next Thursday."

"I'll get them, Tim." His mouth opened and no words came out. "Don't worry." His mouth closed. "I've spoken to their manager a few times. We just have to set something up. Do you want me to talk Photo through the piece?"

"That would be great." Some color began to come back into his round moon of a face. I'd been thinking of asking him if an interview was necessary. If the band was going to be so hard to contact, I could make a column *about* them. But for anyone of lesser stature than Madonna or the Arctic Monkeys, a critic's notebook-style essay wouldn't be enough for an Arts cover. Plus, it sounded like he had enough on his plate. So why give Tim a coronary? He and I might not always see eye to eye, but he had given me the column.

Instead, I used our rare face-to-face to bring up some of the other stories I'd been thinking about.

"The process piece, that sounds hot. Behind-the-scenes and all that." I'd distilled some of my thoughts about Monday night's showcase, and pitched a column on how musicians work out their ideas. "See if you can get anyone who people will have heard of. Someone on the radio."

I nodded. It would still be a good story.

"The other thing I'd like to look into, Tim, is the use of designer drugs in the clubs. I've got a source with the police that says they're definitely on the rise."

"Your boyfriend?" He was better connected than I thought.

"Yeah, but I actually saw a girl OD the other night. She was unconscious when they took her to the hospital."

He looked interested in that, his pink lips pursing in thought. Drugs were always sexy. But after a moment's mulling he shook his head. "No, Krakow. It's a good lead, if there is a story there, but I'd rather have one of the staff writers look at it. You know, do some hard reporting. Get some numbers. See if there really is a trend here."

I knew what that meant: Two quotes from the spokesman at Mass. Health, a drug rehab counselor, and a meaningless statement from the police PR guy. It would be better than some of our "trend" pieces, the ones Bunny called "I've found three people to interview." But somewhere in it would be ham-fisted description of the club scene as a subterranean den of vice, a criminal network where Boston sent its youth to be corrupted.

"But I know the scene, Tim. If you send in someone who doesn't, they're not going to know who to talk to." They're not going to get it, is what I didn't say. "There's a whole community, a network of people. If I do it, I bet I can get people to talk to me."

"You're not a news reporter, Krakow. Hell, you're not a reporter at all!"

I bit my tongue. Everybody who came from the news side had the same bias about arts writers. "I do know the scene. I've got access."

That was the magic word. He paused, but not long enough. "Well, I don't like it. It's not in your bailiwick anyway, and I don't think you're the writer for the job." I waited. "But, I'll tell you what. Poke around, see what stones you can roll over." He laughed at his own joke. "Give it a few days and then bring your notes in. I'll give you a tagline. Maybe even a co-byline. We'll see."

We'd see indeed. I'd make this story mine before handing over my notes to a staff writer. But for now I thanked him, standing up to leave. He seemed more relaxed since we'd talked, and I'd done my bit for protecting my turf. I started to say goodbye, but as I did, his phone rang. With a wave, I left the office.

"Krakow! You still here?" Tim's bark caught me. I'd stopped by the desk to chat with Shelley, one of my old comrades in copyediting.

"I'm here." Great, there goes the drug story. But it was too late to hide. I walked back to Tim's office, better to take my bad news in private.

"Good, good. You free tonight?" I wasn't sure how to respond, but Tim didn't wait. "I need a live body for third. Ralph's got some kind of stomach bug."

I thought a hangover was more likely, but decided not to blow Ralph's cover. Besides, a live review was a plum assignment. If I didn't have a column to put together, not to mention some questions to ask about drug use, I'd be intrigued. "What's the gig, boss?"

"Savannah…something. Seals? I have the press release somewhere."

He started shuffling through the papers on his desk, but I was ahead of him.

"Savannah Walruses? They're making their United States debut tonight, at Jato's, right?" The Walruses were a hot new band from England, and Ralph must be seriously laid up to miss them. Or, really, to miss the chance to have the first say on whether the new sensation lived up to its hype.

"Yeah, that's the band." He found a piece of paper and skimmed it over. "The *New Musical Express* says they're better than the Beatles."

He looked intrigued, so I hated to break it to him. "Tim,

the *NME* says that about a new band at least once every six months. Last year, it was the Arctic Monkeys. Before that, the Kaiser Chiefs…."

He'd lost interest. "Whatever." I reached over and took the press release from where he'd dropped it. "But Ralph seemed to think they were a big deal. Anyway, we've budgeted this for third. Forty twills."

"No problem. Jato's sets are early." Writing for the paper's third and final edition, which went to press around twelve-fifteen was always fun. Cranking out the prose while your ears were still ringing, having to compose and file all before bed. When it worked, the excitement of the show made it into the next morning's paper, music transformed into type. When it didn't, the review could be a mess, the kind of story that had you wincing for weeks after. But I liked late nights, forty twills—typewritten lines—wasn't much at all. And, yeah, the opportunity of being one of the first American critics to weigh in on a new phenom gave me a lift. Besides, writing for the third edition meant I'd have to file by eleven-thirty. Hours before bedtime. This new assignment wouldn't really interfere with my column at all. "Forty twills for third! Thanks, Tim."

"And Krakow!" I turned back from the open doorway. "This is just an extra. Make sure you get me Swann's Way. That's what you're supposed to be good at!"

"Have I ever missed a deadline, boss?" He shot me a look. I smiled, and headed out.

"Theda!" I was walking quickly, trying to get my ducks in order. It was too late to reach the Walrus's record label rep. What was the number for Jato's box office? And what was the manager's name—Mike? Bob? Joe? "Theda?"

It was Bunny, running down the hallway. "What's up? Are you okay?"

"Yeah, I'm just glad I caught you. You haven't talked to Tess again, have you?"

"No." I'd tried, but with everything else going on, she had slipped my mind.

"I didn't think so. I just reached her at the lab and it was weird." I waited while Bunny caught her breath. She must have run all the way from the library. "I asked her what happened with the accident, and she tried to put me off. I mean, I know they're going for this grant, but c'mon! I told her what you said, about hitting a divider, and reminded her that she'd told me she hit a truck. And, Theda, she lost it! She said you were spreading stories and then asked why I was so interested in her life suddenly. But she really didn't want to know, you know? She just blew up at me."

That didn't sound like Tess and I said so. "But she has been under awful pressure recently. I mean, I don't think she's had time to work on her music at all, since the whole grant process started. And you know that's not like her."

"None of this is like Tess, Theda. That's what worries me."

"I'll try her at home tonight. And you—no more running. You've got to start being careful with yourself."

"Sure, mom."

"Who you calling 'mom'?" I hugged her quickly, her warm softness reminding me of a cat. "We're on for Sunday, right?"

"Right!" She saluted. "But before then, Theda, I'll expect a full report."

EVEN BEFORE I WAS out the door, I was on my cell. Knowing it was futile, I called the press contact on the Walrus' release and left a voice mail. I had to try every avenue to get in: word was the show had sold out within ten minutes of tickets going on sale. Two more calls got me through to the Jato's box office, and another machine. At least I'd remembered the manager's name. "Mike? This is Theda. Ralph is out sick, so the *Mail* wants me to cover the Walruses, tonight. Can you put me on the house list?" For a show this big, I wasn't going to ask for a plus-one.

The rest of my day consisted of phone tag. I called Mike again, and the label rep for good measure. I tried Tess, too, but decided not to leave a message when she didn't pick up. I even phoned Ralph, wondering if against all the odds he had an actual paper ticket that I could pick up. All I got was his voice mail. Maybe it wasn't a hangover. Maybe he was taking an un-scheduled vacation. I left a message anyway, knowing it was futile, and while I was recording it Mel Baker from Wilson and Crave left me a message. Of course, by the time I picked that up and dialed his extension he was gone—for the day, the week, the year. I left another message, trying not to let my frustration creep into my voice. This was the job. And besides, someone had to call me back.

While waiting, I moved on to my other outstanding assignments: Wilson and Crave were major players, but they weren't the only developers in town. Looking through my notes, I found two more realtors among Patti's contacts. Voice mail again, another try for Tess, and one more message about Swann's Way for Heather. If I wasn't so anxious about getting on the list for tonight's show, I'd be tempted to head out again. Sometimes, actual beat reporting—showing up at someone's office—provided results. But the number I'd left had been my home phone, not my cell. I didn't want to miss anything, and so between messages, Musetta and I played foil ball. She seemed to enjoy it, pouncing on the small shiny thing like it was live prey. After all the dead ends, I was grateful for some kind of interaction. It was after seven before I finally gave up on reaching Tess in person, and recorded my own message for her. If she was pissed off, she probably wouldn't call me back. But it seemed chicken to avoid her—especially if she really was at home and had heard my previous call and hang ups. Besides, I was due at Jato's. Whatever else was going on, the excitement of the gig— the show, the third-edition assignment—had me jazzed.

"Tess? I really need to talk to you. Call me, please. Whenever." Musetta was asleep before I went out again, but my regret at leaving her was the only drag on my growing buzz. I would miss her soft, warm belly fur, and my own cozy apartment, where the heat was once again blasting, but this was what I lived for. Still, going out was a shock. Winter had returned with sunset, freezing the daytime's melt, and I shivered my way along newly icy sidewalks to my car, cursing all the neighborhood SUVs that had taken the parking spaces on my block.

Jato's, at least, would be warm, and I lucked into a spot out front.

"Ticket? You have a ticket?" A thick arm blocked my progress into the warm anteroom.

"I'm on the list." I hoped I was telling the truth, but the second bouncer recognized me. "She's all right." I was through, at least to the ticket window.

"Krakow, Theda Krakow. *Boston Morning Mail.* I should be on the press list?" I could hope. Or bluff. The young box office attendant, with a face like Bettie Page and the black bangs to match, ran one lacquered finger down the typed-up sheet. "Nope." She flipped the page.

"You might just have the *Mail* down. I'm covering for Ralph—"

"Uh uh." She popped her gum and looked up at me, dull eyed and bored. "Nothing on the label list."

"Would you check the house list then? Mike should've put me on." If he got my message, that is. And if he was feeling kindly toward me. But sometimes just mentioning the name of the manager would do the trick, lend some credence to my claim that I really was working press. Bettie flipped another page. "Nuh-uh."

Great. I pulled my wallet out of my jeans. My *Mail* photo ID was six-months outdated, but it had an official look, and it had gotten me into shows before. "Is Mike around? Or is the road manager around?" I slapped the ID on the tray at the bottom of her window. Being a critic meant learning how to get in when you had to. I wasn't leaving.

"Look, the show's sold out. There isn't even a house list for this one." She pushed my laminated ID back through to me. I was ready to beg.

"She's all right." Over my shoulder I heard Mike's voice. He put an arm around me and I turned around, hugging him out of gratitude. Bettie, meanwhile, pulled a stack of green-and-white tickets out from a drawer and with a sigh of resignation began leafing through them. "Here to see the next big thing?"

"I'm working. Ralph's sick, so I'm here for the *Mail*." I could hear the note of pride sneaking into my voice.

"Can't believe Ralph's missing this one. You need a plus-one?" I shook my head. "Okay, gotta run. Enjoy the show."

"Thanks." I took the ticket Bettie had passed through to me. "Thanks to you, too." She shrugged and popped her gum, sliding the remaining tickets back into their drawer.

The air was ten degrees hotter in the music room, steam rising from the packed-in crowd. I contemplated standing by the door where at least some air circulated, but I was too excited. Besides, not only could I barely see the stage from where I was standing, the sound would probably be distorted by the entranceway's overhang. I dived in.

And immediately got an elbow in the chest. Wow, that hurt, but I slid sideways, making my way toward the bar. I was working, and didn't want to drink, but having solid wood at my back gave me a sense of security and I ordered to justify using the real estate.

"Keep the change." Club staff are a freelancer's best friend, as Mike had just reminded me.

"Thanks, Theda. You working?" I looked up and recognized Graham.

"Graham! I thought you were at the Casbah. Hey, can I stow my bag?"

"Sure." He grabbed my big messenger bag and tucked it behind him, leaving me free to maneuver. "Better money here." He pulled four Budweisers from the cooler and opened them all with two rapid wrist movements. "Little crazy on a night like tonight though." Grabbing a twenty, he whirled and returned with two Coronas, a shot, and another Bud, before wiping up a puddle that had started to seep across the bar.

"Impressive!"

He smiled back at me, and reached for more bottles. "The drug of choice tonight."

"Hey, Graham." His flip comment made me wonder. "Have you been seeing a new club drug around? Something like GBH or some acid-Ecstasy mix?"

Three bottles in each hand, he paused to look at me. "Theda, that's not your thing, is it? I thought you were straight."

"I am." He bent to open the bottles and hand them over to a lace-clad brunette with tattooed arms. I waited.

"So, you're not involved with it, right?" He stared down at the bar, working the rag over the spot where the puddle had been.

"Graham, what is it?"

The crowd was pushing closer, and I had to grab hold of the bar's rounded edge to keep my place.

"There's something, Theda. I've heard things." He looked up and, for a rare moment, stood still. "But it's not us—not the bar staff." I nodded. Too often Graham's colleagues took charge of distributing all kinds of intoxicants. "That's all I know."

"That's all?" Graham was pointing at customers now, signaling for each to yell out their order. This was definitely not the best time for a conversation, but I didn't want to let it go.

"Look, Theda." He grabbed a plastic cup and poured in a two-count of vodka, topping it off with cranberry juice and a lime wedge. "Ask on your side of the bar." Two shots of Southern Comfort filled smaller plastic cups, and then he grabbed more beers. "Some of them have been paying to play, if you know what I mean."

I thought I did, and couldn't help wondering about Ralph. But just then, the lights went black. I felt in my back pocket for my pad. As soon as I had the pen cap off, the drums kicked in with a bang, rolling up to a resounding crash. White spots shone down on a pimple-faced boy who couldn't be more than seventeen. But then the guitars started up, a real old-school rock and roll sound, and I stopped caring.

"Mash up on the dance floor!" The lead singer, who also played guitar, had the kind of accent that made everything sound more colorful. Leaning into the mike, his head turning sideways, he sang of a working-class Saturday night. *"Some bloke's kicked me out the door…"*

I found myself humming along and smiled. Who needed drugs, when you had good rock and roll? Could what Tess felt about her job come anywhere close to this? The next song I'd heard on the radio, and I wasn't the only one. *"Rev it up!"* Half the crowd shouted along and the room began to heave and bob in unison. Another elbow caught me in the chest. I'm just the wrong height, and I tried to back away. I was scribbling notes fast and furious now, noting how the bass player stood so still, his fingers picking out a rapid walking pattern. What was that other guitarist playing? Damn! My pen went flying as the same dancer backed into me. That's why I carry spares, but as I was uncapping it, he did it again, catching me full in the chest. With the bar behind me, I had no place to go. *Woof!* I was slammed again, and looked for an out.

"Graham?" He was at the bar's other end, but looked up, questioning. I smiled and waved him off. To ask for sanctuary, behind the bar, was to risk his job. And to call for a bouncer, well, was I no longer tough enough for the gig? Another shove, as the crowd surged. It wasn't personal, it was the beat. I crossed my arms high. The next time that particular meathead came flying my way, let him back into a sharp elbow. But the crowd had filled in and the wild movement had slowed. I could see why the box office wasn't letting any more tickets out. Forget the fire hazard, I only hoped nobody here had lice.

The thought made my head itch, but I resisted the urge to scratch. Keeping my elbows out and writing notes was hard enough. They'd be indecipherable, half of them, by the time I got home. But the process of writing sometimes helped me remember details, sometimes suggested thoughts or connections. Working on deadline like this, I'd need to have my lead soon after the show ended, and so I kept on scribbling.

"We've got summat going on." Summat? Was that accent real? *"Going on!"* I was singing along now, my momentary panic forgotten.

Who were these guys anyway? Kids, not more than twenty, one of them pudgy, the rest stick thin. The singer, who seemed to be the leader, had that kind of big British nose that looks like it was pinched out of a blob of Play-Doh, with a wide mouth to match. He could've been Keith Moon's illegitimate son, what with that '70s-style brown shag, the bangs and edges now plastered to his face with sweat. "Going, going on!" No, he was far too young; the Who's crazy drummer died in 1978.

"She were grand!" I caught a bit of slang grammar, and the copy editor in me smiled. *"She were awesome!"* I loved these regionalisms. Hell, I was loving this band. The lyrics sounded smart, too, vignettes of life in some industrial city. Maybe that's why they were making their debut here. Boston was, or once had been, such a tough town, a breeding ground for bands. I could hack this. *"Yes, she were!"*

I was bouncing on the balls of my feet, moving along with the crowd's tighter, contained surge. Each upswing helped me see, but it was more than that. The beat had gotten me, so I almost didn't see when I bumped into someone. Carl from the *Independent.* "Hey! You're working?"

He nodded, held up a pad. "What do you think?"

"They're fantastic!" I sounded like a fan. A song ended and the singer reached for his second guitar. I reached to redeem my credibility. "To me there's a lot of Ray Davies in their songs. You know, the whole tongue-in-cheek slice-of-street-life thing?"

"Yeah, yeah!" I looked over and saw him write "Ray Davies." So much for friendship. I had to learn to quit showing off. The new guitar launched a punk-funk rhythm and I bounced away, sidling between two T-shirted hulks both wet with sweat. Ah well, I was sweating now, too. I could shower before bed. *"In the bright lights! Bright lights!"*

One more unison attack and the band quit the stage. The lights came up. But we all knew an encore was in the offing and I only edged toward the entrance as the group came back, guitars blazing, for one more three-minute explosion. I love the scene—my "clubland"—but this was testing even my toler-ance. Working back to the bar, I reached around the side and grabbed my bag. By the time the lights came back on for good, I was the first out the door. That cold air smelled great and I was still moving to the beat as I plotted my review. Should I start with their guitar sound? The accent?

A horn blasted me back to awareness and I jumped back as a rust-colored blur sped by. I'd been in the street, on my way to my car, without looking. Of course the street was busy, the show had ended. I leaned back against a white van and watched the taillights disappear. Breathe, Theda. Don't get that carried away. Take your time. But I was on deadline and as soon as I could walk steadily, I forced myself to cross the street, care-fully this time, and start up my own car. I gave it a minute, telling myself I needed to let it warm up, but my mind was racing. Was that what had happened to Tess? She'd been so pre-occupied by work. Was that what happened to Gail? Out in the cold, a storm coming on and the lives of innocent animals in her hands? My hands were still shaking as I buckled my seatbelt. The world was a dangerous place, but I was not about to give up. I drove home five miles under the speed limit, my eyes on every shadow.

BACK AT HOME, I scooped up the cat while the computer booted up, and tried telling her my lead. What I really wanted was the comfort of her warm body. But I was on deadline. "Without the hype, the Savannah Walruses…no. Don't start with a prepositional phrase." Musetta squirmed and I put her down. "Making their American debut, Britain's next big thing…"

By the time I had a file open, I'd worked through these early drafts and dived right in. Urban landscapes, smart fast takes on gritty city life: that was the key, what the Boston audience shared with these British teens. Forty lines drafted themselves as I talked them out loud. Four songs made perfect examples, each one fitting a point, and I caught myself trying to sneak in a fifth. Don't overload. This is an essay, not a set list. I checked the clock: twenty minutes before I needed to file. A quick Google confirmed a lyric that I thought I'd heard, and let me check the band's birthdates. The oldest was twenty. I toyed with rereading some of the British reviews, but it was quarter past eleven. I saved my file and pushed back my chair.

Between the near-miss on the street and my excitement over the concert, I was pumped. I could feel the adrenaline in my belly, as sour as cold coffee. Three deep breaths and I went back to the computer, re-read my story, and hit the keys to send it in. I'd call the desk in a few minutes, just to make sure it had arrived and to let whoever was working know I was available for questions. I didn't expect any. I was in my element, and despite feeling shaken, I knew the piece was good.

By one o'clock, I was at Bill's. Still driving a bit tentatively, I'd managed a slight detour past my favorite late-night Chinese, and arrived with a bag of moo shi shrimp, stir-fried peapod stems, and some fiery dumplings still hot in hand. He'd eaten hours before, but took a bowl anyway, and listened to me unwind, the adrenaline draining off as I told him about the music, the crowd. I skipped my own scare—and Graham's intriguing comments—and instead focused on the assignment, telling him how I'd woven a little history into my description to give some perspective on this latest phenomenon.

"I don't know where you get the energy." He speared a dumpling. "You're bouncing off the walls still. I'd have been tired out just by the noise."

A bit of that energy, just a bit, was nerves. Which I wasn't going to admit to. "Ah, but it was glorious noise, Bill. I didn't realize how much I'd like them."

"Best band since the Beatles, huh?" I'd quoted the *NME* hype.

"Maybe the best ever!" We laughed and I felt myself relax. Writing for third was fun, like some kind of work-drug, but coming back to earth had its rewards as well. Back to earth…

"Bill?" I still hadn't broached him with Violet's questions. Still hadn't told him about Tess. "Do you think Violet is a suspect?"

He was used to me. I could tell by the way he jumped subjects along with me. "You know I can't talk to you about this, honey." Maybe he'd been waiting for that question. "Here, you can have the rest of the greens."

I recognized my own technique, but took the greens anyway. I love anything stir-fried with garlic. Not that I was going to let the subject rest. "Well, you can tell me about some of the technicalities. I mean, would a van's tire tracks look different from a car's?"

"Yes, they probably would. But, you know, it's not like on TV, darling. I mean, often there aren't clear tracks, or there are too many tracks. Think about it, Theda. How many cars skid and brake on that traffic circle each rush hour? And the road's a mess: sand and salt from the last storm, grease, oil, gas, and who knows what else."

Blood came to mind, and my own near miss, but I knew he was right. "And paint chips?"

"There's a lot of paint on that rotary, honey. But, yeah, they collected some samples, so, maybe, *maybe,* the car that hit her might have been red or black or light blue."

I perked up. "Light blue?"

"Or black or red." Bill was smiling at me now. "I'm sorry I don't have a clear answer for you, babe, but do you know how many fender benders happen on that rotary? And how many are never reported? All the paint means is that someone scraped something in the last week or so."

There were a lot of light blue cars, I reminded myself. And Tess had said that her accident was down by the river. "So how do you solve a hit-and-run?" Even if I didn't have anything to take back to Violet, I was curious.

He bit into the last dumpling. "Most of the time, Theda, we don't."

NINE

THURSDAY MORNING and I felt ready to tackle the day. My own note-taking had reminded me that sometimes if I write things out they make more sense. Why not start jotting down what I knew about Gail's accident, or even Tess's? Maybe I'd see some connections. But first, coffee. I started toward the kitchen.

Thud! I heard a dull crash and a few muttered curses. Bill, trying out his crutches apparently, had beaten me to the coffee maker.

"Sweetie? You okay?" The only thing grinding in the kitchen were teeth.

"Yeah, it's these damn props." The water ran, coffee was in process. I squeezed into the small kitchenette and righted the fallen crutch. Bill still held one under his arm, but he was leaning against the counter.

"They're not forever, Bill."

"I know, but I was watching those para-athletes on Sports Center yesterday—"

"Bill, they're professionals. Well, maybe not, but they've had a lot more time to practice. A lot more than you will." It seemed an inopportune moment to point out that if he spent more time moving around and less watching sports on television, he'd be better able to emulate his heroes.

Bill grunted and stumbled, catching himself on the fridge. I righted the coffee grinder. "It's just for a few more weeks, Bill."

Another grunt. Sometimes it's best to walk away. I reached for the newspaper.

"Yeah, but then I'll have physical therapy and even then,

who knows if I'll get enough flexibility and strength back to go back to the job."

I put the paper down. "Are you thinking of not going back?" He was leaning against the counter, counting spoonfuls of coffee beans and I waited while he finished.

"Well…" The noise of the grinder obscured what he was saying, but he realized it. "Sorry," he said, pouring the water into the pot. "What I've been thinking is, well, I've got twenty years put in. And especially if I'm not able to walk or run at my best…"

"Bill, you know you're as fit as anyone on the department." With his tall, lean athlete's body, he had an edge over a lot of cops, particularly his partner, who ran to flab. But I also knew that he'd worked hard to stay that way, particularly as he made his way through his forties.

"I have been, but…" He reached for the cereal bowls and handed them to me. "It's getting harder. And besides, Theda, I'm bored."

"You're bored *now*. You're just losing it because all you're doing is lying on the sofa watching TV." There, I'd said it. "What?" He was staring at me.

"I didn't think you'd be so uptight about this, Theda." He passed me the cereal boxes. For me, he stocked Raisin Bran, but he was still a Cheerios loyalist. "I mean, you left a steady job. Maybe I want to explore a bit, too."

I started to speak and realized, I didn't know what to say. He was right. Last year, I'd been a copy editor, working regular hours for a paycheck and benefits, and I'd quit to follow a much-less-profitable dream. I hadn't met Bill then, but he'd heard me talk about the decision to leave safety and security for the footloose life of a freelancer. And I took his support for granted. But that was my dream, my risk, and my life. Bill was different. I wanted him to stay the man I met and fell in love with. I wanted him to be steady, solid, and, yeah, employed. The hypocrisy of it hit me. Who was I to block his ambition when just last night I'd been high on the thrill of writing, or living the rock-crit life? I took another breath and let it out.

"You're right, Bill. I'm sorry. I guess I'm just surprised. I didn't know you were unhappy." No, that was a lie. I'd listened to him complain often enough, even when he was mobile. "Or, maybe, I'm just not that comfortable with change. With you changing, that is."

"You and Musetta." He was smiling now as he tucked the second crutch under his arm and made his awkward way around the table to sit with me. "But I'm not changing, not in any fundamental way. I'm just looking at my options."

"Okay." I could deal with this. "So, what are you thinking about? Security? Becoming a PI?"

"Yeah, lying here, I've been wondering about that. Thought about getting some binoculars."

"Rear Window?" I smiled, too.

"Only if you'll play Grace Kelly."

"I thought I did that last night. And Grace Kelly never brought Jimmy Stewart moo shi pork."

"It was shrimp, Theda. But, seriously? No, I can't see becoming a private investigator or doing security. It would be too similar to homicide, only less, you know?" I nodded. "I'm not sure what else, though." He picked up the paper. "Maybe I'll become a music critic."

He just laughed as I grabbed the arts section away from him. I still hadn't even read "Clubland." I had to check to make sure I had the right section: Yes, it said "Arts," but the opening fashion spread—the pre-print—was followed by an interview with a TV star about her clothes, and then something on skateboarding. By the time I found my review of the Savannah Walruses buried toward the back of the section, where the "fresh" copy ran, the coffee had brewed. Moving slowly, so as not to spill, Bill brought me my mug and stayed to read over my shoulder.

"It's good. You were so hopped up last night, I was wondering if you'd really been able to put it together in prose." I shot him a look. "Sorry to doubt you." I reached up and kissed him, and we both turned the page to my column.

My guy was in an appreciative mood. "I really like the second part, on the Monday night thing." He took the paper from me and placed it on the table. "That part, there. It sounds like that was what interested you most."

"Good eye, Bill. It was. But hang on." I was reading over his shoulder now, like a proofreader, line by line.

"Looking for mistakes?"

"Looking for bad edits. The review went in fast, and nobody asked me any questions on it."

"God, you're as bad as a Cambridge driver." The memory of last night's near miss made me look up. I hadn't told Bill everything, but he was calm as he hopped back to his seat. "When you're behind the wheel, watch out. But when you're walking through Harvard Square you expect everyone to stop for you. I mean, weren't you a copy editor just a few months ago?"

I nodded. "Yeah, I know how much damage we can inflict." He did, too. I'd told him the stories. There was the editor who hated contractions, so he changed every "can't" to a "cannot" and every "won't" to a "will not." Only sometimes in his fervor, he forgot to type in the second word.

Bill wasn't buying it. "You're like that driver. You think you rule the road. But once you're on the sidewalk...."

"You're saying I have trouble seeing the other side?"

"I'm saying that you can forget awfully quickly what the view from the other side looks like."

"I'm sorry I questioned you about leaving your job, Bill." I reached across the table to take his hand. Maybe he was right about my club scene, too, but I wasn't going to admit that. "Now are you done with news? I've got no use for the rest of this section."

WHEN I GOT HOME about an hour later, Musetta was nowhere to be seen. A thick rubber bracelet and the catnip-stuffed butterfly greeted me instead, right by the door, revealing what my industrious pet had been up to.

"Musetta? Kitty girl?" No answer. "Musetta?" I dropped my bag and checked the living room. Her favorite chair was empty, as was the kitchenette. But when I went into my office I found her on top of the file cabinet, her black fur soaking up the mid-morning sun.

"Hey, Musetta! What's up?" She gave a big yawn in response, and stretched. But even as she looked up at me, her eyes began to close. "Okay, I get it. Nap time. Hope I didn't disturb you." I needn't have worried. She tucked her nose back under her tail and resumed her beauty sleep.

My answering machine proved a little more responsive. Heather had called, and when I dialed her cell she picked up right away.

"Theda? Excellent. I've spoken with Swann's Way and they're willing to meet with you whenever might be convenient." I was about to suggest that afternoon, but she wasn't pausing. "How about Sunday?" Her words let me know she'd memorized the formula, but not the meaning.

That was pushing it; my column was due noon Tuesday, just in case the section pre-printed. Plus, I had plans with Bunny for dinner and then Violet's set, that night.

"I was hoping to meet with them sooner. Like, tonight or tomorrow?" The line was silent. I didn't want to promise anything—newspaper plans change—but thought I could sweeten the deal. "Look, Heather, there's been a lot of talk about Swann's Way. Some people at the *Mail* are really interested."

"Who?" Now I had her.

"I'm not at liberty to give you details. But let's just say, they won't be sorry they spoke with me." This was all getting a bit cloak-and-dagger.

"Well, I'll ask again. But they were pretty set. Let's schedule Sunday anyway, and I'll get back to you if their schedules change."

So much for offering a carrot on a stick. "Okay, I'll make it work." I thought of my other plans for the evening. "But can we make it on the early side?"

"We were thinking six o'clock. Perhaps we could all meet at the front room of the Casbah?"

I hesitated. An interview at the Casbah would fit my evening plans perfectly. But given my druthers, I prefer to meet groups in their own environment—a practice space or apartment. In addition, the Casbah would be awfully loud if I was going to tape the interview.

"Well, I was hoping for something a little more private, so we could really talk. Maybe one of their apartments—or the band's space?"

Silence again, and I feared the moment was slipping by. "Never mind, Heather. The Casbah will be fine. I'll meet them at the Casbah at six. "

"Very good, then." She'd completely regained her young executive poise. "We'll see you then."

The other messages ran the gamut: Musetta's vet tech was looking to place a kitten, a domestic kitten. I thought of the missing ferals; I'd have to call Violet. My alma mater wanted money, as usual. Mel Baker—I figured we were on a first-name basis by now—had rung again. And Josie, from MuzeArts, had called me back to tell me she had a little information on the Swann's Way booking. The one message I was hoping for wasn't there, and I found myself calling university information to get the number of Tess's research lab. When I said it was personal, the assistant put me through right away. But that wasn't, Tess assured me, because she wasn't busy.

"Theda, hey, I'm sorry I haven't called you back. I've been slammed. In fact, I can't really talk right now—"

She wasn't getting away from me. "Tess, Hang on. Give me thirty seconds. I've been worried."

"No need, babe. I've just been busy. And I've made an appointment to bring in my car like you wanted me to." A nervous giggle, one that I'd never heard before, punctuated her report.

"Well, I'm glad, Tess." If she was having it fixed, that meant she couldn't be worried about what might be on it, right? "But Bunny and I were talking—"

"Oh don't tell me you talked to Bunny about me!" She cut me off. "Theda, you know how Bunny is. She's become a real mother hen since she got hitched. She went positively hysterical when she'd heard I'd had an accident."

"Tess, I don't think that's fair." The Bunny I knew had become domestic, but I'd seen her as warmer, more relaxed with the change. The opposite of anxious.

"Well, you didn't hear the way she was talking to me, Theda. She was getting bent all out of shape. That's why I didn't want to talk about it anymore. It's over. Finité."

"I thought you didn't call because you were busy, or bringing your car in."

"Theda, Theda, Theda." The funny little laugh was back. "What am I going to do with you? Hey, I've got to go."

"Tess, before you do, tell me. What happened Sunday night? Where was your accident?" I remembered my earlier resolve to take some notes. I grabbed a pen and took a deep breath. "What did you hit?"

"I told you, Theda. And I told Bunny, too, even if she doesn't remember it. I hit a patch of ice by the river, near that construction site. I must've smacked one of those big concrete girders during my skid. But I'm fine, and nobody's hurt, and by next Tuesday, if Mike holds to his promise, my old girl will look as fine as she ever did. Now I'm going back to work, okay?"

"Wait!" How could I ask her? How could I doubt my friend? I looked down at what I had scrawled. "You said nobody got hurt, right?"

"I admit it! I got smashed up a bit. But you saw: it was just a shiner. And otherwise I'm fine. Okay?"

"Okay," I said, but I didn't mean it. The way she talked about Bunny, that nervous laugh. This wasn't the cool, competent

Tess I knew. I didn't know what was going on, but I didn't need to re-read my own notes to know she was lying.

I had a bad taste in my mouth and hoped talking to Violet would get rid of it. She could give me an update on the cat we'd rescued and, although Bill hadn't given me much, at least I could tell her what he had and we could chew it over together. The robotic "beep" of her answering machine didn't give me the warm fuzzy I'd hoped for, however, and I left only a terse message. To make myself feel better, I started to follow up on some of the projects I did have some control over. Josie, bless her heart, had been able to confirm that the Swann's Way gig hadn't been sponsored by any of the college's arts or alumni groups. That didn't mean for sure that the band had rented the space themselves, but it certainly made it more likely. She also confirmed that while the two Pauls had attended the college, neither had graduated. This in itself didn't mean much: Musicians are artists, not scholars. A lot of them attend schools or conservatories as much for the connections as to further their education. When those connections pay off in gigs, they move on to their real careers.

Josie's info did give me something to work with, however, and I started to call clubs around town. Had Swann's Way managed the MuzeArts show because they wanted to launch with a splash, or because they couldn't get any other gigs? A few phone calls yielded surprisingly uniform results: Everybody had heard *of* them, it seemed. But nobody had actually heard the band. No tapes or discs had been sent out, no phone calls asking for auditions or opening slots. They had a buzz, but musically—professionally—they were ciphers.

By the sixth call, I was beginning to feel a bit guilty. Nobody else I interviewed got the kind of scrutiny that I was giving the members of Swann's Way. But then, they weren't acting like any other band. Usually, by the time a performer was ready for his or her "Clubland" closeup, I'd seen a few gigs, noted their movement from Tuesday opener to weekend headliner. Even the bands I didn't like—there was a movement to bring back guitar-heavy hard rock that just didn't work for me—would have paid their dues by the time I wrote about them. They'd have proved their worth to their fans. So some of what I was looking for was background, information, just material around which I could structure a column. Some of it, I had to admit, was that weirdly moralistic streak that Vi sometimes pointed out to me: Did Swann's Way deserve the coverage I was giving them? Had they *earned* MuzeArts? I listened to myself and sighed. Maybe paying for it was enough.

At any rate, I'd had enough. Pulling myself up from my sagging sofa, I rolled my shoulders and felt the stiffness. Even my knees clicked as I stretched. Did outsiders realize how much of journalism takes place over the phone? At times I wished I had a secret source that demanded in-person meetings in some underground garage, a "Clubland" deep throat.

Maybe I did: Reed. I had no ideas what hours he worked, or when he practiced. But at least I could slip a note under his door, and that would get me off the couch. Reminding myself that in fact he probably would not be home in the middle of the day kept me from spending too much time in front of the mirror, and when nobody answered my knock I was almost grateful. When I ran back downstairs to compose the perfect note, Musetta greeted me, twining around my ankles. The sun had moved on from her office perch and now shone on the corner of the sofa that I'd just abandoned. She wanted me to join her, but I left her with just a quick pet to slide a note under my new neighbor's door. "Just checking in," I'd written. "Curious if you've been able to find out anything about Swann's Way." I didn't leave a phone number, I was right downstairs after all, and upon my return rewarded both Musetta and myself for my industry with a long petting session in the sun.

TEN

THE PHONE WOKE ME from my doze and caused Musetta to jump off the sofa with a thud. That cat was getting quite round! But hearing Violet's voice on the other end more than made up for being abandoned by my pet.

"Hey, Vi, what's up? Thanks for calling me back."

"My pleasure. Read your Savannah Walruses piece. Sounded like you liked them!"

"I did, to my surprise. They were fun."

"What happened to the lush?" She and Ralph weren't on the best terms.

"He called in sick." I heard her snort. "Hangover, probably."

"Or something."

My ears pricked up, and I recalled what Graham had said. "Violet, have you been hearing about some new club drugs?" My friend had been straight-edge, abstaining from everything from meat to caffeine, for years, but she was still connected. "Something like GBH, but not quite?"

"Oh, yeah, Fantasy Plus or something like that. Supposed to be a good high, and no side effects."

"I don't know about that." I told her about the apparent overdose I'd seen, and that I'd noticed Ralph hanging around the same time.

"You think he missed the show because he was chipping? Or maybe OD'd?" She didn't sound too put out by the thought.

"I don't know. Even if he took the same thing, he's got a lot more bulk to absorb it. And, unless he was unconscious, he wouldn't let a hangover stop him. I wish I could find out what the girl was on. Hey, what's the name of Luisa's mom?"

"Eva. If they brought her to City ER, she might have heard."

"Think you could ask her?" I gave Vi all the info I could remember, describing the young woman's beautiful hair and slender build. I couldn't remember the young blonde's name— Amber? Jade?—and made a mental note to ask. Perhaps I could bring it up casually on Sunday.

"I'll give her a call later." She sounded distracted. "Hey, speaking of drugs, want to give me a hand with our feral gal?"

"Sure. I'd meant to ask about her anyway. What's up?" Violet had become expert at "pilling" cats since taking over the shelter last spring and didn't usually need any help.

"She's a little hellion. I've taken to calling her Exene. But I've got to change her dressing and that's really a two-person job."

"Dressing? Never mind, I'm on my way." Helping Vi was better than waiting by the phone, and the afternoon looked bright with that clear hard light New England gets in January. Walking, however, was a bad idea. Even with a parka, hat, and gloves, my nose and ears were punishing me for my profligacy by the time I let myself in the shelter's back door.

"Honey, I'm home!"

"Hey, girl." Caro was sitting at the kitchen table with a bunch of papers and an aggrieved expression. "Invoices. The part of the job I hate. But Vi's upstairs with that wild cat."

"Wild cat?" I remembered the beaten-looking tabby who had cowered, shivering, in the trap. But as I climbed to the upstairs isolation room, a former bathroom, an unearthly yowl greeted me.

"Violet?" What was she doing to that cat?

"In here. And close the door behind you." I slid into the white-tiled room and made sure the heavy door latched. I needn't have worried. The cat Violet held was swathed in a bath towel, and only her yellow eyes and striped face were visible. Her ears were flat against her skull and her mouth was wide open in mid-snarl.

"Thanks for coming, Theda. Would you hand me that

dropper?" I poked around the sink till I found it. The towel-wrapped cat began another whining growl.

"Want me to fill it?" The ear mite medicine had been knocked over, but the small bottle still held some of the sticky liquid.

"Please." I handed the full dropper over and Violet shifted to take it. Feeling the movement, the cat let out a yowl and hiss. Even folded into the heavy bath towel, I could see her struggling to kick free.

"She seems pretty feisty to me!" Violet managed to empty the dropper in one ear and handed it back for a refill. The tabby hissed and glared, her open mouth showing sharp white fangs. "And her teeth look in pretty great shape, too."

"Only part of her that is." Violet readjusted the bundle in her arms, just managing to avoid a swipe as one paw broke free. "Hang in there, Exene!" She re-wrapped the cat.

"What do you mean?"

"This is desperation you're seeing. Not health. I thought she was just cold and undernourished. I expected the fleas and ear mites, even in this weather. But she's got some nasty bites on her, too. Her fur was so matted that I didn't see them, not till Rachel looked her over and we shaved her. Can you grab that?" Nodding toward a tube of cream on the sink, she continued, "I'd muzzle her if I hadn't had to pill her." I put the tube down on the floor. "Okay, you take her hindquarters. She's got quite a kick. Ready?"

The cat reacted as my hands slid next to Violet's. "Wow, she's strong!" I found myself leaning on the tiny animal to hold her still, while Violet separated folds of the towel around her midsection.

"Only reason she survived." Squeezing out some of the ointment, Violet bared the cat's side. There, where her fur had been shaved, I saw an angry red wound. As she spread the clear ointment on, the cat kicked and spit.

"Did a dog get her? Or could that have come from another cat?" The whole area looked infected, swollen and wet with pus.

"Or a raccoon. Could even be a squirrel bite that went bad. It had formed an abscess. That's drained, but it's a long way from healed. The other sores are doing a lot better."

"Other sores?" The cat had stopped struggling, but she fixed Violet with a yellow-eyed glare.

"Don't hate me, kitty. I probably saved your life. Can you reach the collar, Theda?" With one hand, I reached behind me for the plastic cone that would keep the tabby from licking off the ointment. Another shift, a brief struggle, and Violet had it snapped around her neck.

"Okay, on the count of three, we're going to let her go. Stand up and keep your hands and face away from her. One, two, three!"

We both jumped back, sliding the wrapped cat to the floor. In a matter of moments she was free and backed into the corner. Her eyes never left us.

"This city is not kind to felines," said Violet, packing up the medication.

"Speaking of, have you heard anything about the missing kittens?" I knew it was a long shot.

"The ferals?" She shook her head. "No. I think this gal is lucky to have survived. The blood tests aren't back yet, but we've got everything out there—feline leukemia, corona viruses. You name it. And bites like that get infected so fast, and in winter the danger goes up from exposure, not to mention poisons like antifreeze. Add in all the problems that come from cats seeking a warm place to sleep, like on an engine or in someone's dryer." I shot her a look, but she nodded. "Yeah, I've seen it. This little girl is just lucky she got stuck in that trap."

"What's going to happen to her?" The cat seemed to be following our conversation and looked at me now. "You're not going to put her back there, are you?" I knew that was the policy of many feral rescuers, but Vi made it sound like a death sentence.

"Not if I don't have to. I don't think she'll ever tame completely. Most ferals don't unless they had some experience with people when they were kittens. But maybe someone will need a mouser who isn't a pet." Violet put the medicines into the oversized cabinet Caro had built and washed her hands. The cat watched her every move, licking her chops. All that hissing must have made her mouth dry. "She really has settled down a bit. We didn't even find that bite the first time we tried to examine her. She must have been in such pain!"

"You thinking anymore about vet school?" After filling one of the cat's bowls with fresh water, Violet shook her head and motioned me toward the door. As quickly as we could, we both slipped back out the door, making sure it latched behind us.

"Not really. Not yet. I mean, Gail was helping animals without a medical degree."

The mention of the cat rescuer brought me back to why I'd called Violet. As we walked back downstairs, I filled her in on what Bill had told me. It wasn't much. But even as I confirmed that the cops were unlikely to find out who had hit Gail and left her dying in the night, I could at least pretty much guarantee Violet that she wasn't being investigated for the crime.

"So, you're involved with a cop. Who do you think did it?" Violet had taken a bag of carrots out of the human-food fridge and stood there crunching. Caro had taken off, but her papers still littered the table. Clearly, she liked doing the work more than billing for it.

"Well, I was wondering about some of the folks she'd gotten into it with. With the demonstrations, and all." I wasn't going to mention Tess, but I was hoping to raise some other plausible suspects. At the very least, she'd saved that little feral's life, and maybe lost her own in the process. The question was: why? "Didn't you tell me that there was a developer looking at the bottling plant site?"

"You think he'd…? No, he'd pay someone to do it. Still, that's pretty radical." She stood there, thinking and chewing, looking for all the world like a technicolor rabbit. "Pete Wilson is the devil."

Something Patti had told me jumped into my mind. "So, you knew that Wilson and Crave are looking at the property? I thought it was supposed to be some big secret."

She shot me a look. "Please, girl. What kind of organization would we be if we didn't know the enemy?"

"*We?* Are you working with Animals Now on this? I thought you didn't like them."

"Well, let's just say sometimes our goals overlap."

"Vi?"

"Theda, I'm not going to tell you what you don't want to hear. But you know my credo—do it yourself. Sometimes that means alone. But sometimes it means joining forces with some strange people. Sometimes it means taking the law in your own hands."

I didn't want to hear this, she was right. But if it had to do with Gail's death, or Tess, I needed to know. "Tell me, Violet. What is Animals Now up to? And was Gail back in or not?" I wanted to ask if Gail had fallen out with her former colleagues, perhaps far enough out to be seen as a threat. But I couldn't quite tell where Violet stood, and I needed to be sure of my friend first.

"You should talk to Ruth. She's more connected than she lets on." Violet put the bag of carrots back in the fridge.

"Would she talk to me? I mean, she didn't seem to take to me when we met."

"Oh, that's just Ruth being Ruth. Come on, I told her I'd drop by—and I'll vouch for you. But, hey, do you want to see Lizzy's rat first? It's the cutest thing." In response, I grabbed my car keys and headed toward the door.

WE PARKED HALF a block away from the group's storefront. "Ruth really frowns on unnecessary driving." But either the cold was abating a bit, or I was getting used to it. If I kept myself entirely swathed in wool and polar fleece, I barely lost any sensation. As we walked, Violet filled me in: "Animals

Now is all volunteer, obviously, so it's pretty disorganized. But there is a sense of loyalty and everyone pitches in. Keep in mind, the vocabulary's different."

I looked over at her, unwilling to drop my scarf enough to ask.

"You know, basic stuff. Like if she says 'CD,' it's probably civil disobedience, like a sit in or something. Not a compact disk. And 'demo' is demonstration or maybe demolition. Not a sample." I nodded as we approached the row of shops that held the Animals Now office. "And, well, just follow my lead. You'll be all right."

She pushed open the storefront door and ushered me inside. "Hey, Ruth! You remember my friend, Theda?"

The large woman sitting behind one of the desks shot me a look. She remembered me, all right. I was meat girl. I mustered a cheery hello anyway. She flipped over the papers she'd been looking at and came forward, not exactly in greeting.

"What's she doing here?"

"She's okay, Ruth." I let Violet vouch for me and found myself staring down at the floor. The vintage army boots had been customized with bright red laces. Maybe there was a sense of humor in that tank-like exterior after all. "In fact, she's looking into the riverside project. She writes for the *Mail* and some other places." Did Violet not know that the piece I was working on was for potential buyers of waterfront condos? Ruth grunted and nodded, so I figured this wasn't the time to make that distinction.

"Actually, Ruth, I was wondering if you could help me. I didn't know that anything had been done officially down by the river. You guys are talking about the old bottling plant, right?"

"Yeah." Ruth sat back on the edge of the desk, still effectively guarding its papers, but motioned for us to pull up two of the plastic chairs by the wall. "What about it?"

"Well, I live in the neighborhood, too. Sometimes I can write about these things." She looked at me. "And, well, I was thinking of checking out the city licensing office, see what's been filed for."

"There's been no hearing. Not yet." Ruth gave up words as grudgingly as she gave up the moral high ground.

"Have they filed for a demo permit?" I'd done enough of these stories to know that doing the paperwork for such a permit, allowing a developer to get rid of whatever was on a site, was usually the first, and most contentious, step of a new project.

Ruth shrugged. "Haven't checked."

That was my opening. "Well, I will. I'll go over this afternoon. But is there anything you can tell me? Maybe give me an idea of what else to look for?"

She shook her head. "Wilson and Crave, the usual. Anyone else is silent."

Violet gave me a look. She wasn't going to help. "Okay, then. I'll let you know what I find out. But Ruth?" She looked up. "I also wanted to ask you about Gail. Can you give me any idea of what she was working on?"

Another shake. "Those cats. You know."

"So, she wasn't working on stopping the developers?"

"Shoulda been, wasn't."

"That must have been bad, having her drop out like that." I was fishing. The look Ruth gave me showed she knew it.

"Not so bad. We've got lots of people. More than you'd think. We're everywhere."

Was that a threat? That glare made me wonder, but it was also true that with Ruth's heavy features even an innocent glance could look loaded. Violet didn't seem disturbed by her tone.

"Well, I'm on your side." I chuckled, and could hear the nerves in my own voice. "I'll let you know what I find out." I was repeating myself. Nerves. But the big woman only nodded and moved back toward her seat. Maybe she was simply busy.

"And Ruth?" She looked up. "If you can tell me anything

more about Gail. What she was up to, maybe if she pissed anyone off, would you let me know?"

I got another shrug by way of a dismissal, as Violet dragged me to the door.

"What was that about?" Vi fairly hissed at me. The early dusk threw a shadow over her face.

"You don't think it's odd? Gail drops out of Ruth's group for all intents and purposes, and then she turns up dead?"

"You're crazy, Theda. You don't know what Ruth's about." She stalked away.

"I know what she sounds like." I was tall enough that it was easy to catch up.

"You know what she *looks* like." My diminutive friend spun toward me and poked her gloved finger in my chest. "You see big, butch Ruth and assume the worst. But I know her. I know that she's been working on a petition to clean up the Muddy and the Alewife, to crack down on garages that dump oil and transmission fluid. All to save some fish that I'd never even heard of before. And just a few weeks ago, she stayed up, like, all night to pick up poison bait that someone had laid out for the possums and raccoons. Someone had actually powdered chunks of cheese and fruit with rat poison. Can you believe that? Horrible stuff. Ruth was up till dawn, and the next day she was at City Hall to protest that new ferret bill. That's what keeps her going. And she's good at it. She cares."

"She didn't seem to care about Gail." I was losing ground, and backed away.

"People express things in different ways, Theda. Look, I wouldn't be working with her, with Animals Now, if I didn't believe in it and the work Ruth does."

"Just how involved are you, anyway?" We were walking again, so it seemed safe to ask.

Violet shook her head. "You're looking for conspiracies. It's not like that. We're a bunch of community activists, that's all. We all get involved in whatever project takes our fancy. For me, it's development. I've seen this city change too much already. Which reminds me, you really going over to the city offices?"

"Yeah, sure. Wanna come?"

"I've never been."

I checked my watch. Four-thirty. Not a good time for municipal offices. "Pick you up first thing tomorrow?"

"That's ten-thirty, right?"

I resisted reminding her of her own wake-up calls. "Right."

THE SUN WAS OUT for a second day when I picked Vi up, closer to eleven the next morning. But with the wind whipping up Mass. Ave., the weather hadn't warmed up much. I'd gotten coffee and muffins again, pumpkin this time, before swinging by the shelter. We were picking at crumbs by the time I parked, mercifully close to the city hall annex.

"Roar!" Violet reacted the same way I did when I first saw the concrete lions guarding the licensing offices.

"Mew?" The two lions, each holding a blank shield, declined to respond. Maybe the years and layers of paint that had flattened their features had muffled their voices, too. But I still gave each one a friendly pat as Violet pulled open the big wood and glass doors.

"Hey, you sure we're allowed in here?" Violet's stage whisper came with a sly grin.

"Yeah. This is all public." I led her to the right, to where a row of windows lined up like bank tellers. "Developers have to file notice."

"I knew they had public hearings. I've been to enough of those." Her widening grin proved she had, with protest signs. "But I've never been in on this end of it."

"Well, come here, then. Time you learned." I grabbed one of the information request forms and filled it out on the counter, then headed for the windows. The clerk looked up from her magazine, but didn't seem too dismayed by the distraction. At any rate, she smiled and told us to take a seat. Forty minutes later, we'd shed the last of our outer layers, and Violet was kicking her high-tops against the wall, when the clerk came back.

"I'm sorry. There's nothing filed about this particular lot. I checked for demo permits, abatements, dewatering, construction, and also for temporary parking bans, the kind they use for heavy equipment. Checked the properties on either side, too. That doesn't mean someone isn't acting on it. It just means it hasn't made it into the files yet. But, you know, before anybody plans a demolition, they have to have a public hearing. There will be notices posted around the property giving at least thirty days notice."

"Yeah, but I was hoping there might be something here."

"Sorry. Try again next week, if you want."

"Thanks." Violet was already reaching for the pile of clothes, donning the wool vest she wore under her parka, and I followed suit. By the time I had my hat down over my ears and my scarf around my face, I felt the weight of the week hit me. Even Violet's usual perkiness seemed to have disappeared.

"Well, that's good news, right?" I didn't want our Friday morning to have been wasted.

"All that means is that he hasn't filed." My pragmatic friend shot me a glance. "I mean, I didn't want to say anything in there. But I've heard enough stories about builders 'accidentally' demolishing buildings, or using forged permits. They pay a fine after, sure. But those are usually just a slap on the wrist. Once a building is gone, it's gone."

"Great." It sounded plausible, and I only had one answer. "More coffee?"

"Definitely." Together we made our way to the Mug Shot.

"Latte double tall and a soy milk cappuccino." As Sarah brought over our order, a steaming pint glass for me and a mug for Violet, I spied a table. Under the steam-covered window, I could almost pretend I was warm again.

"God, you think spring will ever come?"

"No, never." The grin was back. "Thank god for Caro." I

raised my eyebrows. "No, Theda. I mean, professionally! She's got the Helmhold House so well insulated that I swear the cats alone are almost enough to heat it."

I groaned. "I'd trade. In my building, its either boiling or freezing. Sometimes I think they're trying to drive us out."

"Wouldn't be the first time." Violet sipped from her mug and drew back with a grimace. "Hot!"

"But it's not like we've got rent control anymore. I mean, my landlord is making good money off of us."

"Maybe he wants to retire. Sell the building as condos and cash out. You know what they're going for."

I did, and the thought silenced me. "But wait, he's actually fixing our radiators. The super told me. They're putting new valves on them or something."

"That's just letter of the law, Theda. Could be someone complained to tenants' rights, or something."

"Great."

"You know you do have options. You ever need to, you could come bunk with us at Helmhold House. But before that, I'm sure Bill would ask you to move in with him."

"I know he would." I sighed. There was so much going on with him just then, I wasn't sure where to start. "We're getting along good, too. It's just that…" I conjured up an image of Bill on his sofa, watching sports on TV. "He's been in a funk since his surgery. All he does is lie on the couch and watch stupid sports."

"Well, it's not like he can go out for a run."

"I know. But he's in a rut. And it's not a fun rut." Violet took a long draw on her mug. Either it had cooled, or she was waiting for me to hear my own words. "I know I should try to get him out of it. But it just seems like my efforts are not appreciated."

"Well, now is not the best time, obviously. But everything's going to get better once he's back on his feet, and, you know, you can talk to him about it. Plus, if your landlord pulled anything really nasty, you know you and Musetta have his place as an option. Or our place."

"Thanks, kiddo."

She was right. If I wasn't happy, I owed it to Bill to speak with him. And so once I was home, I vowed to try to bring it up.

First, however, business beckoned.

"Mel? Mel Baker? The man himself?" We'd left each other so many voice mails, I felt like we were best friends.

"Yes, I got your messages. What can I do for you Ms. Krakow?" Okay, so the feeling wasn't mutual.

"Mr. Baker, I was just down at Cambridge City Hall, and I couldn't find that you'd pulled any permits for new construction."

"What new construction? What project are you talking about?"

"I may be writing about riverside developments, and I was specifically looking at the bottling plant that abuts Mem Drive."

"Now, what makes you think we have a project planned there?" I could be wrong, but his voice sounded like he was standing. I'd hit on something.

"Newsroom scuttlebutt." Did that sound authoritative? "It's obviously a valuable property for somebody and—"

"Now, wait a minute. Ms. Krakow? Is that your name? I don't know where you're getting your information, but what we file, when we file, is public and all on the up and up. You make it sound like we're doing something unethical here."

Illegal is the term I'd have used, but I couldn't quite see how to work that in. "That wasn't my intent, Mr. Baker. It's just that word is that Wilson and Crave have an interest in that property, and so as a journalist I'd like to know what those plans are and when we in the community—"

"Are you even a journalist at all, *Ms.* Krakow?" The word slid into something nasty. "You sound like a member of one of those so-called neighborhood watchdog groups that don't want anyone else to move in once they've got their piece of land."

"I am on assignment for the *Morning Mail.*" Here's hoping he didn't call Mina and give her a heart attack.

"Well, then, you'll get our press releases along with the rest of the world when, and if, there's anything to report." The snap of a cell switching off couldn't have been as satisfying as a good slam, but it let me know I'd been dismissed. I really had to hope he didn't call the *Mail*. This would not help me get any more supplement assignments. I needed solace.

"What's up, honey?" Bill sounded so chipper I wasn't sure where to start.

"Not much, a lot of dead ends." I rattled on about my day, skirting around the whole Mel Baker thing. I'd been somewhat out of line in my fishing, and I knew it. Only when I got around to my coffee break with Violet did I realize I hadn't asked him anything about himself.

"And what'd you do today?"

"I'm prepping for the Marathon. Only four more months to go."

"Bill…"

"Oh, the usual. I actually had the physical therapist come by today. That was fun. And ESPN has got this great series of classic football. Interviews with the coaches and everything."

"You know, Bill, I've been meaning to talk to you about that."

"About ESPN Classic?"

"No, this constant lying on the sofa, watching sports TV."

"It's not like I have a lot of options here." I could hear his voice growing testy.

"No, I know. I just worry that you're not helping your mood any. And that does affect healing."

There was silence. "Bill?"

"You mean, you're bored, Theda."

"Well…" I couldn't exactly deny it.

"Hey, I have something. I've been looking at the paper. While watching television." I bit back my retort and waited. "Anthony Ragalia is playing tomorrow over at Tech."

"You want to go out to a show? How?"

"The physical therapist said I should start using my crutches more. Try putting some weight on my leg. I was thinking I could call for a cab, ask for a station wagon or a van, so I could stretch out. What do you say, babe? Go out and hear some music?"

"Anthony Ragalia is jazz, right?" I recalled seeing the name on a CD case at Bill's.

"Yeah, you'd like him. He's like Professor Longhair, only updated."

I liked my 'Fess just the way he was, unadorned New Orleans piano. And I knew of at least four rock gigs happening on Saturday that I ought to check out. But what could I say? Bill was getting off the sofa, and it wasn't for sports. "You're on."

"So, you up for a home-cooked dinner tonight?"

"You're going to cook for me?"

"If you'll pick up the groceries."

Much as I was going to miss my kitty, this seemed like an opportunity to encourage Bill along the right path. Besides, he was a great cook. So although my plump pet was napping on top of the file cabinet, I woke her for a good brushing, which turned into a wrestling session. And by the time I headed out for Bill's, by way of the grocery store, we were both played out, and not a little tired of each other's company.

"You spoil that cat." Bill had noticed the scratches on the back of my hands while I was unloading my bags of supplies.

"I was asking for it." I had already explained about the grooming, and how that lead into rough play.

"You know, when I was on patrol, we used to hear the same thing in domestic violence cases. 'He really loves me. I egged him on.' Here, pass me that garlic press."

"Great. So you think I'm abused by my cat?" I passed him the press, a knife, and a cutting board. Although my sweetheart was ostensibly cooking dinner, I'd been enlisted into sous chef duty.

"I think you encourage her worst behavior. Sauce pan?"

"Well, she's my cat, Bill. And I enjoy it, too."

"It's always fun till someone loses an eye." He was laughing at least, and I felt some of my defensiveness drain away.

"She's hardly a man eater."

"She's hardly a *mouse* eater."

"Bill!" He reached for the wooden spoon and I drew it back. "I want an apology."

"Okay, okay. She's a ferocious, wild beast." I gave him the spoon. "But you know she's one of the klutziest cats I've ever met." I didn't say anything. He was right. "And she's getting really fat."

"She's a house cat. And a lot of that's fur. She has a very heavy winter coat." He looked at me with one of those wide grins, but wisely refrained from speaking.

"Anyway, I am aware of her weight. I won't let her get so heavy that it's bad for health."

"Well, it's a good thing she doesn't have to fend for herself." He must have seen my look. "She's a very loved pet, Theda. I know that, and I think it's adorable the way you play with her. Just—make sure you wash those cuts, okay?"

"They're not deep at all. I do keep her claws well trimmed, you know."

"Seeing as how you're her major prey, I'm glad you do. You both deserve a fighting chance."

ELEVEN

THIS TIME, IT WAS a large rubber band waiting for me that let me know that someone had missed me overnight. "Musetta?" I picked up the band, which seemed thick enough so even my orally-inclined pet probably wouldn't eat it. "Is this for me?"

Silence. Either someone was pissed that I'd stayed out all night again, or someone was deeply asleep. "Musetta?"

I walked down the hallway, noticing other little gifts—an eviscerated catnip mouse, the butterfly toy, a kitchen sponge—along the way. "Kitty?"

She looked up from her perch on top of my filing cabinet and yawned. "Jaws of death, Musetta! The great hunter." Having proved her indifference, she jumped down and led me into the kitchen, where more substantial fare was offered and accepted.

"Sorry about this, kitty." I spoke to her broad black back as she lapped noisily at her dish. "I don't like staying away from you, either. It's just that Bill isn't really mobile right now." Should I take my pet with me? She seemed so at home in my apartment, her little kingdom. No, we'd both just make do until circumstances changed.

"Was that good?" I couldn't figure out how she had become so rotund. Having eaten only about a third of her can, as usual, she'd sat and begun washing her face. "Are we happy now?" I scooped her up in my arms, disrupting her routine, but was rewarded with a purr that turned into a full-on rumble as I dug my fingers into her thick, warm fur. I flipped her over to rub her chest, with its downy white coat, and she lay back in my arms, eyes closed and paws extended, kneading the air. My cat did miss me. "Oh, kitty. I'm being a bad person, aren't I? Maybe I should get you a playmate." I realized with a twinge that I'd be out again tonight, with Bill. Well, I'd make it up to her at some point.

For now, work beckoned. Still holding the cat, I managed to reach the phone. My answering machine was strangely dark, and I had questions.

"Patti? Glad I caught you." Saturday was one of Patti's busiest days, the best day she had for showing the conventionally employed places that would absorb their money. But although I'd expected to get voicemail, it was her eternally perky voice that picked up.

"Oh, Theda." Her voice fell. I heard a thud and a loud sigh.

"Bad time?"

"No." She sounded breathless. "I'm just…peeved. I had set the entire morning aside to drive around with a client couple and they just backed out on me. I was already almost out the door to pick them up, too."

"I'm sorry. That's really rude." Patti worked on commission, sort of like freelance, so I related.

"Thanks. Thought I'd use the time to rearrange my living room. But the carpet shows the wear too much." Another loud huff. "So now I'm moving everything back."

Poor Patti. None of this would be a hardship to me, but in her mind, she still inhabited the upper-income bracket of her married days. How impolite of reality to intrude.

"Well, want to take a breather and talk with me a bit?"

"Sure." I heard a final huff, but this time it sounded like Patti sitting down.

"The bottling plant. Nothing's been filed with the city yet. No demolition permit, nothing."

"Theda! Didn't I tell you that was all hush-hush?"

"Sit back down, Patti. I'm not spreading anything around." Well, that was true: Violet and Ruth already knew. "But I was down at the city office yesterday and I thought I'd see what had been filed. It's all public knowledge, you know."

"Well, I wish you hadn't. Some people are very aware of who is looking into their business, you know."

Some people? "Patti, I'm not sneaking around here. This is all city regulations. Just as a member of the public, I'm allowed to look."

She snorted at that, if such a ladylike exhalation could be called a snort. "Well, just don't say I said anything."

"Patti, I'm not even talking to anyone." Mel Baker wasn't human, so he didn't count.

Patti knew me too well to believe my denial. "So you say. But remember, Theda. These are big boys and they can play rough. And, please, you said you wouldn't bring my name up in it."

"I got it, Patti." I looked at the names and numbers she'd given me for other developers. Nobody would be in the office today, but that didn't mean I couldn't do a little footwork. "Hey, you have any interest in driving around, looking at some properties?"

"For you and Bill?"

"Forget it, Patti. I mean for my story."

"Well, there's no point in hanging out here. But if anyone calls, I may have to run."

"It's a deal. And if nobody does, I'll buy you lunch. Pick you up in ten?"

"In your car? No thanks, I'll drive. And if anyone asks us, you're looking to buy."

"Got it." I had time to change into my better jeans. I'd showered that morning, but if Patti was going to try to pass me off as a potential client, I didn't think the torn Levis would pass, even if the rest of me was swathed in down.

"Sweet." Patti's Audi had heated seats, which were well warmed when I slid into the passenger side. "A little unnerving, kind of like when you're a really little kid and I couldn't hold it…"

"Watch your mouth, Theda. I love this car." I looked over at my friend, her pink wool scarf and hat matching the trim on her long parka, and was glad I'd thought to dress up a bit.

"I know, Patti. I know." Underneath that neat, preppie exterior beat the fierce heart of a struggling single woman, not that different from me. For Patti, I'd put on lipstick, just in case we ran into a real potential client.

"You look nice." She glanced over at me, then back at the road, now mostly clear, but still slick. "A little color perks your face right up."

"Thanks, mom." This was going too far.

"Well, it does." I bit back my response. "Now, where shall we start?"

"I wouldn't mind looking at the bottling plant."

Her look lasted a little longer this time. "Theda, are you sure this is just for a *House* supplement? There's really nothing to see there right now."

"I know," I lied, remembering the deep grooves of heavy machinery in the frozen earth. "But I'd like to see it through your eyes. Have you explain to me how it could be developed into housing."

"Well, I was thinking of Maverick Square. But I guess making a quick stop before we hit the Pike won't be a bad thing. Besides, Maverick Square is almost ready for occupancy, so it will be a useful contrast."

I sighed and told myself it wasn't going to be that bad. All things considered, doing these kinds of service features was pretty easy. Minimal creativity was required, in fact, more than once too much had gotten me into trouble. The editors of such stories, whether they were discussing real estate or bakeware, didn't want poetic imagery. They wanted me to contact a bunch of sources and to double-check my information. But even if the only creative part of the piece would be the lead, I knew I had to go around to at least some of the sites I'd be writing about. Just being able to describe the bend of a river or the sailboats at dock below would make the article just that much livelier.

But my tour of prospective real estate was not to be. Patti's cell rang as she pulled up to the bottling plant, and so I left her in the car and poked about on my own. The old building, with its granite base, looked as desolate as before, the dry front grounds still empty of anything but brush and trash. I kicked at some branches, and wandered around to the back. The wooden shed was still standing, its faded paint the only touch of color beyond the low evergreen hedge. Nothing looked different, but I jumped when I heard footsteps crunching through the dry leaves behind me.

"Theda! There you are. I thought you'd run off without me."

"Sorry, Patti. I didn't know how long you'd be on the phone and I wanted to get a sense of the place." No need to tell her I'd already thoroughly explored the grounds.

"No problem. But I am going to have to cut our rounds short. That couple called, and they do want to see the Avon Hill property." She looked as smug as her two cats combined. "I think they were trying to cut me out, and just maybe they learned that you do need a real estate professional for access, as well as expertise."

"Well, good for you, Patti! Give 'em hell." Before she could respond, I followed up. "So, throw some of that expertise my way. What should I be seeing here?"

We started walking past the windy courtyards. With Memorial Drive traffic whizzing past, it was difficult to imagine the kind of luxury Patti described. But she drew quite a picture. High enough to avoid the noise of traffic, above a full-service gym and various small convenience shops, the condos-to-be would take in the sweep of the river, including two of its most picturesque bridges. It would also take the glare right off the water, but I didn't say that. Instead, I looked behind me at the empty windows. Blank behind the growing midday glare, they stared out at nothing.

"Spooky, huh?" I pointed at the row of glass. As clouds whipped past, they alternated between black emptiness and a high-intensity shine.

"Be worse if they were all broken." Patti was practical. "There are a few boarded up, but basically this place is in decent condition. If the building were entirely empty, there might be vagrants living in there. Some of the places being developed have had lawsuits from those so-called squatters. And, no, I'm not telling you anymore, Theda!"

"I didn't ask. But, so, the plant isn't vacant?"

"There are still some subletters, I think. But it's all on the up-and-up. Tenancy at will, leases that go month to month. Just enough business to keep the place safe, but nobody who will cause trouble when Peter is ready to move."

"Hmm." I thought of those squatters, otherwise homeless people who had found some shelter in buildings like these. From what I was learning about Peter Wilson, I wouldn't wish him on any of them.

"You think anybody's home on a Saturday?" I walked up to one of the courtyard's legs. Closer to the river than the windy courtyard, its brick was bleached to a light russet. The doors set into it were less picturesque: gray, unpainted metal with small, wired windows set high.

"Theda, I don't think…" I pulled the handle of one, and then the other but both held fast. Locked tight, and when I stood on tiptoe to see inside the wire-laced glass, all I could make out was my own reflection.

"You know, we don't really have permission to be here." Patti shifted her feet, the kitten heels of her zip-up boots sinking into the crumbly, frozen earth. "Technically, I mean, I should have put in a request to Peter Wilson."

"But he's not the owner yet, is he?"

"Well, technically, he's not." I stared at her. "Technically, it's still owned by some trust that's in charge of keeping the property safe and clean. But realistically, nobody else cares about it."

"So you think anyone would notice if it disappeared?" I was thinking about what Violet had said: Demolish now, pay the fine later. "If someone just happened to act a bit precipitously?"

"Theda! I don't know where you get these ideas of yours. No, I *do* know—"

"It was just a thought, Patti. Just a thought. You know there was a colony of feral cats living here?" That's what was getting me, the quiet. I wouldn't expect many animals to be out in the middle of the day, even a sunny day, in January. But all I could hear was the buzz of traffic. No birds, no beasts, and the lack of living noise was unnerving. Patti wasn't so easily spooked.

"Ferals?" The realtor's berry-red lip curled, but the love of her two pets, former strays from Violet's shelter, softened the snarl. "Well, better than other animals I could name. And they'll keep the rodents under control."

"That they would, if they were still around." I walked over to another window, a wide low stretch of glass that seemed cleaner and clearer than most. "But they took off."

"The cold probably." Patti looked at her watch with the kind of broad gesture I was supposed to notice.

"No, not the cold." I pulled at the window's metal frame. It looked like it ought to be able to open. "They found shelter here. Had kittens, and everything."

"Kittens? Out here?"

"That's just it. There was a rescue worker, a woman who worked with ferals. She said the cats had a good place here, but for some reason they were moving away. Leaving whatever shelter they had, and in this weather, too. She said they seemed to have lost some of their kittens."

"Do you think there are wild dogs out here?" She looked about nervously.

"I don't know. She never figured it out." I was tempted to tell Patti the full story about Gail, about how the tiny, wire-haired woman was killed near here while working with the cats. But my realtor friend was so defensive about the property, about Wilson and Crave, I couldn't tell how she would react. Patti was a good soul, but nervous. Hearing that a woman had died, perhaps been murdered, so close to a property like this might be too much. I looked around and saw a haunted old building, a remnant of my city's past that had witnessed some bad times. For her, it meant serious income and another step away from her own hard times. I couldn't press it. Besides, she was stamping her pretty boots now, rubbing her gloved hands together.

"Theda, I'm freezing my buns off out here. And I've got to get changed before my twelve-thirty pickup."

"Okay, sorry. I get carried away. But why do you have to change? You look great." She did.

"Oh, you young girls!" She laughed, but I could tell she liked the compliment. "If I go to meet potential clients without freshening up my suit and makeup, I may just scare them into the Charles!"

TWELVE

"Wow!" The sound from the other side of the door was clearly annoyed. "Wow!"

"Hang on, kitty." I fumbled with my keys and pulled off the note stuck to my door: "Radiator work scheduled. Call me." I recognized Julian's scrawl, if not his cell number.

"Meh!"

"I'm coming." I'd stopped by the grocery store on my way home, but try explaining that to a cat. I used my shoulder to bang the door open, so of course the bags slipped. I watched apples roll down the hallway, following the path of Musetta, who headed for the hills as the first fruit landed with a soft thud.

"Great. Why is it always the apples?" I placed the other bag, containing Musetta's cans, on the counter and went to gather my scattered produce. "Musetta? Dinner?"

No reply. It was early for her, but I knew I'd be staying with Bill tonight and didn't want to forget her evening can. "Musetta?"

From the end of the hallway, a black and white face peered back at me. "Musetta!" I held up a can and she came trotting, noise forgiven if not forgotten. "Come on. Sit up! Do the gopher."

My cat eyed me as if I were nuts and then looked around. One apple was still rocking in an enticing way.

"Pss…pss…psss." I held the can directly above her head and she obligingly sat up. "Good—" "Girl," I'd been about to say, before she batted the can out of my hand. Now this was fun.

Ten minutes later, I'd fed the cat and gathered my errant fruit. How do women with real children do it? I guess I'd find out soon enough, vicariously. Just then, the phone rang.

"Bunny! Speak of the, nevermind. How're you feeling?"

"Great, Theda. I'm pregnant. Not sick." I could hear her crunching on something as she spoke.

"I know, I'm just asking." Now didn't seem the time to inquire about her diet. "Any morning sickness or anything like that?"

"Nope. I seem to be healthy as a horse. Still eating like one, too."

"Well, your body probably knows what it wants." Your mouth, too, I thought, as I walked the phone into the kitchen. Cheddar cheese rice cakes or the caramel ones? Actually, the apples looked good.

"Seems to. Anyway, I was wondering. Have you talked to Tess yet?" I cut out a brown spot and started slicing the fruit for quieter consumption.

"Yeah, I meant to call you." And tell her what? That our mutual friend had accused Bunny of hysteria? "She says you got it wrong. That she did hit a girder, like she told me. And, well, that you're overreacting." Bunny started to protest. I cut her off. "But I don't believe her, Bunny. Something's wrong. Tess doesn't sound like herself."

"Thanks, Theda. I know what I heard." Bunny was crunching away again. The sound of thinking. "Dropping out of sight, and this thing with her accident, it is weird, right?" I nodded, my own mouth full. "I mean, Theda? Is this just my hormones?"

"No, I don't think so." I choked the slice down. "Tess is acting odd. I'd wonder if she'd been drinking or something. But I don't think she's done anything but work recently."

"Me neither." We both crunched companionably. "I haven't seen her in ages."

"Maybe there's something else we haven't thought of?" I knew Tess cared about her job, but this was too much. "Like, maybe she's got something going on with one of the guys in the lab? Maybe they were making out while she was driving?"

"Nah. That we would have heard about. Something's going on. But if she doesn't want to let us in, I don't know what we can do." Bunny was hurt, I figured, by Tess's accusation. But she was also right. I grunted and reached for another slice. "Hey, you hearing anything about Ralph?"

"Other than the usual, that he's a drunken lech?"

I grunted. That was a given. "I think he got the flu that's going around. But half the office is wheezing and hacking. I'm taking echinacea like it's going out of style."

"Gotta love the winter." I didn't miss the *Mail*'s recirculated, overheated air. "But you feel okay? We're still on for tomorrow night, right?"

"Violet's band? Most definitely, I've got to party while my nights are still my own. Shall I pick you up?"

"No, I'm actually doing an interview first. But it's at the Casbah, so I'll meet you there."

"Sounds like a plan."

I THOUGHT ABOUT all the calls I should make. Not that anyone would be answering on a Saturday anyway, and ended up rigging up a new toy for Musetta: a wad of aluminum foil attached to the end of a string. The idea was that I could sit and maybe even read while she played. But my stationery tossing and retrieving didn't interest my cat once she realized that the bare hand holding the string was more vulnerable—and got a bigger rise out of me. A couple of flying tackles, paws wrapped around my wrist and just the touch of teeth, got me on my feet and playing in earnest, as my hunt-crazed kitty lashed her tail and jumped at every movement.

Ten minutes later, we were both exhausted. I collapsed on the sofa and Musetta leaped up to join me. Bill wasn't due till six, but the apple hadn't held me.

"What do you favor, Musetta?" I reached for the phone. "Mushroom and pepperoni? Or should we go for olives?" Disgusted by my taste, she promptly fell asleep.

WHEN THE CAB HONKED two hours later, I was asleep, too. Sated and warm, the idea of venturing forth to hear jazz had less appeal than the three slices of mushroom, pepperoni, and olive that sat congealing on the table in front of me. Still, I'd promised Bill. And I did want to encourage his interest in anything outside the tube.

"Hang on!" My voice probably didn't carry through the closed window, but I waved to the taxi below and threw the remaining pizza into the fridge. Nothing beat cold pizza for breakfast.

Bracing for the weather, I was still wrapping my scarf around me when I got downstairs. The cabbie reached over and unlatched the passenger side door.

"Miss?"

"Thanks." I looked over and saw Bill stretched out in the back. The way he'd propped himself up, his leg stretched across the seat beside him, didn't look comfortable, but he managed a smile. "Your chariot, madame."

"Onward!" I climbed in, exchanged a smile with the driver, and off we went.

To DO HIM JUSTICE, the cabbie did his best to get us close to the show. Held in one of the nicer lecture rooms at Tech, Cyrus Hall was buried in the warren of buildings that made up the institute. Very few of them adjoined an actual city street, but our taxi had driven up on a service road as far as he could.

"Sorry, mon."

"No problem." Bill sat up with an effort to pay the driver, and I wondered how we'd proceed. But somehow we slid him off the seat and onto his crutches.

"Can I do anything to help? Do you want to lean on me."

"No, just watch out if I fall."

"Fair enough. I think it's this way." I pointed to a long, low building. As far as I knew, Cyrus Hall was in there, somewhere.

"Okay, here we go." He took a step and swung his bad leg. "One step at a time."

At this rate, we'd miss the show, which didn't really upset me. But I knew Bill wanted to see it so I took a breath. "You sure you don't want a hand? Or a leg?"

"A leg I could use. But, seriously, no. Let me just get the hang of it."

Fifteen minutes later, we were in the building, and less than ten minutes later we'd made it to the hall. The lights had been lowered, but I could see well enough to tell the place was packed. This was not going to be good.

"Bill!" Someone stage whispered from the back row. "Over here!" A chubby bald man waved us over and I saw that he'd spread a coat over two adjoining seats. "Take the aisle." He slid over two seats and I grabbed the middle seat, holding Bill's coat while he lowered himself down, his leg stretched out in what was probably a fire hazard.

"Thanks." I started to introduce myself, but just then the music started.

At first, it was fine. The hall smelled of damp wool, but it was warm and the seat was comfortable. The pianist, a skinny older man with wild gray hair, didn't look like he was enjoying himself. But he was amusing as he pounded down on his instrument like a man possessed. The sound was strange, ugly even, and I couldn't make out a pattern, much less a tune. But I was enjoying it, enjoying his Brillo-topped vigor and the satisfying dissonance. It was almost punk, really. Passion aiming to provoke.

I smiled at the thought and looked forward to sharing it with Bill. Hey, I do get jazz after all! But that distraction was too much: I missed a transition, or some kind of connection. The pianist had stopped the delicious noise and was playing chords, big dense things that didn't let me in, and I was lost. A quiet section followed. Was there a melody in this? Something plaintive? I didn't know, couldn't find any part of it to follow, and soon I was drifting.

The warmth didn't help. What had been welcoming was now stifling. My eyes began to close and I jerked myself up. Try to find a rhythm, I told myself. Start counting beats. But counting beats is only steps away from counting sheep, and I was lying when I told myself, "I just want to rest my eyes." The applause saved me, startling me up before I realized, no, that was just one number. The wild-haired man was going to play more.

What kind of name was Ragalia anyway? Italian? Maybe something Eastern European? The tousled gray curls looked like they'd been black to begin with, and his pale face wrinkled around a bulbous nose. Ukrainian? I felt my lids growing heavy again and forced myself to sit straight. By tilting my head, I could begin counting ceiling tiles. Really, it was quite fascinating. This being a lecture hall, there were rows and rows of acoustic tile, set in sets of six. Eight sets on each wall. These rimmed an inner section of some harder material. Could it be wood? These must provide just enough echo for resonance, which would explain why the hall got booked for concerts. The piano was certainly ringing.

Just then Brillo-top shifted. The upper keys made a sound like Musetta pouncing on a live rodent, and I found myself paying attention. Was someone snoring? No, that was the pianist, singing to himself in low, guttural tones as he played a lot of notes, very fast, and in no apparent order.

This was ridiculous. I was here, stuck, for the duration. I might as well put the time to good use. Sorting through the problems of the last few days would do me more good than memorizing the arrangement of ceiling tiles, no matter how intricate. And besides, I'd never know for sure what that central section was made of.

Swann's Way. That was the biggest weight on my mind. Probably I'd talk to them tomorrow and everything would go fine. I'd have Monday to write, Tuesday to read it through, and I could file by noon easily. But I didn't like it. I'd never written about a band that I hadn't heard play before, at least in their practice space. And the way they'd put the interview off worried me more. What if they canceled? Tim was expecting this story.

Beyond that, it was a point of pride. Theda Krakow made her deadlines.

I'd get the interview. It would be fine. But just in case, I needed to see if I could dig up a smidgen more background. If they blew me off, I'd still be able to write about them—and reminding them of this might just give me leverage if they sounded like they were going to back down.

So what was next? Tess. Well, Bunny and I could confab about this tomorrow. If our friend was becoming a workaholic, or something worse, we would do an intervention. We didn't know why she was being so evasive about her accident. For now, all we knew for sure was that she was hiding out and spending too long at the lab. That wouldn't kill her, right?

Gail. I didn't know what to think about the diminutive cat rescuer, but I found myself almost missing her dark-eyed stare, her shrill voice. She was intense, but maybe she had good reason. And that Animals Now group might have its heart in the right place, but something about its methods made me queasy. The fact that Violet seemed to be getting so chummy with that Ruth woman, too, didn't bode well. I'd have to talk to her about it, sometime when we were both sitting down and not wrestling with half-wild animals or digging through an urban ruin. Then I could talk over the whole development deal. Despite what Patti had said, I felt comfortable spilling to Violet. She knew it all, anyway, and if we were face to face, I could convince her to keep it close. Between the Animals Now folks and that developer, there could be a lot of bad blood, and I didn't want her getting stuck in between. Besides, maybe she'd have talked to Eva. Found out something about the girl from the club. And she knew more about the drugs than she'd told me. I had to get her to talk. Dinner, that's what we needed.

My stomach rumbled. Why had I eaten so early? But wait, everyone was standing. I did, too, and nearly fell over as my sleeping leg buckled on me. "Whoa, girl!" Bill caught me. He, at least, was solidly propped on his crutches. I applauded madly. It was over!

But no, the pianist sank back down on his bench, and my heart followed suit. An encore. Well, at least I was getting some planning done. I did need to talk to Violet, but I also remembered what she said. If nobody from Animals Now had a car, then the chance that they'd hit Gail with one seemed unlikely. Unless, of course, they were masterminds looking to hide their crime and had borrowed a car for the occasion. No, I was going about this wrong. Maybe it wasn't who Gail was, or who she'd pissed off. Maybe it was *where* she was. I knew what Patti had said about Wilson and Crave and their league of lawyers. But that didn't mean they were above dirty tricks, just that they could get away with them. Pay a fine and be cleared. And feral cats or no, if Gail had stumbled over something going on at the plant … I remembered those deep equipment tracks. If Gail had mouthed off to the wrong person….

Suddenly everyone was clapping, and for a moment I felt proud. Then I realized that the applause wasn't for my minor mental breakthrough. The concert was over. We were free to leave! I clapped and hooted along with the crowd, stopping only when it became clear that the wild-haired man was considering another encore. The promoter saved me; he must have had a time limit on the room. He thanked us all for coming, and then I was helping Bill get up onto his crutches and meeting his friend, Phil, who introduced himself as a member of the New England Jazz Club.

"Good to meet you!" It was good to meet anyone who got my guy away from the television.

"You as well. Wasn't that wild?" I nodded, smiling, and was saved when Phil turned to my beau. "Can you believe he couldn't get a club date?"

"Amazing." Bill was glowing, and I didn't think it was from the overheated room. "Where did the promoter try?"

"Everywhere. Riverbend. Maple Room." He listed every jazz bar I'd heard of in town. "Man, did they miss out. There must be a hundred people here tonight!"

Barely enough to make it worthwhile to open the bar at most rock clubs. Especially when the crowd, filing past me now, looked to be middle-aged and cerebral. These folks were not serious drinkers.

"Maybe they figured this isn't a bar scene." I felt like the voice of experience as we waited for the foot traffic to pass.

"Doesn't matter." Bill, usually silent on club issues, chimed in "A performer like Ragalia draws from all over New England. These tickets were a steal at thirty bucks." Thirty bucks? No band I knew commanded that, not on this level. "And this may not look like a drinking crowd." He smiled at me, guessing at my thoughts with an eerie accuracy. "But I bet they'd have been up for a two-drink minimum. No, somebody missed a bet here."

"I didn't realize." Bill smiled at me as we followed the last stragglers into the long hallway.

"It's a bit different from your scene. Not that much, but a bit. Hang on." Out in the hall, Bill called for a cab, specifying that he needed a station wagon or van.

"He said he'd meet us out by Ames." Bill was walking better. It could have been practice and getting the hang of the crutches, but I suspected that the concert had been good for him. "So, what did you think?"

"Well…" I paused. Should I tell him life is too short? That I hoped never to sit through something quite like that ever again?

"Wasn't it outrageous? I know he got really out, especially the second number. The passage with the syncopated eighths, but I figure you've got the musical sophistication to hear what he was doing."

"I…" He smiled. Did he know he was appealing to my musical vanity?

"I mean, that whole inverted structure was just mayhem."

"That it was." Finally, something I could agree with. "And you know, Bill? It was a fascinating evening. It really made me think."

THIRTEEN

"You heard Anthony Ragalia? Cool!" Violet was not commiserating as I'd expected. "I didn't know Bill was into anything that rad. Did he do that thing with the syncopated eighth notes, where he deconstructs the melody?"

"Yeah, he did. I think so, anyway." Back home after a leisurely brunch with Bill, I'd ceded the Sunday paper to my purring cat and made good on my promise of calling Violet. But if she was going to go on about abstract jazz, I was going to have to work the magazine out from under Musetta's butt.

"Nuff." With a grunt my kitty rolled over, exposing her belly and effectively spreading herself across the entire *Mail*. I'd picked up the paper for my personal use, but clearly my cat didn't see it that way. After leaving her alone for yet another night, I lacked the heart to move her.

"Yeah, it was pretty out. " At least hanging with Bill I'd picked up some of the vocabulary. I reached over to bury my fingers in Musetta's downy fur. "Ow."

"What's that?"

"I got bit. Musetta is sensitive about her tummy. Hey, speaking of—how's that feral? What are you calling her, Exene?"

"She's doing all right. She may even be taming a bit. She's stopped lashing out and biting anyway. She still growls at me. But I think it's more habit that hostility. Hey, you still coming tonight?"

"Yeah, I'm bringing Bunny. Can you guest list us?"

"No problem. Ruth might come, too."

That was my entry. "Violet, I've been meaning to ask you

about her." I didn't get much further. Violet and I were close, but she could be as stubborn as I was. As soon as I raised the question of legality, she shut me off.

"Theda, Theda. Come on, girl. What world are you living in? No, I know. You're almost as straight edge as I used to be, at least where the law is concerned. Maybe that's a good thing, considering Bill. But I've got to be practical. When things need doing…." She let it hang.

"Vi, I'm with you. I don't want the neighborhood priced out by some big luxury condo thing going up. Not when we need affordable housing and more parks. But, well, this Peter Wilson sounds like he plays rough."

"You got that right."

"Well, that's just it. If Ruth and the other Animals Now folks escalate, someone might get hurt. Maybe somebody already has gotten hurt."

"Theda, I've been taking care of myself since I was sixteen." She paused, and I realized that what I said had sunk in. "Hey, you think that's what happened to Gail? She wasn't really working on that campaign."

"Yeah, but she was down there. And, you know, if someone saw her poking about in doorways and looking in windows, they might have gotten spooked."

"So, now you *do* believe that Craven is up to something!"

I noticed the play on the developer's name. "Subtle, Violet." She chuckled. "But, yeah. I mean, you saw those tire treads. Something is going on there. And Patti—" Damn, I'd meant to keep her out of it.

"Don't tell me Miss Pink is handling the sales?" Patti and Violet got along, grudgingly. They were neighbors. But they'd never be close.

"No, not yet. And, hey, I'd promised her I wouldn't mention her name. But she did hint strongly that Peter Wilson had his eye on the plant. So when we didn't find any papers filed, well, I wondered."

"That maybe they'd act first, file late, deal with the fines? 'Spossible."

"So, well…" What I wanted to do was warn Violet off. Keep her from getting too close to a conflict that might have already escalated into violence. But how could I say anything that didn't sound like I was just bashing Ruth? "Well, I just wanted to throw the idea out there. You haven't heard anything from Ruth, have you? I mean, nobody's threatened Animals Now, have they?"

"No. If anything, Ruth seems to think Gail had lost it, gotten distracted from 'the cause.' But put this way, maybe she'll decide that Gail was martyred."

"That's a bit strong, Vi. Come on. If those developers were somehow involved in Gail's death, it wasn't martyrdom. It was murder."

As soon as I'd hung up the phone, I realized I hadn't asked Violet whether she'd had a chance to ask Eva about the girl from the club. The ER nurse was a long shot, but I just felt like I had too many feelers out and none of them were giving me anything back. I rang Violet back, but the call flipped to voice mail and I had other duties. Especially with no good leads coming in, I was finding it difficult to get to work. Of course, it was Sunday. That didn't help. But even if the interview tonight went wonderfully, I was going to have to write my entire column tomorrow. I could do it—hadn't I filed a review for third on Wednesday?—but a lot had been going on, and I was sorry I hadn't made any headway on anything else in my life. I was tired, I missed sleeping in my own bed, with my own cat, and I just didn't want to risk having an off day. Besides, how often was my column ever going to be on the Arts front? Time to do some work.

The good thing about covering clubland is that weekends are workdays. Fridays and Saturdays, "amateur nights" when everyone came out to play, are the nights that filled club coffers, making our scene possible, and odds were good that on a Sunday someone would be cleaning or counting. I felt too lazy to trek around town, but that didn't mean I couldn't let my fingers do the walking. First call was over to Amphibian.

"Hey, Theda, love of my life. What's shaking?"

"Not much, Tony. Just working on a piece. You remember I called asking about that band, Swann's Way?"

He laughed at the name. "Yeah, the mystery group. But I still haven't heard anything about them beyond the buzz. Maybe if they changed their name…"

"Not likely with this crew." It was so pleasant chatting without having to worry about anyone that I was loathe to hang up. That's when it hit me: I could follow up on one of my other stories while I had him on the line. "Hey, Tony. I've been thinking. Are you hearing or seeing anything about some new club drug that's hit town?"

"Whoa, that's a shift. What's up?"

"I don't know. That's the problem. I saw a girl having some kind of reaction, maybe even an OD. And I'm hearing dribs and drabs of some new drug—Fantasy Plus—going around the clubs."

"I wouldn't be surprised, Theda. These things aren't that hard to make. The big problem—and this is all hearsay, mind you—is that the labs stink from all the chemicals."

"Yeah, right." Tony might protect his clientele, but I thought he saw a lot more of what was going on than he'd admit. "But I thought the smelly stuff was in meth labs?" I vaguely recalled a PBS documentary that likened the stink to burning aluminum foil.

"Same diff. But, you know, some of those student-y neighborhoods over in Allston? Maybe nobody would notice."

"I lived over a curry house for a year. By the end, I didn't smell anything when I came home."

"I bet you smelled delicious."

"Tony…."

"I'm not going to apologize for the truth. Hey, I'll tell you what though. I'll ask around. You still at the same number?" I murmured yes. "So you haven't moved in with that boy yet? There's still hope?"

I sighed. He was teasing, wasn't he? "See you, Tony."

"Bye, love!"

WOULD RALPH HAVE anything to say? He tolerated me as a colleague, flirted with me out of habit. I thought of him as a goofball, as outdated as his skinny pony tail, but he was out almost every night. He had to hear things. And if the hefty staff writer truly was sick in bed, with the flu, maybe he'd chat. I tried his number next and got a machine. If he was home, he was asleep. Two more calls yielded live bodies, but no more info. Everyone had heard rumors of a new drug, Fantasy Plus, but nobody could—or would—hook me up. By four I felt like I'd done as much work as could reasonably be expected on a Sunday. That still left two hours to kill. I could don some layers and go running.

A quick peek out the window nixed that idea. Not yet four-fifteen and the sun was nearly gone, the early dusk looked as cold and dreary as, well, February. Inside was cozy and warm. My already round cat had curled into a circle on her favorite chair.

"Come here, kitty, and comfort your mama."

My sleeping pet protested slightly as I pulled her into my lap. "Eh." But soon she rearranged herself to her satisfaction and I pet her until we both fell into a doze, the perfect way to finish the day.

FOURTEEN

WALKING UP TO the Casbah a few hours later, I realized I didn't know what to expect. Despite all my calls and queries, the band that was to be my next column, and the Arts cover, was a blank to me. As I'd gotten dressed, I'd played the four songs on their Myspace page until I knew the words by heart. Even as I jammed my gloved hands deeper in my pockets and trotted the last block up to the busy Central Square club, I found myself singing. *"Madeleine, Madeleine, your sweetness falls like rain, rain."* But, like that press kit, the tune was too slick, lacking that certain undefinable tension that would make me chew on it, that would set the band apart. I hummed the hook again. If I weren't on my way to an interview, I'd wash my ears out with some good college radio. As it was, I had a tune in my head that was going to get very annoying very soon, and no real idea what I'd be writing about.

But what could I expect from a baby band? Of course they had no press: they hadn't played out. Hell, they hadn't released a CD yet, which these days often came before the gigs. Reed hadn't gotten back to me, but from all my calls around town I was pretty confident Swann's Way hadn't even sent out audition tapes. I'd just have to see what I could get from the musicians themselves—and try not to be too harsh on them. Maybe they would be great one day, and maybe they had found a shortcut to stardom. With any luck, the next hour would give me at least a clue.

"Rain, rain…" In the bustle of the Casbah's front room, I couldn't hear myself, but I realized I was repeating the refrain.

Maybe it was better than I'd thought. "*Madeleine, Madeleine*—Hey!" Ralph was weaving through the crowd. The front room wasn't that busy, not yet, so I credited the pint glass he was carrying. It was full, but I doubted it was his first.

"Hey, gorgeous." I turned in time to take his sloppy wet kiss on my cheek.

"Hi, Ralph. Glad to see you're feeling better. You working tonight?" Violet could use the press.

"Might check out the opener. Once I'm fortified!" He hoisted the pint, losing a quarter of it in the process. I stepped out of range and smiled, looking around for my particular assignment.

Heather was standing over by a table, and, as I made my way through the crowd of early diners and drinkers, I recognized the two young men flanking her.

"Theda, these are the masterminds behind Swann's Way. I'd like you to meet the two Pauls, Paul Berman and Paul Wexner." On cue, they stood to greet me. Both taller than I'd thought and equally thin, Paul Wexner had the edge in the looks department, with his baby face and dark hair. Both were also sporting the kind of identical sullen looks that I'd come to associate with self-conscious rockers, or spoiled kids. But then they tossed their heads, clearing the bangs out of their eyes, and laughed as they saw themselves mirroring each other. Their laughter was friendly, their faces clean and fresh, and I found myself smiling back.

"Hi, Pauls. Good to meet you. But I've got a bone to pick: I've got 'Madeleine' stuck in my head." The last trace of temper vanished as they accepted my dubious compliment, Paul Berman ducking his sandy-brown moptop in mock humility while Paul Wexner, definitely the chick magnet, smiled more broadly and thanked me. Couldn't hurt to warm up the interview subjects, could it?

We sat and I explained my procedure, putting my minicasette recorder on the table as I did. "I'll be taking notes, as well. Partly for myself, in case other questions pop up while you're talking. I don't want to interrupt something you're saying. And partly for backup. This isn't the ideal venue for taping an interview."

"Should we take turns speaking into the machine?" Paul Wexner picked up the little recorder and turned it over in his hands. "Or lean into it to speak?"

"No, not at all." I took it from him and placed it back on the table. "This is sensitive enough to pick up your voices, and I'll be able to tell you apart. Just try to forget it's even there. Besides, this interview is only one part of the story." I had their attention now. "I know you guys haven't played out yet, but I always try to get some other feedback on an artist. You know, reviews, when they're available. Outside opinion. It's like triangulating a spot on a map." All three of them were looking at me and I realized I wasn't making sense.

"Let me try again. I figure if I just talk to you, then it's my opinion. If I was writing a critical piece, that would be fine. I'd be speaking in my voice, based on my background, experience, whatever. But this is a feature, so I don't want it to read like an 'as told to.' So I'm doing research, too."

"You've got the press kit Heather put together." Although Berman was the primary composer, Wexner seemed to be the spokesman of the bunch, and I made a quick note in my pad to find out if the sweet-faced singer also wrote the lyrics. He leaned forward. "What are you writing?"

"Just a note to myself." I smiled again, forcing it a little to reassure him. "Now, let's start at the beginning. Did you two meet at MuzeArts, or did you already know each other?"

By the time my tape had run out, ninety minutes later, I was wiped. I'd exhausted every possible avenue of inquiry, from their childhood influences to their rehearsal habits. This one was going to be like pulling teeth. It wasn't that they were dumb, or even particularly evasive. They admitted that they argued. Wexner leaned toward a heavier, almost metal sound, they'd explained, while Berman—whom I now thought of as "the quiet one"—pushed for the pop hooks. And since both wrote the lyrics for Berman's tunes, things could get tense.

But that was innocuous stuff. Background. When I moved onto the topic of their MuzeArts gig, the conversation had seemed over. They looked at me, both blank faced, and for a moment I floundered. I didn't have much to press them with, admittedly. Still, I've been a journalist long enough to know that a hint can serve as leverage, and after a pause those instincts kicked in. "It's not like I couldn't find out," I said, with more confidence than I felt. "I've been making some inquiries into the economics of what you're doing." That was it. The two Pauls exchanged a look that said it all. When I followed up with a direct question—"So you're renting the hall for the upcoming gig, right?"—Berman looked again at his partner, who nodded.

"You see, our sound doesn't fit with the Boston punk ethos." Once he'd acknowledged it, Berman was happy to share his rationale. "Everything in the clubs these days is punk derived. Either it's emo or some loud hardcore thing. We're beyond that. We're into a more complete, evolved sound, and not only would it be difficult to get a break in a club like, well, this." He gestured around to the increasingly crowded room. "It wouldn't present our music as it should be heard. So, yeah, we're taking a risk. But we think that once people hear why, they'll understand."

It wasn't a bad argument; I'd heard musicians with years of touring under their belts make the same case. Boston was a rock town—punk, garage, you name it—and pop was never the sound of choice. The problem was that Swann's Way were so young and inexperienced. I suspected they were throwing their money away. Then I remembered that they'd managed to hook my editor. Maybe it wasn't a bad strategy.

At any rate, it was on tape now. I'd transcribe it in the morning and find some way to stitch a story out of it. It wasn't like I hadn't written with less before.

"I've given your contact info to our photo department." I'd

stood to shake hands with them, and looked around for Bunny. We were due to meet here soon, and I wasn't going to give up a perfectly good table. Besides, I was starving. "I'm sure they'll be contacting you."

"Okay, great, thanks!" Berman smiled and made his way out, and Wexner turned toward me. "Heather and I are going to have a drink. Want to join us?"

So that was the connection. "No, thanks. I'm meeting a friend for dinner in a few. Enjoy!" I looked around again for Bunny or, failing that, a waitress with a menu, but saw that Heather had the grace to blush slightly as the baby-faced singer led her away to the bar.

LUCKILY, I ONLY HAD to wait about five minutes before Bunny showed up, swathed to her eyebrows in a peacoat and great purple shawl.

"I can't believe it got so cold again." She took off the matching hat and shook out her curls. "Or maybe I'm just getting more sensitive to it."

"You're nesting." I reached for her shawl and folded it over the table's third chair. "I took the initiative of ordering an appetizer sampler."

"Great, I'm famished." My friend lowered her considerable self into her seat just as, as if on cue, Risa the waitress came over with our platter: hummus, baba ganoush, and some rice-stuffed grape leaves. "I'll be back in a minute with your pitas," she said. We didn't wait, both of us grabbing the rolled-up grape leaves as soon as the plate was on the table.

"Blessed be, these are good." Since her handfasting last fall, Bunny had relaxed in her observance of the nature-based Wiccan religion. It still came up when she was happy, though, so I took the traditional greeting as a good sign. That and the way she was licking her fingers. "Now, I need a drink!"

I sat up straight, but before I could even begin to speak, Bunny was on it. "No, no! I mean soda or juice or something. I'm just parched. You know how the heating system in the *Mail* gets."

I did. With one big, antiquated system responsible for the enclosed environment year-round, the *Mail*'s newsroom was usually colder in the summer than in the winter, when the heat blasted so hard that plants left on windowsills on Friday were guaranteed to be dead by Monday. Bunny took a tube of moisturizer out of her bag and pushed her sleeves up to rub some on her elbows, and I recalled what it could do to skin, too.

I grabbed another grape leaf. "Of course, you could just rub some of this olive oil on your skin." It was drippy, but awfully tasty, with a hint of mint.

"Not anymore. Don't laugh, but since I've found out, my skin has become so sensitive. And my boobs...." She leaned in, not that anyone could hear us over the general bar noise. But I was saved from further detail by Risa, who dropped off a basket of pita triangles. I reached for one; it was still warm.

"Drinks?"

"Club soda with lime for me."

"Ditto." What the hell, it was going to be a long night. Risa raised her eyebrows. "We're being healthy tonight," I explained, but she was off.

"Am I that much a creature of habit?" Now it was my turn to lean in.

"Well, you do love your Blue Moon."

"I guess." Much as I liked having my own research down cold, I prefer to think of myself as unpredictable. So much for that illusion. But then Risa came back with our sodas and a saucer full of cut-up lime. We gave her our orders, and Bunny and I got into it for real.

"So, what's up?"

I filled my friend in on Bill and his leg, and managed to make the jazz show into a funny story. But Bunny was looking at me in a way that made her cat's-eye glasses glitter.

"Something's on your mind, Theda. Spill."

She was right.

"I don't know, Bunny. The Tess situation is really bothering me. Did I tell you, she's got this funny little nervous laugh now? I know she doesn't want me to pry, but I'm worried."

Bunny took a swig of her soda and made a face. "Man, everything tastes different when you're pregnant." She reached for another lime. "So, you don't believe her?"

"No, I think she's lying about telling us both the same story, and I'm trying to figure out why." Our plates arrived and Bunny began digging into a moussaka stacked like an architectural model. I took a bite of my own eggplant and lamb dish, shikel mishi, and tried to reason out my own instincts. "I feel like she went on the offensive, attacking you and me for our concern. And that makes me think she's hiding something. In part, because, well, her story doesn't match up. And in part—God, I hate to even *think* about this—but because of Gail and the lab and everything."

"Hold on." Bunny held her fork up like a traffic sign. "Rewind. What are you talking about?"

"I didn't tell you about Gail?" She shook her head and started to eat again, gesturing with her knife for me to go on. I took another bite—the spicy harissa worked wonders against the earthy eggplant—and gave her the story from the beginning: Violet's call, Gail's death, the evidence that suggested whoever had hit Gail had not tried to stop, and the subsequent inquiries into who might have wanted her dead.

"And Tess's lab was almost closed last year because of those protesters." Bunny had stopped eating again, even before her plate was empty. This was serious.

"It was? I knew there was something going on at the university."

"Yup. And it was her lab that was the focus. Her precious lab that's been taking up all her time recently." We both looked at each other. Suddenly, the food in my stomach felt too heavy. All that lamb, turned to lead. "This is bad, Theda."

Risa broke the silence by bringing us another round of sodas. I reached for a fresh lime and squirted myself in the eye for my trouble.

"Yow. I guess that was self defense, right?" My eye stung like the dickens.

"Exactly."

"Anyway, what are we saying? Tess wouldn't have hit somebody and driven off, would she?"

"No." Bunny said with a bit too much emphasis. "No, she wouldn't," she repeated. I wanted to believe her, and nodded in agreement. But as I reached for my wallet, I remembered one tenet of my friend's religion: thoughts and acts were all part of a larger whole, and whatever you send out comes back to you threefold. Even though Tess had insulted her, Bunny would consciously try not to believe ill of anyone, particularly a friend.

"I just wish…" My voice trailed off. We'd said it all. Bunny looked at me, willing me to be happy. "So, you're up for some music, mama?"

"Mama to be, and yes!" She stood and grabbed her coat and shawl. "This baby's going to rock!"

IT WAS EARLY ENOUGH so that the downstairs was still nearly deserted. Taking advantage of the space, we walked up to the side bar, where the edge of the stage stuck out far enough for nonperformers to sit. I threw our jackets behind us and looked around. The Casbah had worked hard to become the premier club in town. Other places might charge more, but night after night, this is where the best bands in Boston and Cambridge played.

Not that it looked like much. Over the raised stage, where a young Asian woman was assembling a keyboard and amp combo, red theatrical lights glowed. They would've warmed the grimy gray rug and black linoleum, if that were possible, but they couldn't do much for the black-painted walls, piled high with amps and instrument cases. Happy with her setup, the keyboardist started soundcheck. "One-two, one-two," she said into her mike, until Ken, at the back of the room, gave her the thumbs up. Then it was the keys, and the tune she began to pick out had both me and Bunny watching her.

"Who is that?" I shook my head.

"I don't know—and I should." Bunny shot me a look. "No, really. We're going to hear her and if she's any good maybe I could get a column out of it. Hang on."

The young musician had moved on by then, but I walked back to the soundboard, where Ken was playing with light switches.

"Hey, Ken! How're you doing?"

"Hey, Theda! What's up? I really liked the piece this week." He smiled, but didn't elaborate. Whether or not he read it, saying that was friendly.

"Thanks, I try. Hey, who's the piano player? I liked just that little bit."

"Isn't she hot?" He flicked a switch and white spotlight focused in on the black keyboard. I gathered she didn't have a band backing her. "I forget her real name. She goes by Kitty Cat."

"Well, that works for me. Hope some more people come in before she goes on."

"Here she is now." I looked up and saw her walk back onto the stage. She'd donned a newsboy cap and baby-T that made her look even younger. But she started to play, and then to sing—a wordless scat—that had me nodding along. The sound from the back here was perfect. A few more people joined us and soon we were all mesmerized. I watched as the Kitty Cat began to work out a left hand pattern, then reached back with her other hand to adjust an effects box propped up on her amp.

"What's she going for?" As I asked, I heard it: The little keyboard seemed to turn into a vintage organ, giving out wheezy chords that rocked like it was 1966. What had been fine before was now amazing, a trip back in time. "Wow."

"Great, huh? I'm hoping she can move up to Fridays or Saturdays soon." Up in front of us, a long-haired girl started to dance. "Hey, what's with your friend?"

It wasn't that I'd forgotten Bunny. We'd both tended to treat the Casbah as our own living room. But when I looked over, through the sparse crowd, I saw that I shouldn't have. My friend was still sitting over on the side, but now she was bent double, holding her belly and rocking back and forth.

"Bunny! What's wrong?" I ran over to her and grabbed her arm.

"I don't know. I don't know. I don't feel so good." She wouldn't look up. "Theda? Theda? Are you there?"

"I'm here, Bunny. What is it? Do you want to go to the bathroom? Do you need some air?" I'd never known the Casbah to give anyone food poisoning, but then I didn't know anything about the sensitivities of pregnant women, either.

"No, I don't want to move. I just feel, ugh." She stopped rocking and hunched over further. I wrapped my arms around her and tried to think.

"I think we should get you out of here." I reached back for her jacket and shawl and started pulling them over her shoulders.

"No, no. I don't want…." Her voice faded and I missed what she said next.

"What is it, honey? Come on, Bunny? Do you want me to get some help?" I glanced up and two guys turned away. Bunny must look like a drunk, ready to heave. "Do you want me to call Cal?"

I heard what I thought was a sob. "That's it. I'm getting you out of here. I'll call a cab." I reached for my own coat. My cell was in my pocket, though I'd probably have to go up to the restaurant level to get a signal. "Can you walk up with me?"

A sob again. Or, no, I leaned forward. Bunny was giggling. Then laughing, as her shoulders started to shake. I pulled her closer to me and tried to see her face. She was flushed, her eyes closed. "Bunny? Bunny? What's going on?"

"I'm so *thirsty…*" She turned up toward me, her face red and sweaty. And then she collapsed, sinking through my arms to the floor in a dead faint.

FIFTEEN

THE WORLD WENT CRAZY. Still holding Bunny, I yelled for help. Ken came running, and the bartender called over that she was dialing 911. In a moment, we were laying my friend flat on the floor and other hands were covering her with coats. Somehow, suddenly, people had gathered around us. One woman—that keyboardist?—raised Bunny's feet, pushing more coats under them, and my friend's eyes flickered. By the time the EMT team showed up, she was coming around, trying to talk and shaking her head, as if she was trying to push through whatever had gotten her. But when one EMT started in with his questions—"Ma'am. Do you know where you are? Can you tell us your name?"—she just mumbled.

"Her name's Bunny Milligan, Barbara, that is. Barbara Milligan. I'm her friend, Theda. We were just—"

"What did she take?" His question threw me and I paused. The EMTs hoisted Bunny onto the stretcher and began fixing straps around her. "Club drugs? Ecstasy? What?"

"Nothing! We had dinner, that's all." He and his partner exchanged a look.

"Drink? Smoke?"

"Nothing, nothing. She only drank soda. She's pregnant." The EMT guy stared at me, then yelled something at his partner. The import of what I'd just said hit me. "She's pregnant!" I didn't know what was happening, but I knew how much my friend wanted this baby. They had to know, too.

"Got it." The other EMT finally spoke. "Are you her partner?"

"She's married. I should call her husband. Where are you taking her?"

"Cambridge City. You can follow. One, two!" With that, they lifted Bunny, still mumbling and shaking her head, and headed for the exit.

I followed them up the stairs, knowing I should phone Cal but not wanting to let Bunny out of my sight. Upstairs was mobbed, bright and loud, an entirely different world. The crowd parted for the EMTs with only slight dropoff in volume and I was left standing there.

"Theda! What happened?" It was Heather. Could so little time have passed?

"My friend collapsed. They're taking her to the hospital."

"Oh my god! Can I do anything?" She looked honestly shocked. I grabbed her hand.

"Yes. Do you have a car?" She nodded. "Would you give me a ride to Cambridge City Hospital?"

"Uh…." She paused and looked around. I remembered she was there with her boyfriend, and that she was a business acquaintance. Someone I hardly knew.

"Don't worry about it. I'll get a ride." I patted her hand and started to walk away, skimming the room for familiar faces. There was Ralph, he must have missed the opener. But as I looked over, I saw Risa hand him another pint. No way did I want to catch a ride with him.

"Theda, Theda, wait!" Heather was at my side again, her black clutch banging against my arm as she reached for me. "I'll give you a ride. I just had to get my things."

I figured she was really looking for her errant boyfriend, but I was in no position to argue. Besides, I couldn't blame her for wanting to preserve the image of a professional relationship.

"Thanks." I followed her out into the frigid night and over to a sky-blue Mini. "Thanks so much. This is really out of the ordinary." As desperate as I was to follow Bunny, I was also aware of the awkwardness of the situation. "You know where

Cambridge City is?" She nodded. As she pulled out from the curb, I dialed Bunny's home number. Cal wasn't there and I had to listen to their happy voices laughing into their machine.

"Cal, It's Theda." I paused, then realized that the silence would cut me off. "Something's happened. Something's happened to Bunny. She got sick after dinner." How could I say she'd collapsed? "She fainted at the Casbah. An ambulance took her to Cambridge City Hospital. I'm heading there myself to be with her. Call me if you want, or come find us. I'll be with her." I left my cell number and the time. Had only two hours passed? I watched Heather drive, realizing I had commandeered an almost perfect stranger. "Cute car." It was the best I could do.

"Thanks. It was a present, actually. My boyfriend—" She stopped, and I suspected it was more from embarrassment than because she was having trouble with the gears.

"Is Paul Wexner your boyfriend?"

She shifted aggressively, weaving around a cab. "Yeah." She glanced over at me. "Is it that obvious?"

I nodded. "I've had a lot of friends who've worked with their boyfriends' bands. And, yeah, I know it can be difficult to be taken seriously." I wasn't going to share horror stories, not now.

She pushed through a yellow light. Either my sense of urgency had gotten to her, or she was more aggressive on the road than in person. "It's just a great experience for me. I mean, I was pre-business, but no class can teach you about running an enterprise like Swann's Way."

"Enterprise?" Maybe she really did need to hear from some older, wiser women in the field.

"Yeah, you're handling an investment, basically. You've got taxes, outflow, day-to-day expenses, and long-term planning. You name it."

This was not your ordinary baby-band management. And for me, it was just too tempting. "So, where does the money come from, Heather?"

"Oh, it's Paul's. Both Pauls' actually. They're North Shore

boys. But why shouldn't they invest in their dream? I mean, they believe in it as a growth opportunity."

So they were rich kids. Violet was right. Up ahead, I saw the glowing sign for the emergency entrance. "You can drop me up there." She signaled to cut across Cambridge Street and down into the lot.

"I hope your friend is okay!" She was Heather again. Young, determined, a little scared.

"Thanks." She pulled up behind an ambulance, and I started to climb out. "Whatever happened to your friend? The one who OD'd?" I'd forgotten about the young blonde in all the confusion. "She okay?"

"She's still in the hospital, but she'll be going to rehab next week. They say she'll be fine." We looked at each other. I thought of Bunny. Please, let there be some justice in the world.

"Well, thanks again." What else could I say? I closed the door behind me, took a deep breath, and headed into the hospital.

At first glance, the scene inside the automatic sliding doors was more Romper Room than Emergency Room. Brightly colored posters covered the walls, greeting me in every language I recognized and several I didn't, while actual kids' drawings filled a glass display case. Only the kids here tonight had played rough. On one yellow vinyl couch a woman cradled her sobbing child, barely able to hold back tears herself. On another, this one red, a tired-looking man stretched out his legs, the denim of his knees torn and bloody, while across the room two grizzled brawlers eyed each other, the purple bruises on their faces almost matching the plaid upholstery.

"Excuse me?" Trying not to stare, I'd almost walked into a nurse. She was wearing a tunic with aggressively cheery pink and green polka dots.

"Sorry. I'm looking for my friend? An ambulance would've brought her in—"

"Triage." With a firm hand on my back she turned me toward

another glass wall. This one had a window and a person behind it. "You can check in there."

"Thanks." I turned back, but she was gone. Crayola color scheme or no, this was a city hospital. Already another ambulance was pulling up, its back doors popped to unload additional casualties of the night.

The woman behind the triage window was also dressed in bubblegum colors, but her face looked tired as she asked if she could help me.

"Yes, I'm looking for Bunny, I mean, Barbara Milligan? An ambulance was supposed to bring her here?" Something about a hospital just makes me unsure of myself.

She punched a few keys on her computer. "And you are?"

"Theda, Theda Krakow. I'm the friend who was with her when she collapsed." That wasn't the right word. None of this sounded right, but I didn't know what else to say.

"Not family?"

Only in my heart. "No."

"I'm sorry, then. You'll have to wait in the seating area. Family only." She turned back toward her computer.

"But…" I wanted to explain that Bunny and I were family to each other. That I didn't know where Cal was. That I didn't know if he even knew what had happened yet. I was interrupted by a familiar, retro ring. I grabbed my phone out of my pocket as the triage woman turned back to me.

"Outside!" She was tapping on the glass of her booth. Another one of those bright posters, this one featuring a red-barred circle, told me that I was in a cell-phone-free zone. "Outside!" In case I hadn't gotten the message, her jabbing finger now pointed me toward the doors.

"Hello?" Since I was walking that way anyway, I figured it was okay to answer.

"Theda! It's Cal." He sounded breathless, as if he was running. "Where are you?"

"I'm in the emergency room at Cambridge City. Well, just

outside." I was seriously missing the warmth of the waiting room. "You got my message?" I moved toward a small huddle of women, five of them, under a big No Smoking sign. They were smoking.

"Yeah, yeah, I'm on my way." He was definitely running. "Where exactly are you?"

"On the Cambridge Street side. Right outside." I looked around for a landmark. "Uh, the sign says 'Ambulances.'"

"There you are!" I turned around and saw Cal, phone in hand, racing toward me. "Where is she?"

"She's inside, but they wouldn't let me in. Go up to triage." I reached out to him, but he was already past, and I ended up just patting his back as he ran indoors. I was about to follow, see if I could tag along, when my cell rang again. It was Bill.

"Theda! Where are you?" He sounded nearly as distraught as Cal had.

"I'm fine, Bill. I'm at Cambridge City, though, because Bunny—"

"I know, I know. Cal called here 'cause he thought he had your number wrong. What happened?"

"I don't know, Bill. I don't know. That's what's so horrible. We had just had dinner, you know, at the Casbah, when she just got sick and collapsed." The evening flashed back with all its terror and confusion. "It was horrible, really horrible, and she's pregnant, and I don't know if she's going be okay or what's going on or if the baby—"

"Hold on, Theda. Take a breath." I did. "Now, you're at Cambridge City? Right now?"

"Uh-huh."

"Okay, babe, wait right there. I'm coming over to get you."

"But, Bill, your leg." Even on the edge of panic, I knew this didn't make sense.

"I'll take a cab. I'll be fine. I'm trying to put more weight on it anyway."

Now I felt silly. "Bill, I'm fine, really. I just lost it a little."

"Hang up and go back inside, honey. I'm on my way."

I had to confess, it felt better to be inside again, actually waiting for someone, rather than pressing for news. Cal was gone when I went in—they must have taken him past the swinging metal doors. But within minutes, a cab lumbered up and Bill, awkward on crutches, swung through the doors. One of the pink-and-green nurses walked quickly up to him, and I saw him wave her away. He wasn't a patient this time. By that point I was right beside him, and somehow even with balance issues and several pounds of protective casting, he managed to hold me tight in a hug that restored most of the warmth to my body.

"Oh Bill!" I felt him shift and realized that I'd been leaning on him. Not a bad habit under normal circumstances, but not now. "Here, come on over to the chairs." We started to hobble together over to the seating area, when he broke off

"Give me a minute, Theda. Let me see what I can find out."

With an impressive hopping waddle, barely using the crutches at all, he made his way over to the triage window. But if I'd expected him to get the same brushoff I had, I'd forgotten his badge. Cops and emergency room personnel have a long-standing relationship that goes beyond professional courtesy, and so I bit my lip and sat down as the triage nurse buzzed him into the metal doors. I knew he'd tell me everything when he emerged.

THE CLOCK SAID IT WAS only fifteen minutes, but it felt a lot longer before Bill finally came back out. I ran up to him, but he was already swinging along on his crutches, his face contorted with the effort. As soon as he collapsed into a chair, however, he smiled, and I learned to breathe again.

"She's okay." I leaned in toward him, and got a crutch in the shoulder. "Hang on." We readjusted, and he continued. "She's going to be okay."

I nodded for him to continue. "Bunny was conscious but

disoriented when they brought her in. High as a kite, according to the resident on duty. But because they didn't know what she was on—"

"*On?* Bunny wasn't *on* anything. We had dinner, and then she got sick. She fainted! Maybe she had a stroke?"

"No, no. They checked her heart and other vital signs. Her temperature was elevated and her electrolytes were off, but basically her vitals were good, so they just hydrated her and she's already coming out of it."

"They just hydrated her?" This wasn't making sense.

"Gave her an IV. They're keeping on her, but they say they've been seeing a fair number of cases like this."

"Like what? Is this a virus? Food poisoning?"

"They think it's drugs, Theda. Probably some new hybrid of MDMA, Ecstasy."

"But that's ridiculous." I pulled away, sat up straight. "Bunny didn't take anything. She wasn't even drinking. She's pregnant."

"Yeah, they said you'd told the EMTs that. Actually, I'm glad you did. Sometimes they'll try to counter the OD with other drugs. But because she seemed to be coming around, and because of the pregnancy, they kept it simple and opted to observe her."

"But why do they think it was drugs?" My panic was ebbing now, anger taking its place.

"All the symptoms are there." He reached to pull me closer to him again. "And, you know, honey, you were in a nightclub. Just because you didn't knowingly take anything, doesn't mean—"

"Bunny wouldn't. That's not her style."

"No, no, Theda, I wasn't going to say she was getting high without telling you." He settled for draping one arm over me. "What I'm saying is, you were in a place where people have been known to abuse substances. You were eating and drinking, and, well, it's quite possible you were slipped something."

I collapsed against the back of the sofa. Truth was, the

warmth of his arm felt good. "But why? Why would someone drug a pregnant woman? And, I mean, neither of us…."

"They didn't know she was pregnant." His face turned serious. "And, darling, they may not have meant that dose for her. You know how I feel about some of the clubs you hang in."

I didn't have the energy for this old argument tonight. "Please, Bill. That scene is my home, my living room. My… place where I belong. And I'm not a child."

"I know, Theda. But sometimes you can be awfully trusting." I glared at him.

"Who would do this to Bunny, to *me?*" He stared right back, waiting for me to answer my own question. "I had just done an interview, but the band wanted the press. I saw Ralph there—" I paused. The portly writer did keep coming up. But I'd known him for years, a harmless lush. "No, anything he had, he'd take himself. We had dinner, different dishes. All we shared were the appetizers, and the limes. We had a plate of cut limes for the soda."

Bill looked at me. "Did they taste funny? Did anything?"

"Not to me. But Bunny said something. She thought it was hormones." The last few days came crashing down. "I don't know, Bill. I wasn't paying attention. I give up."

"Okay, okay, babe. Let's back up. What else is going on?" Bill knew how to read me.

"It's nothing. Or, okay, it's small things. I keep thinking about those kittens, the ones Violet and I heard were missing. I wish we'd found that third trap. And, well, hanging with Violet, I've learned that she's sort of close to that Animals Now group." Bill raised his eyebrows, but kept silent. "I don't like it either. And then Tess is acting really strange. She's been lying to me and Bunny about her accident—"

Too late, I realized I'd revealed her secret. I might have my fears, but Tess was a friend. And Bill was a cop.

"Her *accident?*" His voice was still warm, but he pronounced the word with care, separating the syllables in a way I recognized. Bill was slipping into cop mode.

"Tess had a car accident. The night of the ice storm." He looked into my eyes. "Yes, the same night that the cat trapper was killed. Now, I know Tess. If she'd been in a serious accident, she'd have told somebody. She would have, really. But I've asked her about it, and so has Bunny. And, well, she told us different things. That scares me."

"You think she could have been involved in the hit-and-run that killed that woman?"

"No." I was adamant. "Or, well, maybe. I don't want to think so. But how can I help but wonder when she's not being straight with us?"

Bill smiled and chuckled a little, turning away to wipe his hand over his bristly chin. "What?" I had thought he'd go on the offensive. "Bill?"

"I don't doubt your instincts, Theda. Really, but I think Tess might be off the hook for this one." I looked at him, afraid to speak. "You see, the latest is that the woman probably was targeted and not just a random hit-and-run victim. The autopsy results came back."

I stared at him. "It's routine, Theda, whenever there's a suspicious death. And this is precisely why. Gail Womynfriend was poisoned. The autopsy revealed a trace of strychnine in her system. It hadn't killed her, not yet, but she was a small woman, and it probably would have. So we're not looking for a drunk driver anymore, or even a bad skid. Someone still hit her and drove away, and her injuries killed her. But she was done for, anyway. Your feral cat lady is dead because somebody *wanted* her dead."

Horrible as that was, relief flooded me. Gail's murder had been premeditated. Not the result of an accident, a tragic skid in an ice storm. Tess's fender bender was probably just that. Even if there was something she didn't want us to know, something embarrassing maybe, it wasn't that she had driven into a human being and ended her life. Someone else had done that, and done it intentionally.

"But poison? Why?" The new reality was sinking in and,

even as I asked, I remembered all the people Gail had pissed off. Including Tess. With her job, her grant, the big new project at stake, Tess had more reason than most to want Gail out of the way. And working in a lab, she had access to all sorts of chemicals. I looked up at Bill. He was smiling now, convinced that he'd put my mind at ease, and I felt sick. Pushing away from him, I ran toward the door marked "Women" and managed to stumble toward a toilet before losing my dinner. The night—and all my friendships—seemed to be going horribly, horribly wrong, and so I lay down on the cool tile floor and let blackness slip over me.

SIXTEEN

I CAME TO WITH a throbbing headache and a mouth like flannel. Sitting up made the headache worse, but I didn't want anyone to see me lying on the bathroom floor, like some junkie or, worse, like a sick person. Instead, I splashed water on my face and rinsed my mouth out the best I could before wobbling back out to Bill.

"You okay, honey? I was beginning to worry."

I smiled, unsure whether I could respond. "Yeah, just the stress, I guess." I sat back next to him, landing a little heavier than I'd intended.

"Look at me, Theda." I did. "You're really pale. Are you sure you're okay? We are at the hospital already, and if you got dosed, too…"

"I'm fine, Bill." At any rate, my headache was receding. "It's just a lot to deal with. Besides, if I'd been given Ecstasy, I'd be happy, right?"

"Not necessarily, darling. But I'll take your word for it. You can come home with me, tonight, right?" He was speaking softly. There were still a few others in the waiting room, but I smiled up at him.

"Is that for my health?"

"I may have some ulterior motives." We were both smiling now, and I burrowed into his scratchy-warm sweater. I could've gone to sleep right there, but just then the metal doors swung open and Cal came out. Thank goodness, he was smiling.

"She's awake. She's fine. She's going to be fine." He came forward and I jumped up to hug him. He sobbed once, then let loose and I held him till he pulled away, wiping the tears from his face. "I'm sorry. I was so frightened, Theda, when I got your call. But she's okay, she's going to be okay." I hugged him close again, and this time, when he pulled back, he was smiling.

"Can we see her?" Bill was struggling to his feet, and I reached to help him up.

"No, she's sleeping. But she was awake and herself again, just exhausted." Cal looked wiped out himself. "They're going to keep her for observation, probably just overnight. But it seems like everything is going to be okay."

"And the baby?" My voice dropped to a whisper, but Cal's face said it all. "Oh, I'm sorry."

"It's not that—" He paused, swallowed, the smile gone. "The doctors just don't know anything yet. They said we'll have to wait and see."

"Do you need anything?" Barely on his own feet, Bill had a practical—and generous—mind. "Is there anything we can get for you, or do?"

"Could I bum a ride?" I'd forgotten that Cal didn't drive. Neither had we.

"We could share a cab." He nodded, and we grabbed our coats. The clock showed midnight, the witching hour, and as if on cue the double doors slid open and five men came running in. Three of them were essentially carrying their friends, one of whom seemed to be bleeding badly from the belly.

"Come on, kids." Bill swung his crutches and led the way past the bloody newcomers, to the cab stand and home. For me, this had been an early night, but I had more trouble than Bill climbing the stairs to his place, and before he had fetched a glass of water for the nightstand, I was dead to the world.

THE NEXT MORNING, I couldn't remember what had hit me. Groggy, achey, with a ringing head, I sat up in an empty bed.

"Bill?" My mouth was parched. "Bill?" The glass on the nightstand was empty.

"Ah, you're up." My lumbering beau, fully dressed, swung into the bedroom doorway. He was getting better on those crutches. "I was wondering when you'd wake up."

"What time is it?" I looked over at the bedside clock, but the glowing numbers hurt my eyes.

"Close to noon. But I don't think you're getting out of bed today."

"Oh c'mon. It's Monday, I've got work to do. I can't believe you let me sleep so long." I started to sit up and immediately regretted it. Bill thumped over to sit on the edge of the bed.

"You were tossing all night." He reached over and brushed my hair off my forehead. His hand felt marvelously cool. "Unless I'm wrong, you got a dose of whatever Bunny had."

I did feel ill, with a head throbbing as if from a three-day bender, but not drugged. "No, that doesn't make sense. I didn't get sick like she had." Then I remembered passing out in the hospital bathroom. "I mean, I didn't get all dizzy or high or whatever."

"You were fairly agitated last night." I grunted and lay back down, in no mood to argue. "And you were pretty sick by the time we got home."

"Maybe I have the flu." Bunny had said a bug was going around.

"Maybe, but I should've insisted that the doctor look you over last night. Here, at least let me get you some OJ. You should stay hydrated." Before I could object, he pulled himself up, pivoted neatly on one crutch and thumped through the kitchen. He was getting pretty good at that. I should tell him about the virus going around the newsroom. Did he know that was how I'd gotten last week's gig? Unless Ralph hadn't had the flu. And I had seen Ralph last night. But before Bill could return, I was fast asleep.

The next thing I knew I was face down on a wet pillow, drenched with sweat. But there, on the nightstand, was a large glass of orange juice, a paper napkin over the top. I downed it in a moment, and fell back on the pillow. The clock said three, and I could hear discordant squawks from the other room.

"Bill?" My voice came out as a croak. I wished I had more orange juice. "Bill?" I started to sit up and had to pause, dizzy. A few more breaths and I managed to stand. Walking to the doorway was a challenge, but I felt better knowing I could, and besides I had to pee. I grabbed Bill's worn terrycloth robe and made for the bathroom. "Bill?"

"Hey, you're up!" The music, if that's what it was, must have covered the sound of flushing, but I wobbled into the living room to find him on the sofa, a variety of CDs spread out around him. "How's my sleeping beauty?"

"Lousy." He moved his leg to rest on the table, and I collapsed on the sofa beside him. "I feel like I was hit by a truck."

"Violet called. She'd heard about Bunny, and I told her you, uh, got a dose of something, too." He looked me over. "Could you eat anything?"

I was about to protest when it hit me, I was famished. "Yeah, definitely. What have you got?"

"Wait here." He reached for his crutches and lumbered down the hallway, but I was close behind him. "Hey, I thought you were sick."

"Food is a great motivator."

He stopped and looked at my face, then reached to feel my forehead. His hand felt normal now, warm and dry. "I don't think you have the flu, Theda. I think you just sweated some poison out of your system."

"Food poisoning?" He shot me a look. "You think we were both drugged. But why?"

"Fun? Malice? You give anyone a particularly nasty review recently?"

"No." A thought was creeping up the back of my head. "In fact, all I've done are features the last few weeks. Except for that Walruses review, but that was a rave." The thought surfaced. "Bill, do you think Ralph is threatened by me? Do you think he's jealous of my work?" My work! "Bill, did I have my bag last night? I've got an interview to transcribe."

"Yeah, you'd dropped it in the ER, but I kept an eye on it. It's on the foyer table." I turned, too fast, and had to reach for the wall. "But why don't you sit down first. Eat something. I think you've been through the mill." He pulled a carton of eggs from the refrigerator and poured me more orange juice.

"Now, tell me about Ralph. He's the fat guy with that little ponytail, right?"

"Yeah, and he's in the union, so he's got no reason…"

"Unless it's personal?" Bill began whisking eggs and my stomach rumbled in response.

"No, we've always gotten along." I didn't even think he'd want to sleep with me, not really. I'd be too much trouble. Not a thought to share with Bill. "No, forget about it." The thought of that night, of my inconclusive interview, of the dinner, and Bill's bombshell was eating at me. But so was my hunger, and so I sat and let myself be entertained as Bill balanced eggs, crutches, and himself before a skillet well moistened with butter.

"This is great." Twenty minutes later, I was sopping up the remains of four sunny-side up eggs with my third piece of well-buttered toast. My personal chef and savior brought two more slices over and took a seat beside me. "Thanks, Bill."

"You're welcome, and since you asked, Bunny is doing better, too." I gulped down the toast. It wasn't that I'd forgotten. It was just that the day had started in such a domestic way, and work had been a factor, and besides, I'd been hungry—and sick.

"I was going to ask…" He waved me off.

"I know. But I beat you to it. I called the hospital this morning. Cal was there, and Bunny is awake. She seems to be fine, feeling a little beaten up, but that's about it." He poured himself some of the juice. "But she has no memory of most of the evening. Knows that you two were going to meet for dinner and remembers seeing you and, maybe, getting a table. But after that it's all a blank."

"Weird." Looking back, the night was fuzzy to me, too. Bunny's collapse. Something with Tess. Too much had happened.

"Maybe not. Bunny had all the symptoms of an Ecstasy overdose, or something very like, and you had some of them."

I reached for another piece of toast. "Any word about her pregnancy?"

"No. To be honest, I didn't ask, but neither Bunny nor Cal offered. Maybe they don't know, but I also think that's more of a girl thing."

"Yeah, I should get over there." The food had been great, but the idea of walking still didn't particularly appeal.

"You're not going anywhere today, honey, and they're keeping her in one more day, too. If you're up for it, you can join me in the living room. You can even use my computer, but I don't think you should try for too much more than that today."

I stood up. The room shifted slightly. "I've got to go feed Musetta."

"Theda." Bill reached up for my arm. Was I swaying? "She's a cat. I know she'll miss you, but she'll be fine. I bet she won't even finish her dry food."

I looked over at him. "Bill, she's not a cat, she's my cat."

"Tell you what. If you're not better by tomorrow, we'll take a cab over. But let's play today by ear."

I was going over there, but I'd argue this later. Besides, standing was tiring me out. "Well, let me shower and get dressed, then we'll see what's up."

"Okay, babe. But remember, if you keel over, I'm not in the best shape to pick you up."

I laughed and reached over to kiss him. But I did pay more attention than usual to where I put my feet as I made my way slowly down the hall.

MUCH AS I HATED to admit it, Bill was right. The shower made me feel clean, but standing under the rush of hot water used up all of my energy. Another nap gave me the energy to join Bill in the living room, but by then it was dark, and the cold night did not look welcoming. A pile of take-out menus did, and we spent a companionable evening on the sofa, with pad thai and a green curry that had us both downing lots of water. I suspected that was part of Bill's motivation, when he requested "extra hot," but I enjoyed it as well. As I drifted off on the sofa, I did feel a twinge of guilt about Musetta. My little kitty was so social, I hated leaving her alone for a full day and another night. But Bill was right. She had dry food and water aplenty, and she'd just be that much happier to see me in the morning.

ANOTHER TEN HOURS of sleep and I was myself again, which did lend weight to Bill's theory. Was Fantasy Plus or whatever I'd been given supposed to be a fun drug? I didn't see it. But whatever the cause of my 24-hour misery, a fresh morning had dawned and the sickness was gone. My deadlines, however, remained, and it was past ten by the time I'd showered and dressed. So after bolting Bill's good dark roast I grabbed my bag. "See you later, sweetie! Thanks for taking such good care of me."

The air was crisp, but not deadly, and I half jogged down Inman Street, looking forward to the day. If I could draft my column quickly, I could get to the hospital by noon. Bunny would be released today, Bill had told me, and I wanted to be there. Besides, she might need a female friend to talk to.

But first, I owed someone a can. "I'm coming, kitty!" My lock was half off the latch, and a note emerging from under the door explained why: Yesterday, Monday, the handyman had come by and replaced my valves. As far as I knew, city law required that landlords give tenants 24-hour notice before they enter an apartment. But I had been running around like crazy the last few days, out more than in, and Julian was basically trustworthy, though the thought of him alone in my bedroom did make me cringe.

"Kitty, I'm home!" I fiddled with my key and the door

opened of its own accord. One of these days, I'd have to get Julian to fix this, too. "Musetta!" Instead of the black-velvet linebacker I expected to come pounding into my shins, I was greeted by silence. Two catnip toys and the belt of my terry-cloth robe were piled by the door, and I wondered what Julian had made of that. "Kitty?"

She had to be pissed. Well, no, I knew that was my imaginative take on her mood. In reality, she was probably enjoying a mid-morning nap. "Musetta?" Dropping my bag, I picked up one of the toys, which had a tiny bell attached. I shook it. "Kitty?" Nothing. Maybe she *was* pissed. I walked back to my office, but the cushion on top of the file cabinet was empty, despite a strong beam of sun warming its paisley velvet surface. "Kitty?" A flattened circle showed where she'd slept on my comforter. "Musetta?" She wasn't on her favorite chair, or the sofa either.

The workmen must have scared her. She had good instincts for a house cat, tending to hide rather than run out of any open door. I got down on the floor but found nothing under the bed beyond some dust bunnies and a sock. "Musetta?" Nothing in my clothes closet, either, despite a neat nest in the back made comfortable by an old flannel shirt that had fallen off its hanger.

"Kitty cat, where are you?" I checked the coat closet, and under my desk, then every cabinet in the kitchen. Maybe the repairmen had been looking for a pan to catch water from the radiators, and had locked her in. Nothing, and I was back to the closets, under the bed. Her favorite cushion still sat empty, warmed only by the sun. I returned to the living room and back again to the office, the bedroom, the closet. "Musetta!" I was yelling now, in a tone more likely to scare her than draw her out of any possible hiding place. But it was no use. My cat was gone.

SEVENTEEN

"DAMN JULIAN!" I YELLED out loud. Inwardly I cursed myself. How could I have left Musetta for more than a day? Why hadn't I put a note on the door, "Don't let cat out." Why hadn't I even said something to Julian? He must know I had a cat, permitted or not. Why hadn't I barricaded her in my office or borrowed a crate from Violet. Or, or…. Dizziness forced me to lean on the wall, but it was emotion not sickness overcoming me. Succumbing to panic would not help.

I took a deep breath, and then another. What did I know about lost cats? Musetta was a hider, not a runner, so if something scared her out of my apartment, maybe she'd found another cubbyhole to burrow into. Maybe she was still in the building. Hoping against hope, I carefully closed and locked the apartment door behind me, pulling tight until I heard it latch, and made my way up floor by floor.

"Musetta?" I tried to visualize some neighbor recognizing her, letting her in. "Musetta?" I stopped at each door and listened. "Kitty girl?"

But there was no answering "mew," no scratching from inside a neighbor's apartment. "Musetta?" By the time I hit the sixth floor, the top, I had to face facts. She wasn't up here. Still, tracing my own footsteps back down, I repeated my ritual, calling gently for her, stopping by every door to listen for her voice, for the sounds of movement, of scratching or playing. Without hearing anything, I went back by my own apartment and past the main entrance, down to the bowels of the building.

Someone would have had to have propped the basement door

open for my cat to have gotten in here. But anything was possible, particularly if repairmen had been working on the radiators.

"Musetta?"

The basement was warm, but loud. The furnace, a car-sized metal box painted an absurd aquamarine roared in a way that would have sent my sensitive pet running. But the furnace wasn't on all the time, and a scared cat might not necessarily run toward the door. And so I looked behind the three boilers and around some boxes and tools that must have dated from the Reagan era. Nothing.

"Musetta? Kitty?" An open doorway connected the working basement with the tenants' storage room. Our storage spaces were stacked cages, their mesh walls too small to allow my portly pet through, and flush to the wall. "Kitty?" She was not on top of the cages, nor in any of the corners. For good measure I looked through the wire mesh, trying to see between bicycles and boxes of books. Nothing. Unless my pet was fast asleep inside a neighbor's apartment—I could hope—she was not in the building.

I raced back up to my apartment. Time was wasting. And just for a moment, I had the thought, the fantasy, that as I pushed open the door, I'd see her there, sprawled on her back with her white tum exposed for pets. She wasn't of course, and the wave of feeling that hit me made me realize how real that fantasy had been. I made myself sit for a moment, trying to figure out a course of action. First, I should make a poster, just a flier to hang downstairs alerting the other tenants about Musetta. Maybe one of them had taken her in. Maybe she *was* happily asleep on one of my neighbor's beds. But then I should go out looking.

Violet had schooled me well: Most lost cats don't go far. Cats, especially house cats, tend to be frightened and disoriented when out of their familiar surroundings. Odds were that she was within a few blocks of our building. She might be hiding, she might even have wedged herself into some tight

space and gotten stuck. Violet and Caro and I had done our
share of rescues and found neighborhood pets in some of the
oddest nooks and crannies. But I also knew that time was of
the essence. Most lost pets are found within a day or two, or
never. And the dangers presented by the frigid weather were
just too terrifying to count.

I quickly wrote up a note on a piece of printer paper and
grabbed my parka. Taping it to the inside of our main front
door, I stepped out, zipped up, and made myself think. You're
a scared cat, fleeing the noise and strangeness of big loud
workmen who are banging on pipes. You find yourself outside.
Where do you go?

To my right was a long, low hedge of some kind of evergreen. That would be perfect cover. But across the street was
another big, bushy holly, its glossy leaves offering the sem-
blance of protection—and if Musetta had darted across the
street, she might have dashed under that holly, or even climbed
one of the trees behind it. To my left, an alley led behind my
building, and suddenly that looked tempting, too. I needed help.

"Helmhold House!"

"Violet, Musetta's gone!" In breathless tones, I rushed
through my morning's discovery.

"You're sure she's not just hiding? Not under a radiator or
in the back of a closet or something?"

"No, no. She's gone!" I could hear the panic in my own
voice. So could Violet.

"Okay, hang on, Theda. Are you feeling okay? You've got
to be calm here. You calm?"

"Yeah." I was crouching by the evergreen hedge. No green
eyes peered back. "She's not under the hedge."

"Where are you now?" I told her. "That's good, Theda. You
know, most indoor cats who get out don't go far. They hide."
I nodded, then realized she couldn't see me.

"Uh huh." I walked over to the alley. No sign of movement.
"Musetta!" Nothing.

"Theda, Theda, are you with me?" I could tell she was repeating my name as a way of grounding me, bringing me back. But I didn't want to listen to her. "Bill said you'd been sick, Theda, so keep in mind that you might not be yourself yet." I had nothing to say to that. "Theda, she won't have gone far."

"Musetta!" I started down the alley, and I could hear the cell signal flicker as Violet talked. I didn't care. I wanted my kitty back. Musetta was a soft, pampered house pet. The temperature alone would be a shock. "Musetta!" Someone had squeezed a car into the alley. I looked underneath, noting a poisonous shimmer of green on the asphalt. Hadn't I read that antifreeze tasted good to cats?

"Theda! Are you listening to me?"

I stood up. "Yeah, Violet. I just can't stand here talking. Will you help me?"

"Sure, honey. Let me just get dressed. You're outside your building?"

"Yeah, I'm heading toward Mass. Ave."

"Okay, I'll find you. Just remember: she's probably freaked out. Whenever she quit running, she would have headed for the smallest, safest-seeming space she could squeeze herself into. She probably hasn't gone more than a block."

I closed the phone and tried to take heart. What Vi had said made sense. I had to be methodical. I had to think. So where was I? Halfway around my building, so I may as well continue. Across the alley, behind the parked car, were two recessed basement windows, the glass set back in leaf-filled wells. My soft fugitive wasn't in either, and neither window moved when I pushed on them, so she wouldn't have been able to wiggle her way back inside. Behind the building was all dirt and pavement, bordered by a high chain-link fence that I doubted my round cat could climb. Two more window wells got my hopes up, but neither held any sign of her. Two ground floor porches proved empty as well, although one of my neighbors had left out a rattan settee that Musetta would have loved to get her claws on. Slipping through the narrow dirt alley on my building's other side, I saw nothing that could conceal even a smaller cat. No window wells, no holes in the fence. Not even any plants.

I should be grateful I wasn't finding other burrows. That talk about fishers had scared me, even though I knew that a city cat faced more dangers from cars and humans than from four-legged predators. My pet was round and soft. Easy prey, probably. But she was also so lively, so full of personality, I just couldn't stand the thought of anything hurting her.

Out on the street again, I stared in each direction, desperate to see her distinctive bouncing jog. Nothing, nor did another peek under the hedge reveal any traces of her. "Musetta?" Time to move: Violet had said that a scared cat wouldn't go more than a block, but I hadn't checked that far yet, and began to walk in the direction I'd told her. Which had been stupid, I realized. Massachusetts Avenue was three blocks away, and loud, a major artery. Wouldn't my cat have run in the opposite direction? I'd go to the corner and then start the other way. Violet would find me.

"Musetta! Musetta? Pss-pss-pss." One building over and another hedge, I crouched in hope, peering under its gray stick base. Dark green ivy formed a thick carpet behind it, piled into lumps and caverns that would have attracted me, had I been a small animal. Had I been a mouser, it would have seemed like heaven. I found a breach in the hedge and waded carefully through, all the way to where tendrils started to climb a brick wall. Nothing. The rest of the foundation planting was bare, gray-brown in the cold, and dead to the eye. "Musetta? Kitty girl?" I knew that cats hear sibilants better than any other sound, but I hoped the sound of my voice, of my familiar names for her, might draw her out from some hiding place, some warm haven that I hadn't seen. "Kitten love? Pss-pss-pss." The neighbor's elm showed a squirrel nest, high out of reach, but that was it.

I reached the corner and readied to turn around when— wait!—a movement, halfway down the block. "Musetta? Kitty?" I was calling softly now, terrified of spooking an already frightened cat. "Musetta? Pss-pss-pss." Bending low, I walked softly toward what I'd seen, a flicker of movement, cat high.

"Musetta?" There! Under a bush. But the face that looked back at me was white, with yellow eyes. A cat, but the wrong cat. And after a second of face-to-face, she turned and disappeared. I sat down, hard, the sidewalk cold through my jeans. How could people let their cats out in the city? In this weather? At all? How did they stand this?

And how could I have let my sweet, soft pet get out? She'd trusted me, her person, to take care of her, and I'd failed. I'd never thought of myself as an irresponsible pet owner, as one of those careless types who didn't properly consider the needs and responsibilities of cohabiting with an animal. But I'd been lax, I hadn't thought, and I'd failed her. I'd stayed away overnight, knowing that workmen were due. I hadn't made any provisions for her safety when they came in, even though I knew they were coming, sooner or later. I never put a collar on her, either. Did I even have a recent picture, one of her full grown, with which to make up a poster? Would I ever see her bright round eyes again?

My phone rang and I grabbed it. "Violet, where are you?"

"Theda, it's Bunny. What's wrong?" I'd forgotten all about my friend.

"Bunny! How are you? *Where* are you?" Shaking off my Musetta misery, I tried to focus for a moment on Bunny. I couldn't let anyone else down today. "Have they released you?"

"No, not yet. But they're doing the paperwork. But, Theda, they had a cop come in to talk with me. They think I was drugged."

"That's what they were saying when they brought you in." Silence. "Don't you remember?"

"No, Theda. It's all sort of foggy. We were going to Violet's gig, right?" I made an affirmative noise. "And then I was really dizzy and really hot, and then I was here. I can't even remember for sure how long I've been here, even though Cal's told me it was just two nights, at least I think that's what he said."

"Yeah, Sunday and Monday." Bunny usually had a bounce that carried through to her voice. To hear her meandering and confused was worrisome. "Are you sure they should be letting you out today?"

"Oh yeah, everything is good now, I just can't remember. I thought if I talked to you, maybe it would come back. We did have dinner, right?"

I love Bunny. She's one of my closest friends, but just then I wanted to get off the phone. I wanted to look for Musetta, to find my pet before a car or dog or any of a million chemical or mechanical dangers did. A sudden flash of sympathy for Gail shot through me. Sometimes animals do seem more important. But as much as I loved my pet, I was not Gail. Bunny had just been through hell. I could spare her a few minutes. And so I stood up, brushed off the seat of my jeans, and talked Bunny through the missing time, through the evening we'd gone out together and the next day, everything I knew and everything I had learned, filling in as many of the blanks as I could. Yes, I did walk down the block, occasionally catching my breath as a squirrel made the underbrush move, or a sparrow rustled some low pile of brush. But I tried my best to focus on my friend, reassuring her that, yes, she was not unconscious for long. And, no, I had no idea what—or who—had essentially poisoned her. It took forever, or what felt that way, but finally her questions ceased.

"So, Bunny?" I was afraid to ask, afraid to upset her if she hadn't thought of it. "Did the doctors say anything about the effects of whatever it was?"

"On my baby?" I nodded, unable to speak. "Yeah, we talked." I heard her sigh. "The horrible part is, they're not sure. They started to give me something when they hydrated me, but they say that won't hurt her. Or him. And, well, I'm not bleeding or anything, so that's good. But someone drugged me, Theda. Someone gave me something that messed me up and knocked me out, and we're just going to have to wait and see what the effect of that is."

I nodded again, and realized that she couldn't see me. "Bunny, I'm so sorry. You've been so careful. I'm so sorry I got you to come out with me, that we went to the Casbah, that—"

"Cut it out, Theda. You did nothing wrong. You hear me?" Her voice was full again, almost like it should be, and I agreed out of relief. "Seriously, Theda, you didn't drag me anywhere, and I can't stop seeing my friends and going out. I'm going to be a mama, not a hermit."

"Fair enough, Bunny."

"And, you know, things happen. I'm going to take the best care I can of myself and this baby, and we'll just trust the goddess to handle everything else."

"Amen."

"You know the rule that says that what you send out, you get back times three? Believe it. Because I'll tell you something, Theda. Forget Cal, if I ever get my hands on whoever did this to me, to my baby, I'll make sure he gets his three-fold back again. With interest!"

Pacifist as she was, Bunny's anger sounded healthy and heartening and when she rang off to greet Cal, and head home, I felt better than I had since I'd come home. One lost friend was enough.

My phone rang again. "Violet?"

"No, it's Shelley. I'm on the desk." She was whispering and it hit me. Today was Tuesday. My column was due.

"Theda, your copy isn't in the queue. Is there a problem?"

"Oh, Shelley, you don't know the half of it." I tried to think. Work seemed very far away right now. "Are we pre-printing?"

"No, you're in luck. Is something going on? Is there something I can do?"

I shook my head and sighed. "Nothing really, thanks. But, Shel, can you buy me some time? Say I called in and 'cause there's no pre-print, I really wanted to follow up on something?"

"Sure thing. But Theda? Tim's already been looking through the queue, looking for your piece. He wanted it early, because it's the lead, even if we aren't going to press today."

This was all too much. "I can't, Shelley. I might, maybe, get it in later." If Musetta turned up. If she was found.

"Don't worry, kiddo. I'll swear you're on the trail of the hottest story in town."

"If nothing else, I'll get it in tomorrow, Shel. Early. I promise. And thank you."

"Theda?" When I shut the phone, I saw Violet walking toward me. In her hand was one of those big wire cages, like we had freed the feral from. A trap—to trap a cat. I thought of Gail, her broken body lying in the street, and all the sad homeless animals that she had tried to save. Those missing kittens. The reality of my situation hit me hard.

"Vi!" I heard my voice cracking.

"Don't worry, babe. We'll find your kitty. She's tougher than you know."

I shook my head. Musetta was a plump housecat, and a not overly agile one at that. "The trap?"

"She might be freaked out, Theda. I've done rescues where a cat refuses to come out for anyone. But we'll put some food in this and put it by your place, and when she gets hungry, we'll get her."

When she gets hungry.... "You mean, you don't think we're going to find her?"

"We might not *today*." She looked up at me, and took my arm. "But we will. I can almost promise."

You're lying, I thought. Instead, I said. "But a baited trap... won't it attract raccoons and other cats? Or fishers and coyotes?"

"Theda. Theda, calm down. We're in Cambridge. Yeah, we've got raccoons and skunks, but most of them stay pretty much to themselves this time of year. We're looking for one spooked kitty, who is used to having her meals served up regular. Right?" I nodded. "Plus, she's micro chipped, so if she shows up in one of the shelters, you'll get a call." I'd forgotten about the pea-sized nib in my pet's ruff. "But I don't think it'll even get to that. Now, where have you looked so far. Let's make a circuit together, help me get the lay of the land."

We turned then and walked back, past my building and up the way that I realized my kitty would have run. If only I had gone that way first.

Two hours later, I was near tears again, and Violet packed me off by promising that she'd keep on looking. We'd already left the trap, baited with Musetta's favorite treats, under the hedge by my building. "She's probably right around here, Theda. She's probably dug in and watching us right now, trying to figure out what to do."

To get me to leave, Violet gave me a task. I had to make up a poster, and so when I heard footsteps on the stairs behind me, I ignored them.

"Theda! I've been looking for you." It was Reed, but who had the time?

"My cat got out." The everyday hassle with the key was beyond annoying.

"Oh, yeah, I saw the sign. I'm sorry. I'm sure she'll turn up." For a minute I hated him and focused all my attention on my lock. Why was it locked now, when it was too late? "Hey, I dug up some info on those MuzeArts guys you asked me about. Not much, but it's sort of curious…"

"Reed, I can't deal with this now. I'm busy."

"Oh, okay." I should've felt bad when I shut the door in his face, but I knew I was about to lose it. The quiet of the apartment hit me, and I leaned back against the door. Where was the little pat-pat-pat of her feet as she ran down the hall? Where was her insistent mew? I sank to the floor and picked up her catnip butterfly. Where was my cat?

I could have let the tears flow, then, but Violet's instructions echoed in my head. A photo, recent if possible, and more than one if I had them. My breath caught as I went into my office—no, there was no round, warm body on top of the file cabinet—but fifteen minutes of searching turned up two snapshots that would work. One, a closeup of her face, framed the round green eyes and the off-center white star that made Musetta's face so kissable. The other, with her stretched out on a windowsill, showed her plumed tail and medium-long fur to advantage, as well as the white boots and belly that completed her description. Five more minutes to dig up a magic marker with which to write up my poster, and I was off to the copy shop. I could buy a couple of rolls of tape there and plaster the neighborhood on my way home.

"Theda." I looked around as I locked the door. Reed, again, looking concerned. "I'm sorry if I was brusque before. May I be of help in any way?"

"Thanks. I'm off to make up some posters. My buddy Violet is out looking for her now." I showed him the photos. "If you see her, take her in, will you?"

"Of course. I can help look, too. I've got to get to work right now, but if she doesn't turn up tonight, you let me know."

I hadn't wanted to ask, but his offer made me tear up again. "Thanks, Reed. I appreciate it." I ducked my head and made for the front door.

"We'll find her, Theda. She'll come home to you." I waved to avoid trying to speak, and sprinted the five blocks to the copy place. It was only afterward, as I wrapped thick plastic tape around a telephone pole, securing yet another reproduction of my pet's sweet face, that I felt the first drop of rain.

"Theda!" I heard Violet yell from the end of the block, but found myself looking up instead. Sure enough, the sky had turned too dark even for a January afternoon. The clouds looked ready to sink: low, gray, and angry.

"Hey, Theda! Give me some of those." Violet ran up to me

and took a bunch of fliers. "Good photos. Any luck?" She looked at me and I didn't have to answer. "Well, I put some more Pounce in the trap, and I've been searching, too. These posters will help."

"Violet, it's starting to rain." I looked at the drops darkening my parka sleeve. They were thick and splattered as they landed. "Or sleet." The air was cold. As the sun set, whatever form this precipitation took would surely freeze.

"Maybe it'll pass." As if on cue, the sleet started down, heavier, along with clods of wet snow. "She's a smart cat, Theda, and she's got a thick coat."

I remembered the feral we had rescued only the week before. I remembered what Violet had told me about the combination of freezing temperature and wet fur.

"Come on." Violet could see it all on my face. "We'll put up some more posters and start poking around basement doors and recessed windows. Maybe she ducked into someplace warm and is having trouble getting out."

I handed her one of the rolls of tape and we each took a side of the street, working methodically down the block. Five poles down, I saw another cat's face looking back at me. "Have you seen Binky?" The cat, described as a five-year-old indoor-only calico looked pampered and round, a perfect house pet. "She slipped out during a party and may be hiding in your garage or basement." The poster was dated December 23. A month ago. Had Binky been found, or had the holidays been particularly bleak and lonely for one of my neighbors? I taped my own poster under theirs, and tried not to think about the faded handwriting, so full of hope, and the sweet, spotted face it framed.

FORTY-FIVE MINUTES LATER, Violet and I were soaked. We'd circled my block and two in either direction, wrapping the tape around and over our posters to protect them from what was rapidly becoming heavy, wet snow.

"I'm bushed, Theda." Violet crossed the street toward me.

In the streetlight, I could see how red her nose and cheeks had become.

I nodded, shivering, unsure how much of my exhaustion was emotional and how much from the storm. "Let's go in." I croaked, and we trotted back to my apartment without speaking.

Once again, the emptiness threatened to floor me, and to avoid it I got busy. While the water was boiling, I grabbed towels and dry sweats for us both, and hung our soaked jeans and coats over the tub.

"Cocoa?" Violet nodded. "Want something in it?" She nodded again and I reached under the sink, pulling out a bottle of rum and another of brandy. The hot chocolate was from a mix, but this would jazz it up.

"Have you told Bill yet?" We both had hot mugs in our hands and, curled up on the sofa, I felt something like life returning. I shook my head, no.

"I've been in panic mode. And, well, what can he do?"

"Comfort? Man the phones?" I waved my cell in response.

"Well, what if someone tries your home number?" She had a point. I'd put both on the poster.

"It's just hard to even talk about."

"I know, but he's your partner. He'll get it."

She was right. Telling him would make my loss real, somehow. But sharing might help. "Do you mind?" I reached for the my reliable land line.

"Bill?" The tears burst out then, and it took all my strength to explain. No, I was fine, physically, and no, it wasn't Bunny or Violet. It was Musetta.

"She's—she's gone, Bill!" I started sobbing for real then.

"She's *dead?* What happened?"

"No, no." I choked back my sobs. "She got out. Outside, and it's horrible out there."

"Oh, darling. She'll be okay. She's got nice, thick fur."

"Bill!" I was furious, suddenly. How could he presume?

"You don't know. She's a house cat, all soft. You said so yourself. It's dark out. And the sleet and the snow…they soak into fur, and it's freezing. It's getting colder every minute!"

"Theda, darling. I'm sorry. I know it's cold out. But she'll be okay." He was desperate to calm me down. I could hear it in his voice. "I just meant, she's still got her instincts. She's a smart critter. She'll be fine. I promise."

"How can you promise?" I was too miserable to be comforted. Plus, my nose was all stuffed up.

"I just have a good feeling about this, Theda. Call it my cop's instincts." I sniffed. "Did you call Violet?"

"She's here now." I looked over; my friend was pulling her boots on.

"And she's going out looking with you?"

"Uh-huh, and we put up posters. And Violet put out a trap." The word stuck in my throat.

"Well, there you go, Theda. You'll find her, or one of your neighbors will. I promise." I nodded, tired and finally ready to be consoled. "You want me to come over?"

"No." I did. I wanted the comfort. I didn't want to be alone. But I knew what the last few nights had taken out of him. I missed my cat and I was terrified to think of her out in a winter storm. But Bill was hurt and healing, too. All I really needed was moral support. "Don't come over. I just wanted to talk to you."

"Well, I'll talk all night, darling." Violet had her coat on, by then. It was still soaked and hung like a blanket from her shoulders. She was gesturing to me.

"Hang on a minute, Bill."

"Theda, I've got to get home. Caro's on a job and I've got to feed everyone, change Exene's dressings. I'll check the trap on my way out and I'll come by again tomorrow. It's right out and to the left, under that heavy yew, if you go out again tonight. And call me if you hear anything, even if you just want to talk. But, Theda?" I nodded. "Try to get some sleep. Musetta's probably dug in some place, and even if she does get soaked, she'll be okay. We'll find her tomorrow. Maybe someone will even call tonight."

"Thanks." I waved as Violet let herself out. There was no need to get up and lock the door behind her.

"I'm back, Bill."

"Good. Now have you eaten anything?"

I wasn't hungry. I felt like someone had slammed me full on into a wall. But I let him talk to me as if I still cared about meals and by the time we got off the phone, I'd humored him by making a turkey sandwich that tasted like paste.

"I love you, darling. Do you have something to keep your mind busy tonight?" I thought of that stupid tape, the column that was due, and grunted.

"Well, whatever it is, try not to worry too much." Like that was going to happen. But he must have heard my silence. "Try to get some sleep, okay?"

"I'll try, Bill. I love you, too. Thanks."

I made a stab at transcribing the tape then, though the work goes slowly when you turn off the machine at every noise. But there were no calls, and no familiar mews kept me from finishing every fatuous word of it. God, the Swann's Way guys were full of themselves. Writing would have been impossible, and by then my eyes were barely focusing. The bed was too empty for comfort, but I must have dozed off on the sofa. When the phone finally rang, I found myself tangled in the afghan that usually lies along the back. I nearly ripped it in my haste to grab the big, old phone's receiver.

"Hello? Hello? I'm here!" Please, god, let it be someone with news of Musetta.

"We have your cat." I went dizzy with relief.

"Oh, thank god! Where did you find her? Where are you? I'll come out and pick her up." I reached for my glasses and started looking around for a pair of dry shoes.

"No, you don't understand." The male voice on the line was

muffled but clear. Still, his words confused me. "We have your cat. Back off with all the questions, and she'll be all right."

The line went dead in my hand and I was left staring, the only sound the buzz of the phone and the soft patter of wet snow against the window.

EIGHTEEN

I FELT NAUSEOUS. DIZZY. My stomach and head both reeled from what I'd just heard. Someone had kidnapped my cat? Because of something I was asking about? Someone had taken Musetta?

I hit *69, desperate to know more. To demand the return of my pet. "The number you are trying to call is unavailable or private." I tried again, over and over, listening to that damned recording each time before finally accepting that I couldn't simply ring the caller back. I couldn't reach them—him—for answers, for details. For my pet.

Putting the phone down, I made myself think. This was insane. What had the caller been talking about? What was I asking questions about? What would have endangered my pet? And who would do such a thing?

This was crazy. But, okay, assuming crazy rules. Whom had I pissed off?

There was the developer. I'd been completely within my legal rights to inquire if any permits had been filed or requested. But Mel Baker hadn't liked my questions and from what Patti had said, maybe Wilson and Crave didn't care about legal rights.

Maybe they knew that I'd also been talking to the Animals Now group, and thought I'd planned some kind of sabotage?

Or what about Animals Now itself? Could Violet have let something slip about me writing a real estate story? Told someone I was wondering if Ruth and her colleagues might have been involved in Gail's death? Or maybe they were just so secretive, they didn't like me poking around. My friendship with Vi wasn't a secret either, and if she was joining forces with them, maybe they saw me as a threat.

This possibility was actually comforting. The Animals Now folks were crazy enough to do something like this, but they wouldn't hurt an animal. Then again, Ruth seemed to have no love for domestic cats, and my Musetta, my plump little friend, was certainly domesticated.

Oh, this was horrible. And as I gave in to the horror, other ideas flooded my head. Maybe Bill was right, and some band I'd panned had been looking for a way to get back at me. I'd been threatened before, but the harsh words had always been aimed at me, not my cat. No, the caller had specifically referred to my questions. Not criticisms, reviews, or judgments. Questions.

I'd also been asking about Swann's Way, of course. But there was nothing threatening there. Obnoxious, maybe, but that's not dangerous. And my questions had all been standard operating procedure; they were a baby band, and I'd wanted some background. Even if they had originally tried to maintain some kind of mystique, some kind of control over my coverage they'd been as psyched as any newcomers would be when they heard they might be on the Arts cover. Yeah, they cared more about the photos than the interview, but for post-MTV types, that wasn't unusual.

Still, it could be someone on the scene. I shivered, but it was true. I'd been asking about drugs. Specifically about that new drug, the so-called Fantasy Plus. It was quite possible that it was being made locally; it certainly had hit the clubs hard. But had I threatened somebody? Had I gotten close enough to hit a nerve? I mean, I hadn't really gotten started. I'd only questioned a few bartenders, a couple of club staffers. I'd asked about Ralph. These were people I knew.

Or did I? How well did I really know Graham, a man I only saw at night, serving drinks? And Tony at the Amphibian, for all his flirtatious manner: how did he really feel about me? Even

Ralph, goofy Ralph, whom I'd dismissed as a joke, a lush, a harmless boor, could easily be more. All these men I'd considered colleagues. But I had been asking questions. I was a journalist looking into illegal activity. And I was a college grad, too, while many of them were not, and with the rising rents in the city I knew class tensions were heating up. Most of the guys I hung with were blue collar working stiffs; the club scene the pinnacle of their lives. They could easily see me as an interloper. A tourist, or worse. Had I pissed off someone in the scene?

I'd been so trusting. I thought of all the times that I'd tossed my bag behind the bar, as if each club were just another friend's living room. I'd been thinking that the workmen had let Musetta out, or that they'd not known how to coddle an unfamiliar lock and left my door open. But I'd been gone so long I couldn't really say when she'd disappeared. Been taken. Had someone targeted me and had my own careless behavior made it easy? Did someone have my keys? Was someone out to get me, out to hurt my poor, sweet pet?

Bill was always worrying that I didn't take care of myself. Violet had as much as told me I was naive. Without any blood relatives in the area, the club crowd had become my family of choice. Could I have been so wrong? Everything was in doubt.

Bunny. She'd been drugged, but maybe Bill was right. Maybe I'd been the intended victim. We'd both been drinking club soda, both from identical tall tumblers, both taking lime slices from one plate. Had someone on the scene already tried to scare me off? Or was the call from the developer? Was big money worried that I would uncover something that would make them vulnerable to legal action? Or had the underground group seen me as siding with the enemy? Could Violet be involved? She'd never hurt Musetta, she knew how much my pet meant to me. But maybe she'd said something, told someone specifically how much my round black-and-white cat meant to me. Even Tess had been acting weird, and, well, I'd certainly been questioning her.

My thoughts were circling. Nothing was making sense. The night was dark, the storm was getting worse. And I'd never felt more alone.

"BILL? PLEASE PICK UP." I knew I was whimpering, but the sound of his answering machine was the final straw. "Bill?" The clock said four, but this was an emergency. *"Bill?"*

"I'm here. I'm awake." My guy didn't sound awake, but I trusted the habits of years of police work. Besides, I needed him to be there. "Bill, someone's taken Musetta! She's been…" I started to say "catnapped," but that sounded so ludicrous. "She's been taken."

"Theda, babe? Are you okay? You're not making much sense."

"Musetta's been stolen. Catnapped!" It did sound as silly as I'd feared, and it didn't help that I was starting to cry.

"Theda? Sweetie? Can you take a deep breath for me?" I nodded, not caring that he couldn't see me, and inhaled through my mouth. He must have heard. "Okay, now can you blow your nose?" I reached for a paper towel and complied. "Good, now, Theda? You there with me? Let's start at the beginning. Last thing I remember is that Musetta got out, and you and Violet were looking for her."

God, that sounded so long ago. So safe. And so, remembering to breathe and stopping occasionally to wipe my nose, I filled him in. "And they said they had my cat, Bill. *They have my cat.*"

"Maybe. Maybe not." That was not what I expected and it stopped my sniffles. "I mean, Theda, it is quite possible, even likely, that this was a prank call."

"What? Why?" Bill wasn't making sense.

"Think about it: You don't have any proof, right? They didn't, I don't know, they didn't describe her to you or tell you something that would make you sure they had her." They hadn't. I'd told him everything. "And, you know, a lot of people in the city will have seen your poster. It's got your name and number on it, right?" He was right. "Well, there are a lot of sick people out there. Maybe someone is playing a joke on you. Not a very good one, but, I don't know, you've given some pretty tough reviews to bands over the years, right?"

"Yeah, but…." A part of me wanted to agree with him. The idea that my darling cat was simply lost, was only out alone in a winter storm now seemed preferable to the alternative. I started to relax, but some latent editorial instinct held me back. It was the choice of words. "Bill, they didn't say, 'Stop writing' or 'Clean up your act' or anything. They said, 'Stop asking questions.' Specifically questions. And, Bill? I have been asking a lot of questions about things recently."

He sighed, and I could tell that he was really, truly waking up. "Maybe, Theda. But, well, it is odd."

I didn't say anything. He knew me well enough to understand that odd is not that unusual for me.

"Do you want me to come over?"

I did, how I did. But I should have given in to that urge earlier, if I was going to. The idea of my long tall beau stretched out in a cab at this hour was just too much. "No, that's okay. You don't have to."

He didn't argue. "Well, Theda? I know this is going to be difficult, but maybe you can try to get some sleep?" He heard my silence loud and clear. "In the morning, darling, I promise. I'll call over to the station, see who I can get to look into this."

"Bill, it can't be anyone obvious. I mean, they've got Musetta."

"I know, darling. I know you believe that. I hope you're wrong and it's just a really bad joke, but we'll take that into consideration. Look, try to get some shut-eye, and I'll call you as soon as I've raised anyone over at Central Square, okay?"

I had no choice. "Okay, Bill. I know you don't believe me, but thanks."

"Good night, sweetie. Try to get some sleep."

Fat chance of that. But Bill wasn't my only friend, was he? Sure, it was late, but Violet was sympathetic. Even Caro would understand a call like this. I started to dial and then stopped.

What if this had something to do with Animals Now and with Violet? No, that way madness lay. Violet would never betray me, would never threaten my cat even if she and I had had the mother of all fallings out. I punched in some numbers, then disconnected again. What if she hadn't realized she'd betrayed me? What if she was in so deep with Ruth and her crew that she didn't know when to stop, or what not to say?

Rubbish, I started to dial again and once again put the phone down. It was all too much. I could wake Vi, and Caro, too. But right now none of my friendships seemed as sound as they once had. And what had I been warned against? Asking questions. My instincts to uncover, to investigate were maybe, just maybe what had gotten me into trouble. I wrapped the afghan around me and stared out the window until the night started to pale.

WHAT A SHOCK, then, when Violet's voice woke me. I'd reached for the phone automatically, not realizing that I'd been asleep, and time blurred together as she began speaking.

"So, Theda. Has anyone called?"

"Why? What do you know?" My voice came out in a bark and I jumped to my feet. Full daylight streamed in the front windows, but I could see nothing on the street below. The storm had ended, leaving the world slick and bright. I didn't know whether to wish my pet out in this brand new day or not. "Violet?"

"Theda, what gives? Did I wake you? I'm sorry. I was just hoping somebody had called."

"Somebody did." I hesitated. But this was Vi, not some chatty bartender. As calmly as I could, I explained the late-night call, and, to be fair, also gave her Bill's interpretation of it as well.

"Wow. Well, if that's a joke, it's a pretty sick one. But, you know, Theda? He may have a point."

"But why, Violet? And, who would do that? I mean, does someone just go around making prank calls off all the lost pet posters in the city?"

"No, but…" She was holding something back. I was in no mood for games.

"Violet. Tell me."

"Well, Theda? After we called it a night, I made some calls around, too. You know, just to see if I could get some other folks from the scene to start looking. They're all night owls anyway. So, maybe, like, I called the wrong person, gave someone an idea?"

"Great." So she thought I had enemies, too. Enemies among those I worked and played with. Enemies I didn't know about. But, perversely, the idea that perhaps the call had been a joke, a mean, nasty joke, helped. It meant Musetta was out there. Cold, probably wet, but not held hostage by some sicko with a grudge. It meant my happy little cat was free.

"Hey, Theda?" I grunted that I was still on the line. "That's the other thing. How could anyone have stolen Musetta?"

"My front door was open 'cause the radiator guys were working."

"Honestly, how bad do you think the repair guys are? I mean, would they have been so hard at work that someone would have been able to sneak by them and grab your cat? And, besides, how would anyone have known that your apartment was being worked on?"

"I think they left it unlocked, Vi. The lock's pretty hinky, and it doesn't always latch."

"But how would anyone know that?"

"Maybe someone had my place staked out? Or, well, you know how I tend to throw my bag behind the bar wherever. Maybe someone snatched my keys? Copied them?" In the light of day, none of these ideas made much sense, which I liked. "So you think that maybe it was a prank call?"

"I think it's likely, Theda. I mean, those are a lot of coincidences. I bet she's still out there, probably huddled down somewhere, waiting to be found. I've got the morning free, why don't I keep looking for her?"

Action was preferable to this. "Good idea. Can you swing by the Mug Shot? I'll meet you on the corner by Mass. Ave. and we can work our way back up."

"You don't want to wait by the phone?"

My stomach dropped out. "So, you think maybe it wasn't a prank?"

"Well, just to be sure."

She was right. The caller—the catnapper, whoever he was—had used my home number.

"And, hey, Theda. Maybe someone will call 'cause they found her."

She was right. Both my numbers were on the poster. With my fresh-minted optimism somewhat restored, I agreed. The problem now was how to make each painful moment pass.

If only there was some way of finding out information. Of digging without asking questions. Who could I call? Whom had I already spoken to? Ten fifteen. Not ten minutes had passed since Violet had called, and I was going nuts. For lack of anything better to do, I opened the file with the tape transcription from last night. I had never felt less like writing, but I needed something routine right now.

Had the band sounded this vapid when we'd met? Had I? I read it through, and printed the file. "Well, that's a useless—" My automatic dialogue with the kitty, a ritual whether she answered or not, caught me up short. The cushion on top of the file cabinet was empty. The sun illuminated the fine web of fur that coated its velvet cover, but I knew if I reached over the surface would be cold. I missed her with an ache like a body-sized bruise and paced the apartment, trying not to look at her favorite spots. Trying not to miss her little movements, her sounds.

I had to keep myself busy, but after typing and retyping a particularly lame paragraph, I gave up. There was no way I could write. I itched to call Violet. Why hadn't Bill touched base? I reached for the phone. But both had said they'd check in, hadn't they? Was there any other lead I could follow up on?

Anybody who might know something, might be able to help me work things through? Anyone, that is, who wouldn't be threatened if I called?

Bunny. No, she had enough on her plate. I couldn't drop this on her, too. Tess? Smart, cynical Tess? Whatever had happened with her car or with Animals Now, she couldn't be involved in this, could she? I didn't have that many friends left. I looked at the clock again. Ten forty-five. She'd be at work, and she might still be pissed at me. But this was an emergency, an emotional one anyway.

"University bio labs. Professor Henneman's office." The professionally cool voice put me in my place. Weren't they filing for that grant soon? Well, I'd already interrupted someone's day.

"Can I speak to Tess? It's an emergency. Kind of."

"Is Tess okay?" The voice warmed up. "We've been really worried."

"What? No, I'm the one with the—what's up with Tess?"

"We don't know. She hasn't been in since Monday, and she's not returning her calls. I've tried her phone, her cell. Paged her." The voice on the other side was breathless. "This is so unlike her! We're slammed or I'd have gone over to her place yesterday. I might later, if I get out before midnight. Do you know what's up with her?"

"No, but I'll find out." This was beyond strange. She wouldn't have—? No, whatever else was going on, she loved my cat and she was my friend. If she was involved in something, caught up, in trouble, maybe she needed a hand. I wasn't helping Musetta sitting around and worrying, and I sure wasn't writing. So I grabbed my parka and jammed a wool cap on my head for the short drive.

"Theda!" It was Reed. He looked great in that long black wool coat, but I didn't have time.

"Hey, Reed, I'm rushing off."

"Any cat news?" I shook my head, not trusting myself to speak. "Well, I'll keep my eyes open. But Theda?"

I was halfway out the door. Holding it open meant freezing air poured into the building. But how else to stress that I didn't have time for a chat?

"Yeah?"

"That band you asked me about. Swann's Way? Well, turns out I was at MuzeArts with one of the guys, Paul something? He and his buddy had a GB band, playing weddings every weekend. I guess they were pretty good."

"Great, Reed. Thanks." If I cared, that would be a fun bit of trivia. The kind of thing I'd like to have been able to throw out during an interview. Nobody likes GB, general business, gigs. They're a bad mix of standards and Top 40, and the closer you copy the records the more the crowd likes you. But they're the biggest moneymaker out there. If a musician laughed about his struggling past, it showed a certain character. I'd bet the Swann's Way guys would deny even knowing "Hava Nagila."

I nearly wiped out as I ran down the front stairs. Driving was going to be treacherous after a storm like last night's. I bounced my keys in my hand and debated walking. It would be safer. And on the way, I could look for Musetta. Maybe she was out there. Maybe the storm had just driven her into someone's garage or basement. Maybe.

Two buildings down, I spotted an open garage and went in. Nothing, not even a rodent, could have hidden in its clean interior. Who stacked their newspapers so neatly for recycling? A block further, I saw what looked like an open basement window. I still had Violet's flashlight in my pocket and so, lying on my belly, I switched it on to take a look, fully prepared to take the heat from an annoyed homeowner. The casement descended two feet, but the window that had caught the light wasn't the real one. Although the glass stood at an angle, a sheet of Plexiglas blocked access to the house. I brushed off frosted leaves and disappointment and continued on to Tess's. The sidewalk was icy, and even if my search was proving futile, I was glad I'd opted out of driving. Twenty minutes making sure

I didn't slip on the ice; I didn't feel better, but at least my blood was pumping.

"Tess?" I rang her bell and thumped on the door for good measure. I'd been trying to raise her on my cell from a block away. "Tess?"

"I think she's not home." A mailman stopped on the stoop and kicked the ice off his arctic-worthy cleats. "I had a special delivery for her yesterday, and it still hasn't been called for."

"No? Well, I'm a friend." I reached for the door, but he pulled it shut behind him, locking me out of the building's foyer. He also shot me a look. "Hey, I'm worried about her."

"Call her." He trudged down the sidewalk. I hoped his boots gave him athlete's foot.

"Tess?" After one more round of ringing and knocking, I decided to poke around the side. Tess lived on the second floor, but she had to have a fire escape of some sort. One nude elm stood close by the building, and I really didn't want to try it. I vaguely recalled a ladder reaching up to her tiny porch, where we'd broken every city fire code last summer grilling veggie burgers on a tiny hibachi.

"Tess?" Calling softer now, just in case any neighbors were home, I trod carefully around the side of the building. The slick, shiny gloss of ice-topped snow crunched beneath my feet. "Tess? It's me! Theda!"

There it was, a ladder, suspended a good ten feet above the ground. I jumped, and missed. But last night's storm had knocked a few branches off the sad-looking tree and one would do the trick. Reaching up, I managed to hook the branch on the lower rung. With a clatter and a shower of ice, it slid down.

I grabbed it and started to climb. "Whoa!" My shout was unintentional and I was grateful for my leather gloves. The foot I'd put all my weight on had slid completely off the iced rung. This was going to be slow going and I would have to pray for good balance as well as hibernating neighbors. My luck held. Climbing slowly, I made it up and swinging one leg very, very carefully, I reached from the ladder to the porch. There was the hibachi, now glazed with frost.

"Tess?" I knocked on the porch door, trying for all the world to look like a casual visitor who happened to arrive by air. "Yoo-hoo, Tess?" Nothing, and I cursed her silently for the thick orange curtains that covered the one porch window. "Tess?"

If I straddled the porch rail, could I reach around to her side window? I knew her bedroom was back there and, although I felt like a voyeur, I also knew that she tended to keep that blind up. She liked the light, she said, and at least for part of the year that one tree provided all the privacy she needed. If only there was more to hold onto. Risking frostbite, I removed my gloves. Yes, with bare fingers, I could get a good grip on the drain pipe. I could only hope it was firmly attached. One leg over the porch railing, one hand locked on the drain pipe, I leaned over. Slipped, and caught myself. I was leaning on the side of her window. The decorative molding, thank god, seemed to be solid wood. If I could just move my body a little further…

Just then a load of ice rained down on me and by instinct I covered my head. Big mistake, I realized as my off-center weight started to slip off the railing. "No!" I yelled without thinking, and grabbed the railing. For a moment I was stable. I looked up. Nothing there, the sun's warmth must have started to melt the load on the roof, and my clambering about hadn't helped. This was craziness. My hands were red and raw. I could see my gloves soaking up the melt in the snow below.

One more try. Holding firmly to the drain pipe, I let myself slide over, reaching out for the window frame as a brake. There, I was steady. I could strain my head and just see into her bedroom. Leaves or no, the shade was up, but I could see why Tess liked it that way. The walls, painted a happy tangerine, glowed in the sunlight. A bedspread, a warm darker orange, was pulled up, neatly, over a bed. And there, lying face down on the floor, was my friend Tess.

NINETEEN

THANKS TO THE LOGIC of emergencies, I couldn't get a cell signal from Tess's porch. But getting back down that icy ladder was faster, if not easier, than climbing it, and once on the street I was able to call 911. The big white and green ambulance showed within minutes and after I flagged it down there was little time for explanations. Two jumpsuited EMTs, a large man and even larger woman, broke in and removed my friend, still unconscious. Covered up to the chin, she looked so still. Even under their protective sheet, she seemed fragile and small. When had her slim grace become that almost skeletal thinness? But before I could even begin to answer such questions, I found myself in the awkward position of explaining my discovery. A cop car had arrived moments after the ambulance, and as the big woman wheeled Tess out and collapsed the gurney into the back of her truck, he turned me away, toward him and his questions.

"You saw her through her window? Her second-floor window?" The uniformed cop taking the report seemed doubtful, to put it mildly.

"Tess is a close friend. She hasn't been at work in days and she wasn't returning any calls." It sounded weak, even to me. "Besides, she's been acting weird." Whatever the reasoning, I'd clearly made a good call. And as much as my heart ached to keep looking for my cat, it seemed obvious that I had a human friend in more critical need. I gave the cop my info and, soon as I could, trotted home, watching out for patches of ice resistant to the brightening sun. Did I have time to run in, check to see if I had any messages? No, I decided. Tess had been unconscious when they'd left for the hospital. I really had to follow her there.

Safety aside, I found myself dialing and driving. First, to Bill and voice mail. "Bill, it's me. Something's happened to Tess. I found her unconscious. They're taking her to the E.R. now and I'm following. Have you asked anybody about Musetta? I haven't heard anything."

Violet was next, and when again I got voice mail I repeated my news. Someone had to call me back. So when my cell rang as I pulled into a spot at the hospital I grabbed it even before putting my car in Park.

"Theda? This is Shelley at the *Mail*."

"Hang on." The copy desk? I turned off the ignition and gathered my thoughts in the silent car. Of course, my column was due. "Shelley, I—"

"You're in the crapper, is what you are." She was whispering, so I knew she was sitting on the desk, exposed and not far from Tim's office. "Where's your column? You said you'd get it in early. Turns out Tim wanted it for design yesterday so they could work something special up for the front."

"Shelley, I—" What could I say? "I don't have it done yet."

"Hell, I covered and said you were having computer problems. Then today, I was hoping that was true."

"Look, Shelley, I'm actually right outside City Hospital right now. A friend was taken to the E.R. Do you think you can buy me any more time?"

"Wow, is everything okay?" Shelley, unlike my editor, was human. The fact that I hadn't revealed the real reason for my missing deadline didn't make me feel too warm blooded, however.

"I hope so. I'll let you know."

"Well, I'll keep stalling. I've got the art for your piece. Some great photos, and I can use those. I'll go hide out with them in design. But that won't last for long. Tim's stalking around and keeps talking headlines. Look, can you send me a lead soon? If we can start writing a headline around it, that'll buy you an hour at least."

I thanked her, meaning it, and went in. The same bright colors, the same children's artwork from Sunday night made the place strangely familiar. At least, this time I knew where to go for information.

"Tess Easterlund? Are you a family member?"

I almost said yes, but the lie stuck in my throat. "I'm—I'm the friend who called 911. I'm the friend who found her."

I saw pity in her dark eyes. Maybe it was simply fatigue. "Hang on."

Fifteen minutes later, an unshaven young doctor in green came out of the swinging doors. "You were asking about Tess Easterlund?" I nodded.

"She's one very lucky girl. And you're a good friend. She's going to be okay." I exhaled. I hadn't realized that I'd been holding my breath. "To be frank, we think she must have been using quite a long time, and paradoxically that's what saved her."

Using? But the doctor was still talking. "I've never seen blood toxicity levels so high in a still-breathing patient. But it seems your friend has been working very hard at building up her tolerance. A big dose of Narcan and some fluids and she's already coming around. Now, we still have some neurological tests to perform—"

"Wait, Tess OD'd? Was she drugged by someone else, maybe? Was it a club drug? That new one they're calling Fantasy Plus?"

"No, what makes you think that?" He was looking at me strangely and I realized how I must appear after a frazzled, sleepless night. I opened my mouth to explain, but he waved me to silence. "You people. You think you're immortal. No, it wasn't one of your so-called party drugs. It was good, old-fashioned amphetamines."

I wanted to argue. What people? I wasn't even that young anymore, not compared with the doctor anyway. Then it hit me.

The long hours. The secretiveness, bordering on paranoia. The accident. Even the decline of her willowy good looks into something more wan and stretched. Speed. Tess had been pushing herself so hard. Always the perfectionist, the workaholic, she must have begun popping amphetamines sometime during the last crunch period, and she had finally pushed herself over the line. Before I could ask any more questions, my cell rang.

"You can't answer that in here." The young doctor turned on his crepe-soled heel.

"Wait." I turned the phone off. "Can I see her?"

"Family only, I'm sorry." He must have seen the next question on my face. "We found her insurance card in her wallet. They've got all her contact info. I should get back now."

At least the university job was proving good for something. I stepped out to the sidewalk to check on my missed call and saw that another was coming in.

"Hey, Violet! Any sign of Musetta?" Tess had done this to herself, but my kitty was a lost innocent.

"Sorry, kiddo. Nothing. I went around again this morning. The trap was empty, too. No more weird phone calls?"

"Nothing on my cell and I haven't been home since I went to Tess's. I'm at the hospital now. They say she'll be okay, but it was speed. She OD'd on speed." Violet's quiet "huh" didn't sound surprised. "You knew?"

"I wondered. Especially when you said you hadn't seen her for a while. Speed freaks tend to drop their straight friends."

"Am I that straight? And, like, is everyone around me doing something?"

She laughed. "I'm not, Theda. I don't even smoke anymore. But, yeah, you can be a little innocent sometimes."

"Great." My fears from last night hovered. Had I been so trusting, so comfortable in the seeming community of the clubs, that I'd endangered my pet?

"But anyway, I was calling for a different reason. Ruth

called me. They've got word that Wilson and Crave are going to try something down at the plant. We're planning a quickie demo as a response. I know what you think of Ruth, but I thought maybe you could use the distraction. You want in?"

"I don't think so. Thanks, though." At least they trusted me, but all I wanted was to keep looking for Musetta. What I *needed* to do was write my piece. "Hey, Violet, I heard the strangest thing this morning. You know Swann's Way? How we thought those guys were from wealthy families? Well, it turns out they worked their way through MuzeArts doing GB gigs."

She laughed, as I knew she would. Some degree of normalcy had returned. "That must have burned their egos, huh? Think they had to learn 'Butterfly Kisses' and 'Daddy's Little Girl'?"

"Hey, it's part of the gig, right?"

"Makes sense, though. Paul Wexner—the one with the dark hair?—drives the most rundown beater. I just assumed it was some kind of pretentious anti-nouveau riche statement, like wearing taped-up Topsiders. You know, calling a broken-down wreck your 'blue bomber' or something."

"Wait a minute." Things were clicking. "What color is his car?"

"This sickly light baby blue, like something you haven't seen since the '70s. Truly a hideous vehicle."

Baby blue—like the paint chips left in the rotary. Like Tess's car. Bill had never been more specific. But there might be other reasons.

"What is it, Theda? I can hear the gears turning."

"Just thinking about Gail's hit and run." It was time to spill the beans, at least some of them. "I've just been so afraid that Tess did it. I mean, she had an accident of some sort that night, and there were blue bits among all the other paint chips left at the scene. And, well, I guess I'm just stretching for some other suspect."

"And you think, 'cause of the drugs?"

She meant the speed, I knew that. She meant, did I think that

Tess had hit Gail and not been aware, because she was speeding or blacked out. But as soon as she said it, something else clicked. Drugs. Paul Wexner. That late-night call. Right then, nothing else mattered.

"Theda?"

"Hang on, Vi." What had Graham said, "pay for play"? Money was vital in the grab for fame. Drugs meant money. And I'd been asking questions about the band and about drugs.

"Violet, do you know where Swann's Way rehearses?"

"No, I thought you did an interview with them?"

"At the Casbah. They didn't want me at their practice space. But, Violet, I think they're it."

"What? Swann's Way killed Gail?"

"I don't know." Truth was, I'd forgotten about Gail for a moment, and Violet didn't know about the poison anyway. "I don't know if there's any connection there. But think a minute: Swann's Way is new on the scene and they're not the rich kids everyone thinks. But suddenly they have a load of cash, enough to put down at least five grand on MuzeArts and buy cars for their girlfriends. And I've been asking questions about them—*and* about that new club drug—all over town, not realizing that both lines of inquiry might be related."

I was pacing. Excited now. I didn't know how clearly I was thinking, what with lack of sleep and Musetta and Tess. I had to talk it through. "I think they're behind it, Violet. I think they're selling or even making that crap, that Fantasy Plus, in some basement somewhere." I flashed back to that first meeting with Heather. It was her friend who'd overdosed, passing out at the club. She and both Pauls had also been there the night Bunny had been poisoned—I couldn't think of a better word—and both of them had probably heard me asking about the new high, too.

I slapped myself on the forehead. "They put it together before I did, Violet. They think I know, that I've figured out they're dealing. Violet, *they're the ones who have taken Musetta!*"

"Wow." My friend neither laughed nor hung up, so I knew my idea had some merit. "It sort of makes sense. I mean, Swann's Way is totally new to the scene, but, well, everyone does seem to know about them, anyway. And, Fantasy Plus has come out of nowhere."

"It has, right?" I no longer trusted my perception.

"Yeah, that's not a name you forget. Hey, Theda, want me to ask around? If these jerks stole a cat, there are a lot of people who will want to help find them."

"Thanks, Violet, but I don't know." Did I want the club world notified? The old familiar warmth wasn't there. "I mean, who knows who is involved?"

"I'll be careful, kiddo. Let me make some calls. You're going to tell Bill, right?"

Since when had she started worrying so much about me? Still, it felt nice. "Yeah, I will."

"Keep me in the loop."

BILL WAS STILL OUT when I called back, and to make my frustration worse, I saw that the missed call had been from him. "Theda, you okay? That's horrible. Call me as soon as you know more. Or better yet, let me know where you are and I'll come find you. I've got some news for you by the way. Not on Musetta, though." The last, an afterthought, deflated my hopes, as he must have known it would have. "Sorry, sweetie."

I went through my old calls until I found Heather's number. True to the rest of my day, I got her voice mail.

"Heather? This is Theda Krakow. I must speak with you immediately. As soon as you get this, please call me back." It took all my control to not yell or threaten. But I needed her. I needed to find out where Swann's Way would hide one small, frightened cat. Did they have her locked in a closet or closed in a box? Was she hurt? Had they fed her? A dozen images sprang into my mind, none of them what I wanted to see.

But they did spark an idea. "Shelley?" My copy editor buddy picked up on the first ring.

"Theda!" She whispered my name. "Where's your copy? Tim is going bonkers!"

"Shelley, hang on. This is important. You said you had the photos for the story?"

"They're in the system, hang on." I remembered how slow the *Mail* computers could be and tried not to fidget while she called up the files. "Okay, I've got three of them here."

"Can you describe them to me?" It was a long shot. The photos could have been done anywhere, posed in a studio or at a local landmark. But often our photographers met their subjects where they lived or practiced, and it was clear that Swann's Way cared more about their photos than they did my interview. It was also the only thing I could think of.

"Are you still looking for a lead, Theda? 'Cause if you are, I don't know that these will help any. They're pretty plain."

"Just describe them, Shelley. *Please.*"

"Okay, okay. Hang on." I heard the click of keys and knew she was enlarging the computer-screen proofs. "Okay, the first one is four guys. Kind of cute. One of them is wearing a gas station jacket. That's the tall one…."

"No, no, Shelley. Not the band. The setting. Can you describe where they are? Anything around them?"

"Oh, sorry. Well, it all looks kind of generic. You know, post-industrial chic or something."

I was losing it. *"Shelley?"*

"Okay, okay. Sorry. In that first one, they're up against some kind of wall. Red brick. It looks sort of chipped and old. Faded. Nice color actually, but it could be anywhere. That goes for the next one, too. Now, in the third, there's something else, a metal wall. No, I see a hinge. It's a door, a pair of doors, with those little windows in them. Looks like there are wires in the windows, like it's a prison. Boy's school, maybe?"

Or maybe something closer. It was a long shot, a very long shot, but I remembered seeing windows like that.

"Wait, there's another here, too. This one is different.

They're outdoors now. Well, maybe they were before, too, but you couldn't really tell with what they're wearing. But here they're definitely outside, cause there's snow and leaves on the ground, and they're leaning up against a hut of some kind. Really decrepit. It's wood, all gray and splintered. Maybe it was once blue? Yeah, there's still some blue paint on it. Nice shot, actually, lots of texture."

"Thanks, Shelley." My long shot was sounding better. "I gotta go."

"What should I tell Tim? Uh-oh, here he comes again!"

"Tell him I'll have a whale of a story for him soon. Really soon." I hung up and raced toward my car.

It sounded like the bottling plant. That shed, those wired doors. Even as I was telling myself to calm down, that in our red-brick city there were doubtless dozens of wired windows and wooden sheds as well, I wanted to race right over. But I'd had enough of being careless. Swinging onto Cambridge Street, I started to dial Bill's number again and looked up just in time to see the truck headed toward me.

"Watch it!" Window open to the cold air, the driver yelled down at me, a few particularly choice epithets trailing behind him as his big rig barreled away. Shaking, I pulled over. Better to keep my mind on the road. And, besides, hadn't Bill made some reference to a message? I was only about five minutes from my home.

Sure enough, the message light was blinking rapidly.

"Krakow, where the hell is your story?" Tim, I hit "next."

"Hi, Theda. Patti here. I just got the strangest call." Mel Baker. Well, I'd make nice later.

Two more beeps signaled call-and-hang-ups, either telemarketers or Tim, his temper growing shorter. But the last proved to be from Bill.

"Theda. I'm at the station. Not moving quickly, but I got here." So that's why he hadn't been answering his home phone. He'd mentioned touching base with his colleagues, but since he'd been laid up, I hadn't thought to call his office line. "I'm not sure it feels good to be back. But it does feel good to be doing something. Haven't found anything on your Musetta problem." I could picture him in a crowded squad room, choosing his words to sound generic. "But I am asking around. Give me a yell when you can. Let me know how Tess is doing. And, well, I know this isn't the best time, but there's something I really need to discuss with you."

TWENTY

SOMETHING WE NEEDED to discuss? Great. That sounded like relationship talk. Odds are, he wanted to lecture me on my lifestyle and my friends. He didn't know the half of it yet, and I didn't have time to go over it. I called his office line and got voice mail. Not the place to leave a lengthy explanation, but I knew enough not to go off without leaving a trail of bread crumbs behind. I called back and, this time, started talking after the beep.

"Bill, I have reason to believe there might be a drug lab somewhere in the old bottling plant. I think Musetta is being held there, and I'm going to investigate." He'd think I was insane, but at least he'd know where to find me.

The message I left for Violet was a bit shorter. No need to mention the lab, just that the creeps in Swann's Way might be at the bottling plant. She'd be a useful ally if she got it in time, having poked about those premises considerably more than I had.

But so, I realized, might Patti. Breaking my streak, I got her on the first ring.

"Theda? I can't chat, I'm expecting a client to make an offer any minute."

"Well, until call waiting comes through—what can you tell me about tenants at the bottling plant? Are there any areas that you know are occupied? Is there anyway in besides those big main doors or the basement?"

"Theda, you're not doing anything down there, are you? I got a rather annoyed call about you, and I really would prefer you stay away."

"Why? What's up?" I wasn't going to be deterred, but if Mel Baker or his cronies had anything planned, I wanted to know about it. I didn't put anything past them: armed guards, rabid dogs. Land mines.

"Well, maybe you don't know. But *they* know about what those friends of yours have planned." Of course, the demonstration. But wasn't the demonstration a response to something that the developers were already doing? I thought of those tire tracks, sure sign of heavy machinery, but they weren't recent. What did Ruth know? Patti was still talking. "Believe me, nobody is going to let valuable property be compromised or damaged."

"Damaged? But don't Wilson and Crave want to tear the building down?"

"Not necessarily. It's a solid structure, so they may just demo the inside, and then expand it up with the towers. The granite front has got heritage appeal." Patti was always using phrases like that. At this point, her lingo just annoyed me.

"Patti, I'm not involved with any demonstration, and right now I don't even care what Wilson and Crave are up to. But I've got to go check something out. There might be something up and, well, I just wondered if you could help me." I took a breath and decided to trust her. "If I needed to get into the building, and I swear to you I'm not going to vandalize anything or lead the Animals Now crew in, but if I needed to get in, how would I do it?"

She paused and I thought I'd lost her. Had her other call come through?

"Patti, please. It's an emergency. I, well, I think that some real dirtbags may have grabbed Musetta and may be hiding out there."

"What?" I heard a double click. "Hang on."

She was back within a few seconds, but the wait was long enough. "Patti, please. I will explain, but please, for now, just trust me. I need to know: is there any way to get into the old bottling plant without a key?"

"Well, there may be." Another pause. "You promise me

you're not up to something? You won't let *anyone* else in?" I knew she meant Violet, but I agreed anyway. If Violet came to help me, she'd be on my mission. "Well, then, there's no guarantee of this. But around the back there are a set of fire doors at the end of each of the building's wings. They're that thick, gray metal? Hideously unattractive, with little teeny windows set up high in thick glass." I knew them. Shelley had just described them to me. "Anyway, they're the kind of safety doors that can't be locked from the inside. When they close right, they lock automatically from the outside, but it's a catch lock; each door has to be completely closed. But anyway, the far one— you know, like the other end of the 'E' from where we were? Well, in that wing I know for a while there was a tenant, some software inventor type, who always left a little piece of wood propping one of the doors open. He damaged the hinge eventually. Now, I don't think he's still there. All the tenants are supposed to be finishing up their leases, but there's a chance that the back door might still be workable."

It was slim, but it was something. "Thanks, Patti."

"Now, Theda, remember, you *promised*…"

I was saved by the double-beep of her call waiting. "Don't worry!" I yelled out, and she was gone.

Seeing as how I was about to attempt an illegal entry, I parked a block away and tried to look inconspicuous as I trotted toward the brick and granite building. It was still early afternoon, and the first of the rush hour traffic hadn't yet started using nearby River Street as a cut through. I'd have the place to myself, and light, for at least an hour or two. It was cold. Even in my gloves, my fingers had started to go numb. But when I thought of my poor pet, huddled and shivering somewhere in that brooding building, I just rubbed my hands together and walked faster.

I was crossing the frozen grounds when I heard them. Chanting, a group of voices, from the other end of the building. Unsure what was up, I ducked behind the front stairs and peeked out.

The demonstration. When Violet had told me about it, I hadn't realized it was going to happen today. But I hadn't waited to hear the details, either. I looked again. The group was small, but their purpose was clear. At the block's far end a group of about three dozen people milled about and then all turned in my direction, yelling something rhythmic that sounded like it rhymed. I ducked down, but when the small crowd grew quiet I risked another peek. The group was bundled into sexlessness, but I'd wager that the large figure out front was Ruth. She'd raised her hands up, like she was conducting, and turned to address her followers. Two people in front of her held signs. Great, just when I'd hoped to sneak into an otherwise empty, forgotten building, I'd stumbled into the beginning of a march. All I could hope was that on a frozen day like this, such a small protest wouldn't raise much attention.

"Building for housing! Cambridgeport for the people!" The voices were louder now, and I debated my next move. I could move away from them, duck around the back of the building that way. To do so would expose me to any River Street traffic and to anyone watching from Memorial Drive. Patti's warning echoed. The developers were on the alert. I really didn't need to fall foul of any Wilson and Crave legbreakers. I had too much to do. But to try to pass the marchers seemed foolish. "Buildings for housing!"

In for a penny, in for a pound. Head down, hands jammed into my pockets, I tried for nonchalant stroller as I walked quickly around the exposed side of the building.

I was in luck. If Wilson and Crave had set watchers here to keep an eye on the demonstration, they were out front, monitoring the progress of the tiny demonstration. I had no idea if any of Swann's Way were around, and could only hope that the sound might have scared them off, too. Did dealers work on weekday afternoons, anyway?

Brrrinnng! The sound of my own cell phone made me jump, and I reached for it to quiet it down as much as anything. Violet was probably right out front, but maybe this was Bill.

"Krakow? Where the hell are you? Where's my story?"

It was Tim. To call him irate would be an understatement, though it did make me wonder when my column had become his story.

"Tim! It's coming." I hissed, and then realized that I was making myself more conspicuous by whispering. "I'm getting you your story." I was around the back of the building now, the river side, and the blind windows looked on ominously. Was anyone inside there? I talked as softly as I could.

"What? Krakow, speak up! I don't care if your computer blew up. You come down here and type it in yourself. I'm holding up the arts front. The entire section goes on press in three hours."

"Tim." I raised my voice a smidgen. "This is becoming a bigger story. I'm going to have a bigger story for you, very soon." I looked around. The doors I had tried with Patti were about five yards away. I trotted up to them and pulled. They were still locked tight. Their twins, the doors she had told me about, lay across the exposed stretches of two windswept court-yards. "Very, very soon."

"Don't give me bigger. I'm not shrinking the photos for you, Krakow. Fifty twills and that's it."

"No, not longer. Bigger." I paused, not wanting to be over-heard by anyone inside those doors. "Tim, you're going to want to hold the presses for this one."

"Hold the presses! Are you insane, young lady? Have your hormones finally driven you around the bend? This is the features section, Krakow! And you're an on-the-edge free-lancer who is about to lose her gig."

"Tim—" He wasn't listening.

"Send me your copy or get your butt in here to type it up within the hour, or don't even think of writing for the *Mail* ever again."

I CLICKED THE PHONE SHUT. Some things were more important than work, and my cat was one of them. The ground crunched beneath my feet as I jogged, half bent over, to the end of the middle wing, between the two courtyards. Here, too, was the faded brick; here were identical doors. Was this where Swann's Way had posed? Could Patti have been wrong about which wing's doors got propped open? I took a deep breath, grabbed the handles and pulled.

Nothing. They were locked, rusted in place. I looked through the little windows, set high like in the first set of doors, but all was dark. Ducking down again, I ran to the third pair, the last set. The doors Patti had told me about. Taking a deep breath, I almost prayed. "Please…." And pulled.

A slight rattle, and then nothing. These, too, were closed fast. Locked, unmoveable. I rattled them again, and again. But nothing gave. With a sense of growing desperation, I ran my hands around the edges, searching for a nick, an opening, in vain. Despite what Patti had said, the hinges looked untouched. Any wear or scrapes had long since weathered into the general gunmetal gray. I ran back to the middle doors and pulled again, then the first, shaking and punching the cold flat surfaces until my hands felt hot and bruised.

It was hopeless, and the full force of it hit me, sending me sprawling against the rough brick wall. I had no idea if my cat was inside, but it was moot. I was outside, and that was that. My eyes stung with tears and I pressed my face against the cold metal. Musetta, my sweet little pet. What had I brought down upon on your smooth black head?

I don't know how long I stood there, letting my sorrow overcome me. But it was long enough for the marchers to start moving. More a small mob than an organized march if their shouts and chanting were any clue, their voices reached me, rising, waking me from my stupor. They were doing what they could, standing up against a giant corporation. How could I give up?

There were other entryways. There had to be. Maybe I could get the plywood off one of the broken windows. For that, I'd need something to stand on, something I could drag over.

I ran back to the second courtyard, where that tumble-down shed guarded the entrance. Maybe I could break off part of its splintering wood to use as a lever.

I was pulling on the door, desperate to tear off a piece, when I heard the voices, louder and closer. They must have turned the last corner. They'd be coming my way soon and—justified or not—I really didn't want to have to explain myself. I looked into the courtyard. It was as bare as ever, the few trash-strewn bushes offering no shelter for an animal my size. The bulkhead, however, the spider-y one, that was an option. I could hide there while the march went by, and then use its broken doors to ram through a window. As I dashed for it I realized that the broken top, the surface doors I'd propped back into place, were wide open. Had someone been in?

Two steps down and the smell hit me. Stronger than cat urine, too strong if the feral colony had supposedly moved on, the stench grew stronger down by the bottom doors. Doors that were closed but no longer secured by chain and padlock. Doors that were unlocked! Behind me, I could hear the chanting. The marchers were close enough for me to make out words. Something rhyming "save" and "Wilson and Crave." Taking a last deep breath of fresh air and thinking of Musetta, I ducked into the dark.

THE SMELL WAS pungent here, but not unbearable, especially if I breathed through my mouth. The dark wasn't complete either, and in a moment I could see the passageway ahead of me, lit ever so dimly by a high-set casement window half obscured by leaves and dirt.

I began to walk, treading as quietly as I could on what looked like a concrete floor. I didn't have a plan beyond getting into the building. Now that I was here, all I could do was poke around. To my right, toward the main building, all seemed still and dark. To my left—back toward the fire doors—I heard some noise. It could be the marchers, but I had to make a choice and turned toward the sound. A few steps in, the odor began to grow stronger.

I was going toward something, the source of the smell. My eyes began to burn, and I thought of Musetta. With her moist, sensitive nose, this would be torture for her. Then it hit me. That must have been why the feral colony was moving. Gail's notes had focused on feline behavior, but she must have noticed, too. What I was smelling wasn't cat urine at all, but something chemical, abrasive to any living creature's nose and eyes.

"Musetta! Psss, psss, psss." I came up to a closed door, firmly locked. There was no light under it, and no sound from the crack along its side. "Musetta?" I got down on the floor. If my pet were locked inside, she'd respond to my voice, wouldn't she? Wouldn't she mew or scratch to get out? I thought of all the times I'd heard her, impatient, while I'd be fumbling with my keys or my groceries and nearly choked up. "Musetta?" Nothing.

The next door was unlocked, but the room was empty. A janitor's station, probably, back in the days when this building had been filled with life and all its messes. Now only a broken metal storage unit remained, one shelf drooping where a support had buckled. What had been so heavy? A corroded sink stood as dry as a desert. Nothing here for any living creature. I stepped back out, closing the door behind me.

I TRIED TO PICTURE the layout of the building. Was I getting close to the edge of the wing yet? The smell grew worse, a mix of drain cleaner and something burning. It caught in my throat now, making my chest hurt. The low light still showed nothing, but as I followed the hall down its dim length, I thought I saw movement ahead.

"Musetta?" An open doorway was letting light into the hall, and I ran to it. *"Musetta!"* Eyes at cat level, I turned into a pair of feet. I looked up: Paul Wexner, grinning that big schoolboy grin.

"Man, you're as bad as my girlfriend!" The baby-faced singer flicked the light off and was pulling the door shut behind him, but through that door, I could tell, was the source of the stench.

"Where's my cat?" I reached back to punch him. I needed

to strike at him, but I'm not in the practice of fighting and he grabbed my wrists, both of them, easily.

"Calm down, girl. Calm down. What makes you think I have your kitty cat?"

"Because you—" I stopped myself in time. If he knew that I knew, then why would he let my cat go? Why would he let *me* go? That thought, along with his tight grip on both of my hands, struck me in the stomach like cold coffee. I had hoped I'd find my cat, locked in here somewhere. Trapped as a prank. I hadn't thought about confronting her captor, and I was clearly at a disadvantage. Wexner wasn't the pretty boy I'd thought. His smile—that was key—his smooth, supercilious smile. He was proud with a young man's pride. Used to getting his way. I was another "girl." I could get him to pity me, maybe even want to help me. To see me as a possible ally in his great push for fame. "Because it sounded like you. On the phone."

He grinned. "And you, what, traced the call?"

"No, no." I had to think fast, had to turn this around. "I was just at the *Mail,* working on your story. It's the cover story, you know. The pictures look great. They really do. You're going to love it. We're doing an entire spread. But I recognized this place and I thought, 'I bet Swann's Way practices there.' And then I thought, well, maybe it was a joke, right? Like, make sure the critic doesn't get too harsh?" I tried smiling, but between my stinging eyes and my fear, I knew it looked more like a spasm. "You do have my cat, don't you?"

I was pleading, my eyes were tearing up. I knew he didn't buy my line that it was a joke. But he didn't care. I could see that as his smile, a real one, grew broader and more relaxed. He had power over me, and he was enjoying it.

"Well, there have been a lot of cats around here. Not the nicest kitty cats, though my girl and Berman's fell for some of the kittens."

"The feral kittens?" That would explain the crazed behavior of the mothers.

"Feral. That's a good word. I gotta remember that for a song." I blinked and forced a smile. "Mean little things. I'm supposed to be watching over Amber's till she gets out of rehab, but sometimes, I don't know…"

I whimpered. He laughed. "Now, do I look like the kind of guy who would hurt a small, defenseless animal?" I forced out what I hoped sounded something like a chuckle. He bent my arm back so he could stroke my hair. "Hurt something so soft and nice?"

"'Course not." My voice broke.

"Now, nosy little girls who poke around where they're not wanted…." He leaned in toward me, bending my arm farther still. I forced myself not to step back as his face came close to mine.

"I figured it was a joke. You know, me being a critic and all." My laugh this time was more of a croak, but he was enjoying himself too much to notice. "You probably came by to talk with me, and since my door doesn't latch, maybe you came in to see how I was. A little 'welcome home party,' right?" I thought of the Fantasy Plus, how out-of-it I'd been that Monday. I had a flash of what could have happened and made a sick noise. Maybe it would sound like a giggle.

"'Welcome home.' Yeah, you've got a sense of humor." Maybe he was used to scaring women. "Some people don't. I mean, it's just a cat, right? Some people take everything so seriously."

Gail. Suddenly, I remembered the blue paint chips in the intersection. Paul Wexner had that old blue car. He'd hit her; he'd been the one. Maybe he'd done it to cover up the poisoning. Maybe just to make sure she was dead.

I should have known. I'd almost figured it out. It was *where* she was, not what she was doing that had gotten her killed. Not because Wilson and Crave wanted the property for development, but because she'd been here, watching the colony. Day after day, her notes had shown. She'd come to care about those animals, and she saw them being forced out of their shelter, their one safe space. She must have confronted Paul. She must have complained. Not about the drugs, but about the stench. About Paul and his buddies chasing out a settled colony of feral cats. Maybe she suspected that they were stealing the kittens. And Gail was never one to soft-sell what she thought was right.

"It's just…" What could I say? As angry as I was, I couldn't risk repeating Gail's mistake. She must have annoyed him, with her shrill voice and righteous manner. Maybe she even threatened to expose his little business. Wexner wouldn't know that she was as unlikely to go to the police as he was.

"Yes?" He wanted me to beg. I could see that. But how could I reach through that cold smile and make him understand how much I loved my pet? How could I reveal any more of that without tempting him to hurt us both, to hurt us more?

I OPENED MY MOUTH. I tried to think, but just as I was about to say it—to say "please" with a stupid girly grin—we both heard a crash and a thud. Letting go of my left wrist, Paul spun around and pushed the door open, dragging me with him. High up on the wall, one of the windows had been broken. Shards of glass sparkled as daylight and cold clean air streamed in, and through the broken casement I could see the feet of the marchers. I opened my mouth to scream, but Paul slapped his free hand across my mouth.

"Oh, no you don't." He pulled me back against him and I watched the feet go by. In the light from the broken window I could see what was clearly a lab setup. Test tubes and burners, trays of aluminum foil, and thin metal tubing that ran the length of a table. From one large glass flask, resting above a small burner, rose a stream of smoke, the source of all the noxious smells.

"What the—" Paul clearly didn't know about the demonstration, but before he could finish his thought a second window was kicked in. I saw a black boot, laced up high, with bright red laces. And then a bottle came banging down on the table below. It had a rag stuffed into it, and the top of the rag was on fire.

Paul threw me against the wall and as I caught myself from

falling I saw him dive toward the table. The rag was blazing now and the bottle rolling toward that large glass flask. Paul stopped short. We both watched, but the bottle didn't break or even knock over the flask.

"Well, that's a…" But then we both saw it. The first window, the one we'd only heard break, had allowed another makeshift bomb through and over in the corner, where the tubing started, a flame had caught. A cloud of white smoke billowed up into the air.

"Ciao, baby!" I looked back at Paul, but he was out the door, racing down the hallway toward the exit.

I coughed—the fresh air from the broken windows couldn't keep up with the smoke. The smell was changing, too. Heavier, with a greasy feel I could taste. I should run, get out while I could. But what had he said about cats? He had Musetta. He had to have her, everything pointed that way. And she had to be here. How could I leave, not knowing? How could I run without trying to save her, too?

"Musetta! Musetta!" I ran around the room, peering under the tables. I knew my little cat. She'd be terrified, cowering in a corner with all this noise and that horrible stench. Afraid to run. It was up to me to find her in time. "Musetta!"

I was choking. My eyes streamed as I flung open a closet and pushed boxes of glassware out to crash behind me on the floor. On the table, something else caught fire with a whoosh. The smoke was black now and the room was filling up. Where was she? "Musetta?"

"Mrow!" On the floor was a large wire box. The missing third trap—but it was empty.

"Mrow!" Over in the corner, behind a chalkboard, stood a tall cabinet. I shoved the chalkboard out of the way and pulled at the door. It was cheap plywood, but it was locked fast.

"Hang in there, kitty!"

"Mmmrow!"

I spun around, desperate, and saw what I wanted. From the

lab set-up I grabbed a length of metal tubing. It was hot and burned my hand, but it was thin and strong. I wedged it into the cabinet door, down by where I could see a catch, and leaned. Nothing. But the trap was cool and large, and with the tubing in place, I could grab it in both hands and swing. Thunk! Not so easy. In the smoke and in my hurry, I'd simply slammed the trap into the door. The cabinet wobbled slightly. "Mrow!"

I took a breath, choking on the fumes, and stepped back. My eyes were tearing. I paused, staring at the tubing, the lever, the door that kept me from Musetta. And I swung. The tubing bent, but it held. I swung again. The tubing flattened, but it had done its job. Cracks appeared in the door. The lock was pushed out, vulnerable. I dropped the wire trap and pulled the useless tubing out, tossing it to the floor. The fumes were getting to me. I could barely see.

"Mrow! Mrow!" She was in there. The edges of the door were no longer flush and I grabbed the one with the lock, forcing my fingers inside. It was tight, but I had a grip on the edge and I pulled. Something cracked, I pulled again, propping my foot up on the other door for leverage. "Mrow!"

"Musetta!" With that yell, I found more strength and pulled with everything I had until—yes—I heard another crack, and the cabinet door opened. Weak, gasping I fell back against a table, felt the heat of the fire burning on its surface, and bounced back up.

"Mrow!" I slammed open the cabinet door, rifling through it to find only lab coats and a stack of cartons. Had I been hallucinating? Was my cat's cry coming from somewhere else?

I shoved the lab coats aside. Confused, I was ready to lose it. But then, poking out from an open cardboard carton, I saw a familiar black face with an off-center white star. It was Musetta, squeezing her rounded body out between the boxtop flaps. She was holding a tiny tiger-striped kitten by the scruff of its neck, and looking up at me with pride.

"Good girl!" I scooped up both cats and ran out the door.

The bulkhead wasn't far away, and a new strength filled my veins. Out in the hallway, the air was clearer and with the two cats clutched to me, I raced back toward where we'd entered. Paul was nowhere in sight. He was no fool. If he had any smarts, he'd keep running. Even if he now denied any involvement in Gail's death, the room we'd just left was clearly a drug lab.

I raced up to the bulkhead doors and threw my shoulder against them. Musetta was struggling now, kicking against my tight hold, and I didn't want to risk losing her in the smoke. But I couldn't help jarring her and the kitten, who mewed piteously, as I banged into the double doors. They must have gotten stuck, and I braced my feet as I pushed. They gave a little, but not enough. If only I could see… The kitten mewed, and as I readjusted, I remembered: Violet's flashlight. "Hang on, kitties." I shifted the animals to reach into my pocket for the little light and ran its beam around the edge of the doors. Why were they sticking? Nothing held them along the floor. But there, through the slight opening, I could see the heavy chain once more threaded through the metal bolts. The bastard had taken the time to lock the door behind him. To lock us in. I banged on the wood with my one free hand.

"Hey! Ruth! Violet? Help!" The marchers must have moved on. "I'm trapped in here! In the basement!" Nothing.

"Mrow!" Musetta had loosed the kitten by this point, and I was holding them both, awkwardly, against my chest.

"Hang on, kitty." I took the chance of dropping the kitten as I grabbed my hefty pet properly. Such a small animal couldn't run far, I figured as I braced Musetta against my shoulder. But the little kitten held onto me, needle-point claws hanging onto my thigh, and once Musetta was more comfortable, it was a moment's work to unhook her from my denim (and flesh) and hoist her up, too. That freed up a hand for my cell phone. But I was in a basement. There was no signal. I paced, no bars appeared. I punched in 911. Nothing.

Okay, no time to panic. We were together, thus far we were safe. The lab was probably still burning, but the air out here still seemed clear. Somewhere, an alarm had to be clanging away, right? I slumped against the locked bulkhead, listening to the ringing.

"Wrow?" Musetta's green eyes were staring into mine and for a moment, I thought we were in bed. "Eh." She wriggled in my grasp and I realized I'd been on the point of letting her go. The air was worse, I could smell it. I felt dizzy, tired. The situation was unreal. It was almost funny.

"Mrow!" Her claws reached through my coat, and the prick of pain woke me up. I shook my head. There were no alarms; the fumes were getting to me. This was not a wait-it-out situation. I had to picture the layout of the plant, had to think, but the burning in my throat and eyes just made me want to close them. Maybe if I lay down, the air by the floor would be less smoky.

"Wrow!"

"Sorry, sorry." I'd started to lean on my cat, and that's when it hit me. I had to move or we would all die. I had to find another way out. A fire door. What had Patti said? The wired-glass doors opened from the inside. Would that still be true, when so much else in this building had been locked down, if not rusted shut?

I didn't have a choice. Shaking my head to clear it, I made myself picture where those doors were. I'd passed two sets before ducking into the courtyard with the open bulkhead. They were on the edges of each branch of the plant—the "legs" of the sideways "E"—and the closest were back on the other side of the lab.

"Here we go." As if she understood what was happening, Musetta clung tightly to me, burying her face in my neck. I felt the kitten nestling in between us and so, ducking my head, I retraced my steps down the hallway. Even in the dim light, I could see thick, oily smoke pouring out of the lab, rolling along the floor like some poisonous fog. Nothing for it, I took a deep breath of the stinging air and ran, eyes tearing as I pushed through the smoke. The heat was tremendous and I heard, as much as felt, my hair singe and sizzle. But we were through and there, maybe twenty feet ahead was a stairway. Taking the steps two at a time and sobbing, I made it to the ground floor, turned and, yes, there were the small, high windows and, wonder of wonders, the big push bars on the doors.

Turning sideways, I threw myself against one bar and almost dropped the cats as the impact jarred me. Nothing. It might as well have been a brick wall. "Please, god." I rammed my hip into the other bar and felt a shudder. "Please." I thought of Bunny and her Wiccan sense of balance. I had two small lives in my care. I shoved again. There was movement. "Please." Bracing my feet, I pushed with what was left of my dwindling strength. The catch was stiff, but creaked and rattled. "Mrow!" Musetta wailed and I leaped at the door, one more time, out of breath and eyes streaming, and it gave.

We stumbled out into the cold fresh air and I kept going, gasping, falling, the cold as welcome as the oxygen, the light blurred in my eyes. I ran until I tripped over my own clumsy feet on the uneven dirt and fell forward onto the frozen ground, thinking only to roll so as to protect the two dear creatures I still held clutched against my chest.

"Wrow!" Musetta pushed against me and I felt her struggle free. I was beyond restraining her and reached to keep my hand on her fur. But just as I thought she'd run for cover, run once more out of my grasp and away from my protection, she stopped. She froze, staring, and then ducked back into my arms, burrowing into where I still held the tiger kitten as, behind us, a giant boom of sound suddenly made everything bright and burning, and then silent.

TWENTY-ONE

WHAT WAS THAT NOISE? Where was my alarm? Why was my pillow so hard? I woke with a start to feel Musetta pushing at me. Had I rolled over onto the kitty? The paw in the mouth finally fully woke me up, and I realized where I was. Outside, on the ground, my eyes and throat smarting something fierce and my ears ringing painfully loud.

The blackout, if that's what it was, only lasted a moment, but it left me confused. Musetta? What were we doing out by the river on a freezing January day? Another moment—and a glimpse down at her slightly matted fur—brought me back to the present. I relaxed my hold on my pet, shifting so I was no longer laying on top of her, and looked around. Three feet in front of me sat a small tabby kitten. She was trying to wash her hind leg, but kept falling over, balance not yet a strong point in her feline skill set. Still too young to be frightened of the people rushing around, finally the wail of approaching sirens got to her, too. She flattened herself onto the bare ground in response and I grabbed her, carrying her and my precious Musetta step by wobbly step away from the smoking building, from which flames and the occasional spark still flew.

"Theda! Theda!" I looked up and saw Violet running toward me. "Are you okay? I didn't know you were coming but when the place went up we all turned, and I saw you." She was breathless. The explosion must have just happened.

I nodded, not yet ready to speak, and handed Vi the kitten. "You brought a cat? Cats?" She cradled the kitten instinctively and put her other arm around me to walk me away from the smoking ruin. "Wait, is that Musetta?"

I felt my breath return and my steps steady. The back of my calves stung, and I realized that although my parka had protected my upper body, the thin fabric of my jeans hadn't done the same for my legs. Thank god I had fallen forward and shielded the cats.

"Yeah, they were in the lab." I recounted what had just happened. It sounded bizarre even to me, but the two cats in our arms and the burning building behind us were undeniably real.

"Oh man, here, you should talk to a doctor." Violet hugged the kitten to her. I knew she wanted to do the same with me and Musetta, but I didn't have time. The fire engines had arrived. With them, two of the green-and-white EMT vans with which I was becoming a little too familiar.

"Wait a minute." My back smarted, but my memory was coming back. Musetta was using her claws to hang onto me, a forgivable sin, but I shifted her a bit to the side anyway and felt my pockets. No, my cell was gone. "Vi, can I borrow your cell?"

She handed it over and I punched in the numbers with my thumb.

"Krakow? Where are you? Your story has *not* shown up in the queue and unless you're calling to say you are on your way in to type it into the system directly, I don't want to—"

"Tim, Tim, it's on its way. Really, hang on." One of the ambulances had taken off, sirens wailing. I hoped nobody else had been in that building, but didn't have time to think about it just then.

"Where are you? That better be your house burning down or you are in such—"

"Tim, it's not my house, but it does involve Swann's Way." He was silent, for a change, but I didn't think I could it explain it all right then. Not with Musetta starting to squirm again.

Besides, I was freezing. "Look, I swear you're going to get a story from me in thirty minutes. But it's not going to be the story you were expecting. In fact, you might want to pull some wire copy for Arts, and tell Page One that they'll be getting breaking news."

"Page One? What are you talking about. You're a feature writer. You gonna tell me again to stop the presses?"

"News doesn't ship until midnight. That won't be necessary." My editor spluttered. Musetta kicked. "Tim, I've got to go now, but look in the arts queue in thirty minutes. I'll slug it 'SWANN' and call you then."

IT TOOK ME FORTY-FIVE, partly because I ran back to lock Musetta in my car before tracking down the fire chief for a quote.

What he'd said, under his breath and not for attribution, when I told him of the makeshift lab in the building's basement, wasn't printable. But once he recognized both my professional standing and my rather unusual firsthand knowledge of the fire's origins, he took a moment to talk. The blaze was under control by then; the brick shell had contained it, but the wing I'd been in—the one with the lab—had collapsed in on itself. For the record, the chief noted that Fire Department inspectors would be sifting through the wreckage, once it was deemed safe. "But simply from the ferocity of the fire as well as from several explosions early on, I won't be surprised if the origins are ruled suspicious."

With that, he too moved to steer me toward the EMTs. But again I claimed deadline and raced to my car. News would be all over the fire once they heard about it on the police scanner. As soon as that had started squawking, they'd have sent out one of the general assignment reporters who learn the trade by writing up such stories. But I'd been there, I had some serious backstory, and, more important, I'd be filing less than an hour after the first alarm. Still, time was of the essence. I'd parked far enough away to avoid being blocked in by the fire trucks, but the noise was still tremendous. Musetta's ordeal must have exhausted her, however, because she was curled on the back seat, nose tucked in tail, and slept the whole way home. I should have her checked out by the vet, but when I opened a can and watched her wolf it down, my heart lifted. Violet would be taking good care of the kitten, I knew, so when my own pet declined seconds, instead opting to wash her face and set her fur in order, I went to work.

For all that had happened, the story was simple. A little too much "this reporter saw" and "this reporter witnessed" for my taste, and I made sure to stick "alleged" in almost every sentence. But other than that, it wrote itself. A large fire, marked by several explosions, had rocked the Riverside neighborhood of Cambridgeport, destroying the largely vacant bottling plant that had been an area landmark for decades. An eye witness ("this reporter") had been there when it started. A protester, marching against proposed development of the old factory, had apparently kicked some kind of incendiary device through a window. There, it ignited what was apparently a laboratory of some sort. The quote from the fire chief fit in neatly, and the rest was speculation.

I had all the reports of a new drug in town, along with the confirming quotes from club owners and bar staff that I'd been gathering. The fire chief had given me a thumbnail history on the flammable properties of the many chemicals used in the creation of illicit drugs. I had my own eyewitness account ("this reporter" again), describing what certainly looked—and smelled—like some kind of chemical cookery, and as a kicker I felt I could safely say that a local band, known in the clubs where the drug had surfaced, allegedly had ties to the old plant.

It wasn't what Tim wanted, and it undoubtedly wouldn't run in Arts. But the story was clear, and nothing I wrote was libelous. There was more I wanted to say, for sure. About Gail, about the ferals and why she might have been killed. But this was the first-day story, breaking news. It was what I had, and I sent it. When

Tim called, sputtering, five minutes later to ask what any of this had to do with Swann's Way I told him then—all of it—and that my next call would be to the police. He'd get his Swann's Way story all right, but not until the cops were on their way to arrest Paul Wexner and his buddies, and shut down what remained of their operation. Besides, I needed the verification.

"And when do you expect to file *that* story, if I may ask?" His voice still had an edge, but I knew it couldn't last. I'd not only broken news, I was on the edge of a scoop: hype and drugs and rock and roll. He'd have to fill a hole in arts with wire copy, but the other paper in town was going to have a bad case of "Why we no have?" and soon.

"Tomorrow." I'd have something by then. At the very least, I'd have talked to the police, and the story would have moved on from a fire of suspicious origins to the drug lab inside.

"Well, it'll be a second day story…" I knew the drill. I'd refer back to the fire, but make whatever was news my lead. More important was the piece I pitched next.

"And Tim? For my next column, I want to write about how all this came about." Silence. Was he thinking that it came about because he'd stolen my emo band from me? "You know, the economics of being in a band?"

"I was thinking more of a modern-day tragedy. I see a big cover splash: The fall of Swann's Way: What went wrong." I bit back a laugh.

"Tim, they never had it all to lose it in the first place. What went wrong was that they were criminals, looking for a short cut. They weren't famous. This isn't likely to become a VH1 'Behind the Music' special." But, even as I said it, I saw the story he was thinking of—and it got to me, too. "However…." I hedged as the parts came together in my mind. "What if we do it as a two-part story? The saga of Swann's Way, with all the background compared to all the hype?" I knew I could get a bunch of people on record, especially once the news broke. "But I'd like to pair it with a piece on making it, the pressure and sacrifice."

He grunted, which was as good as it got. But there was more. "Krakow, you were right. Swann's Way? Scum."

He hung up and I grabbed Musetta for a quick dance around the room. My body was quickly growing stiff, and in her fur I could feel the mats that indicated the need for a good brushing. But our world was righting itself. And now, I had phone work to do. Much to Musetta's satisfaction, I set her back down and let her continue her own grooming, while I hit the speed dial for Bill's extension at work.

TWENTY MINUTES LATER, I was catching my breath. The good part was a cruiser was coming my way to take my statement. The bad part was that Bill wasn't going to be there. I'd committed a major breach of etiquette going for my deadline rather than the cops, and not only was my guy not able to rescue me, he didn't sound like he wanted to.

"Bill, I had to file. It was my story. And I wanted to get Musetta home!" I looked over the poster that I'd pulled from the building's front door in celebration. My pet's photo stared back at me.

He'd spluttered then, sounding almost like Tim. I'd had the sense not to make the comparison.

"Bill, first and foremost, I'm a reporter. And I was on deadline." That's the tack I took with the two uniforms who showed up. I outlined what I'd thought had happened, explaining how Gail might have been viewed as a threat. I even pulled my notes out to make it more real. It occurred to me, halfway into my recounting, that it wouldn't be much of a stretch to assign me a more active role in the drug lab, and I was grateful for the pages of interviews then. If I was writing about this, I couldn't be in on it, could I? But the two uniforms were young and I looked enough of a mess by that point that I think I got a little sympathy. Musetta certainly did her best to play up to them, rubbing against their shins in turn and purring like an engine.

What they were most interested in, really, was my recounting of the fire. How had it started? Musetta jumped onto the sofa and pushed her way onto my lap. While I stroked her absently, remembering the kick, the glass, and the flame dropping through the high casement windows, she settled in, curled and kneading. But, no, I couldn't shed any light on why anyone would want to start a fire.

Or who? The two young cops were insistent, and those boots came back to me. Ruth wore boots like that, complete with the red laces. But I'd seen those boots through the second window, whatever was kicked through the first was what started the fire. Plus, in the Cambridge I knew, a lot of folks donned work boots, Doc Martens or Army surplus, and a lot of them—us—dolled up our clothes for fun. Ruth was a member of a protest group, with ties to illegal activities. I didn't know exactly what was up, and I didn't want to say anything I couldn't take back. I had no problem turning over Paul Wexner. The man had likely drugged me, before kidnapping my cat and leaving us both to die. But Ruth? No, I couldn't say anything until I thought that one over.

"You know about the developers, Wilson and Crave, right?" I should've known better than to ask. The cops were young, but they weren't giving anything away. "Well, I'd been looking into their plans. For an article." The blond cop and his partner shared a quick glance. "They hadn't filed for demo permits, yet. They'd need a hearing for that. But someone had been moving equipment around the site. And there was a lot of feeling about it in the neighborhood." That was all that I'd give them. Hell, maybe Wilson and Crave had done something underhanded. Maybe they'd paid one of the marchers to torch the place.

"Miss Krakow, everything okay?" Julian, the super, was at the door. "You okay?"

"Yeah, thanks, Julian." It hit me how this must look. "This is about the fire. Down by the river?"

"Oh, yeah. Heard about that. Just checking." He looked over at the cops. "I fixed your door. Did you notice?"

"My door?"

"Yeah, when my guys came in to do the radiators the other day, they said it didn't close right. They couldn't get it to lock and had to leave it sort of propped closed. So I came by this morning, fixed it for you."

The door. It had always been a problem. Paul Wexner could have come in anytime after the repairmen left. "Thanks, Julian."

"No biggie, Miss Krakow. Wouldn't want your pussycat to get out." It was too much. How could he not know? I closed my eyes.

"Miss? We were talking about the fire?"

I needed to focus, to remember exactly what had happened. Yes, I'd seen Ruth's boot through the second window. But had she been the one to kick in the first window, the first Molotov cocktail? The one that had started the blaze? Maybe it was a rival drug dealer. Or an accident, something falling against the chemicals on the burner. Truth was, it had happened so fast, I could no longer swear to what I saw. Glass breaking, sure. And then an explosion. But would an errant rock have done the same thing? A dropped cigarette? I closed my eyes and tried to picture the moment. There was a crash, and a second crash… I shivered. God, I was tired.

"Ma'am?" My head snapped back. Had I nodded out?

"I'm sorry. I'm just exhausted."

"We understand." The were standing now, reaching for their regulation parkas. "You don't have to get up."

But I did, letting Musetta jump to the floor. I saw where they left their cards and made all the requisite promises about calling in. And when they left, I locked the door behind them, noting how easily it closed, before crawling into bed. It couldn't have been more than thirty seconds before I felt the soft "thud" of my pet, jumping onto the duvet beside me. She was still kneading, her paws flexing in rhythm with that deep satisfied purr, when I fell into the blessed blankness of sleep.

TWENTY-TWO

I FOUGHT MY WAY AWAKE. The smoke was choking me. There was no light.

"Hush, now. Hush!" Through the fog of my dream, I heard Bill. He was there, in my bedroom, sitting on the edge of my bed.

"How?"

"I'm a lot more mobile now. These crutches actually work." He smiled, and I remembered. It had been so long, but of course he had keys. And, of course, he'd come over. "Your neighbor upstairs, the new guy? Reed? He helped me with the door. Nice guy."

I had a flash of guilt, from multiple sources. "I tried to call you—"

"And you went ahead alone." He shot me a sideways look. Lying in bed, I felt vulnerable, but a little too tired to care. "Anyway, I figured you hadn't eaten."

Food! He was right. "Wow, lunch."

"How about dinner?"

"Whatever." I struggled to my feet and reached for my slippers. Outside, the last light of early dusk glowed. It couldn't be later than six, five-thirty maybe. "What'd you bring?"

My message light was flashing furiously. The copy desk was probably trying to reach me.

"Dumplings and noodles. I was thinking comfort food. A few other things, including some of that spicy pork and stir-fried greens." The copy desk could wait. For the next half hour, I ate without interruption, moving through white take-out cartons like a shark through a shoal of fish. By the time I slowed enough to call the desk just about everything I'd written had already been confirmed by the poor GA slug who had to follow up on the scanner calls. With only the mildest twinge of guilt, I went back to eating

"Oh, this is good. Did you try these?" I held out neatly-crimped dumpling between my chopsticks, but Bill just laughed.

"I stopped eating a while ago, Theda. After the fried rice with shrimp. But you keep going, honey. It's making me happy to see you back to normal."

So much for delicacy. I swallowed the dumpling in one go and went back to the cartons. Only when my chopsticks scraped bottom, did I finally set them down with a sigh.

"Bill." Time for the reckoning. "I did call you, you know. I just couldn't reach you. But I left messages for you. At home, at work. They had Musetta, I couldn't wait."

"I know, Theda. I, well, I wish you'd talked to the police before rushing off. I'm not the only cop in Cambridge, you know, and you came very, very close to being very seriously hurt. A call to 911 would've gotten the cops there before you, you know."

And would any other cop have cared enough to look for my pet? To keep searching once a fire had started? I let Bill keep on talking. "And then, running away like that? It doesn't look good and believe me, I have done some serious vouching for you. But the fact that you talked to the fire chief makes you look more like a victim and less of an accomplice, too."

"I'm a reporter, Bill." Refueled, I was ready to duke it out.

"I know, I know." He put up his hands, palm out, to calm me down. "It's just…well, never mind."

Time to switch topics. "What did you want to tell me about, anyway?" If it was bad, might as well get it over with.

"I don't know if now's the time." It was bad. "But, don't worry, honey. It's nothing about us." He did know me. "Or, not really." Huh? "Now, why don't you go back to bed while I clean up."

So I did.

By the time I woke up, it was the next day. Paul Wexner was in custody, and his bandmates being questioned. Although the baby-faced singer appeared to be the ringleader, nobody thought this was a one-man operation, so it was only a matter of time before someone decided to talk, and make a deal. Bill had taken off earlier, but he'd left a message to give me the news. And, I suspected, to check in on me. When I called him back, he was out again. Nobody would tell me any further details, at least not when I identified myself as a reporter. But the public affairs officer grudgingly confirmed that several parties had been taken in for questioning that morning. Off the record, I was told that a large quantity of the party drug, Fantasy Plus, had been found with them, some in powder form, some as a clear liquid. They'd impounded Wexner's car, too. If he or the other Paul had hit Gail, sometime during that long frozen night, there would be evidence. The police lab would find it, and maybe some trace of poison, too. Sometimes it's good to be a cop's girlfriend.

The public information officer also shared some other news. Despite the apparent solidity of those brick and granite walls, the bottling plant was going to be condemned as unsafe. In fact, the entire area was cordoned off until the rest of it could be taken down later in the week.

I thought of Ruth again, and of those boots. If she'd had a part in the fire, she'd done her enemy a favor. If Wilson and Crave didn't have to get permission to demolish the old plant, or even gut it, they were one step closer to those luxury condos.

A few more phone calls to the fire department and the state's public health office, and I booted up my computer. Still wearing my flannel PJs, I filed my second-day story. It was straight news again, the drugs and suspects in custody being the only real update. But just to do some damage repair, I also touched base with Tim. He sounded great, chipper even. In his mind, the story was all about Swann's Way.

I guess it was, really, only that part wasn't verifiable yet.

Still, it couldn't hurt to get started, and Tim was full of ideas. He wanted to use the photos, particularly the ones that helped me figure out where they'd hidden their lab, and I agreed to come in and look at them. Set against the condemned plant, they had extra significance now, and he'd probably pull one or two from the fire file for dramatic comparison. I was stiff, bruised, and I never had let a doctor look at the burns on my legs. Plus, I really wanted Musetta checked out by her vet. But Tim was being better than I could have expected, all things considered, so I told him I'd be by that afternoon.

THE IDEA OF DRESSING and leaving the house seemed impossible, especially as Musetta was keeping close by my side. I eased my way into the day with a long soak. Musetta declined to join me there, but curled up on the closed toilet seat like a sphinx. She started a bit when I did, when the hot soapy water hit the raw places on my hand and the back of my legs, but as I stretched my bruised body out, she closed her eyes. I did, too.

I had to speak with Ruth. Had to work out what had happened, and why, to my own satisfaction before I said anything to anybody. That was the thought that kept surfacing, and so after the water had grown cold, I pulled myself out. The splashing sent Musetta scurrying, and the sight of her white booties kicking off down the hall cheered me no end.

"Feeling ourselves again, are we?" From the end of the hallway, she glared, and I laughed out loud.

I'd be going into the *Mail* after, but nothing but comfort clothes would do today. I'd stop by the Animals Now office on my way. I had to see Ruth's face when I spoke to her. I drove the long way around, circling by the fire-blackened wreckage of the plant before heading back to Central Square. My windows were closed, the heat blasting, but I could still smell the smoke, heavy and thick with soot and whatever noxious chemicals had gone up in the flames. Had Ruth done all this? Had she meant to? Whatever her intent, she'd paid. Wilson and

Crave were moving in. The need for secrecy was gone. Already the area was cordoned off with chain link fence. Two huge signs announced "386 Units Coming Soon!"

They must have known, the demonstrators. Five of them were gathered in the Animals Now office when I walked in. Violet made a sixth, the small group huddled around the metal desk, looking as dejected as that sad, smoke-stained brick.

"Hey, Theda. That kitten's looking good." Violet, at any rate, had brightened when she saw me. "She's been scarfing down crunchies." She walked over to greet me, but I raised my hand for silence and turned to the others gathered there.

"I was in that building yesterday, you know. I was in there when the fire started." Three women looked up at me, then settled back, sitting along the edge of the desk. Ruth and the one man were leaning back against the file cabinets, talking to each other. Strategizing, no doubt, about how to control the damage, maybe even stop the development. But it was too little, too late. The stooped posture, the air of defeat that hung over the office revealed what everyone knew. Violet stood by me, which was a comfort.

"I almost died in that fire, and I think I know what happened to Gail." I was standing, facing them all, and my raised voice got their attention. I hadn't planned on doing this. Hadn't planned on making a public statement about what I'd been through and what I'd thought happened. But maybe I needed to tell the whole story as I knew it to someone other than the readers of the *Mail*. Simply talk it through, without an angle or quotes or verification, and so I did.

I started with Swann's Way, and how I'd gotten involved in writing about them and about Fantasy Plus. I told them about my cat, about the phone call, and how I figured out about the drug lab. They all knew about Gail's feral rescue program and I realized I was leaving her out. So I backed up, fitted the intense little woman in: Gail must have figured it out, too, I said. Or at any rate, she knew something was up. Someone had taken two of the feral kittens. Something was disturbing the perfectly good home her feral cats had found for themselves. Gail must have confronted Paul. She'd probably been full of righteous rage. Two of the women nodded. That was her way; they knew it, too. But it had probably gotten her killed.

I could say that here. Nothing had been proven yet, but it all made sense. Paul Wexner was selfish and spoiled. Gail had been an annoyance to him. It didn't surprise me that he'd hit her. That he'd see her in the street, tiny but determined, and run her over without a second thought. Just from my brief exposure to his nasty side, I'd have been more shocked if he'd gone out of his way to avoid her.

What did surprise me was the poison. Violet started at that and I realized, with all that had been going on, that I had never told her about the autopsy. I filled her in, along with everyone else. Gail had been poisoned before she'd been run down. A lethal dose, although it didn't have a chance to kill her.

But why? I couldn't figure that out, but when nobody in the room offered any theories, I supplied my own. Maybe poisoning wasn't that far a stretch from dropping a dose of a "fun" drug into somebody's drink—or onto their limes. The basic idea was the same. But if Paul Wexner had been the one to slip Fantasy Plus to Bunny and to me, and I thought that likely, it was probably more of a prank. A chance to loosen up a tight-ass reporter. A bit of a laugh. Carelessness, callousness—a kind of smug passivity—that was Wexner's way. Not intentional poison.

And Gail hadn't been dosed with Swann's Way's new party drug. As I was talking, the small crowd watching me, I found myself thinking it through. Gail had been poisoned by strychnine, rat poison. It must have been diluted, mixed in with something. Gail had been awake, if not entirely coherent, when she'd been taken to the hospital. She must have been in horrible pain, probably bent over from the cramping, when the car hit her. But she'd been alive.

Which meant that she'd only ingested a little. Could it have been Wexner? Rat poison was certainly easy to buy. But if you just want to use a tiny bit of something, why not use what's at hand? Why not a dose of Fantasy Plus?

Could it have been an accident? Working with the ferals, Gail might have came across the poison, especially down by the river around an old building. A smudge on the hand, a move to push a stray hair out of her mouth… I could see it. The back of my tired brain sparked. I shut up and tried to think. Someone had been telling me about animal traps, recently. About disarming a bunch of poisoned traps meant for opossums and raccoons, as well as rats.

It was Ruth, and Violet had told me. That was one of her stories illustrating how much Ruth cared. Well, Ruth and Gail had worked together, way back when. Could Gail have been helping her Animals Now colleague with the traps? Maybe the poisoning had been a horrible accident. A mistake. And suddenly another memory hit me: Ruth, calling the feral cats "just another one of humanity's mistakes." Unless she was talking about Gail. Or trying to correct what civilization had done.

"Hey, Violet?" She nodded. Every eye was on us. "What would you call someone who was helping an invasive species?" Ruth started. She opened her mouth, but I kept talking. "Would you call someone like that a collaborator? An accomplice? If someone was helping feral cats, helping animals that prey on native species, would you think she was guilty of murder?"

"Huh?" Violet's face scrunched up in confusion. She had no idea what I was talking about. But Ruth recognized her own words. She saw where I was leading.

"I never meant it like that. We're protectors here. Not killers. I never meant anyone to get hurt." She was repeating herself, and started sliding along the file cabinet, away from her friends. Away from me.

"Maybe, Ruth. Maybe you never meant to kill Gail, but I think you did it. I think you poisoned her, maybe using just a little bit. But strychnine is deadly, even a dash. Maybe you only meant to teach her a lesson and to bring her back into the fold. Like you never meant to destroy the bottling plant, but it happened."

Violet looked from me to Ruth. We all did. Her red cheeks were turning white, the color concentrated in spots. "Ruth?"

"She didn't tell you, did she Vi? About the Molotov cocktail she kicked through the window? It was during the march, and it probably wasn't supposed to spread. She certainly made sure everyone knew about the protest. I mean, I heard about it from a realtor! I'm guessing she thought she could frame Wilson and Crave, somehow. Make it look like they were moving ahead illegally with the demolition. But things got out of hand, didn't they, Ruth?"

"Ruth?" Violet was small, but determined. She stepped toward her onetime friend, moving between the larger woman and the door.

"They had people at the plant, measuring. Working." Ruth spit out the words with conviction, but her voice was rising in desperation. "They had equipment there. You saw the marks! They could've started the fire!"

"Except that I saw you do it. I saw you kick through one window, and I bet you kicked in both. I was down there, Ruth, in the basement, when the firebomb came through. I was trapped down there. With two cats, Ruth. You nearly killed us all."

"The cats." She collapsed in a chair. "If only Gail hadn't seen those damned animals. We were doing recognizance, way back in the fall when Wilson and Crave first started checking out the site. She saw one of the cats carrying a kitten, and she fell for it. She got all sentimental."

"And lost her crusading zeal, is that it?"

Ruth looked up at me, but her face was calm now. "When she came by that Sunday and took the last trap, it was too much. She needed to be taught a lesson. Those cats would either make it through the storm, or they don't belong here."

She had a kind of logic, but I no longer wanted to understand. "You can explain it all to someone else, Ruth. Maybe someone else will care."

Two hours later, Violet and I were alone again. A blue-and-white cruiser had taken Ruth away, and more cops had come for the files scattered all over her desk. Violet and I had waited, in silent agreement, while the other Animals Now members slipped out the door. They hadn't done anything and we didn't mention them. After answering the questions thrown our way, we needed nourishment and made our way back to Soup's On for something rich and steaming.

"It was a good group, you know." Violet stirred her split pea without enthusiasm.

"Still is, Vi. This was just one person." I'd dug into my turkey chili at first, but put my spoon down. Violet's melancholy was catching, and we both knew that Ruth's actions would taint the entire organization. "Look, Animals Now isn't the only activist group around. It's not even the only one involved with animals or fighting overdevelopment."

Vi nodded, her purple locks sagging, and took a bite of her crusty roll.

"I mean, the Cambridgeport Neighborhood Association is already on top of the permits. I heard they're filing to make sure some mixed use and affordable housing units are put into that development." She slurped a spoonful of soup. "And those kittens, well, they're young enough to be domesticated. They'll probably have better lives as pets, living with Heather and Amber." Violet snorted. Amber had already called her from rehab, checking in on the kitten Musetta had rescued. "They can't help their names.

"And you and all the people who work with Helmhold House probably do as much good as Animals Now already. Not just for cats, but for all the animals that people bring in." I thought about Lizzy's rat and tried not to grimace.

"But that's animal welfare, Theda. This was an animal rights group. They're different."

"Yeah, well, maybe one is a bit more, shall we say, sustainable? I mean, it would be great if we could go back to pre-Colombian times. But for those us of who live in the real world, is caring for the animals we've got such a bad thing?"

"No." She took another spoonful. "No, it's not." She was eating regularly now. "I mean, I'd hate to live in a Cambridge without cats. Wouldn't you?"

I laughed because I didn't have to answer, and then went to get two of the biggest brownies that they had.

"So, I've been thinking." Violet was picking crumbs off the waxed paper with her thumb. The food had done her good. "Exene, that cat we rescued?"

"The feral?" I'd hoarded the last bits of my brownie.

"Well, yeah. Only she's not a feral. I think she was a housecat once. I mean, she's still skittish, but she's not afraid of people. Not all the time. I was thinking someone should adopt her. Take her to a quiet home, where she could learn to trust again. It would take some time, but I think it would work, and I think it would be worth it. A little kitty rehab. You know of anyone who would be up for that?"

"I might have an idea. Let me work on it."

TWENTY-THREE

I HAD TO GO INTO the *Mail* before I did anything else. Tim deserved that much. But when I reached the Arts department, the reception was not what I'd expected.

"Krakow, thank god." Tim was panting. Red in the face, he waved the file folder he was holding. "Follow me!"

What could be up now? I trotted behind my editor as we weaved through our department and past Sunday. We were halfway to Design before I could get his attention.

"Tim? What's up? I thought we weren't running the Swann's Way story until it was all verifiable. That we were aiming for next week."

"It's not that, Krakow. This is more important."

He pulled me toward a cubicle. Three designers hovered, all seated around Jackie Quan, our fashion writer. On the screen was a proof sheet. Dozens of photos, laid out like a film strip, showed sleek models draping themselves over four boys who looked about sixteen, tops. Skinny, dressed in clothes that barely fit their undersized frames, they looked as scared of the women as they did of the camera.

"It's the fashion spread. It's slated for tomorrow." Dragon's Breath, the emo group I'd wanted to interview for my column. "We're jammed up."

"What's wrong? These photos look…" What could I say? They looked silly to me. "They look authentic."

"It's not the photos, Krakow. It's the text. We need cutlines. We needed them an hour ago. And Jackie's interview tape cut out."

"Theda, please?" The fashion writer looked up at me, teary

eyed. Even if she had written down what the band had said, it probably made no sense to her.

"I thought I was on the Swann's Way story until further notice." I was teasing, really. This would be a piece of cake.

Tim was not amused. "Krakow! This is news! Who cares about next week? I need captions, to spec. Immediately!"

"Sure, boss." With a glance and a small smile, Jackie rose, giving me her seat. I grabbed a pad and started writing longhand. What were some key fashion words? Retro, street, authenticity… "I'll slug these DRAGON. You'll have them in twenty minutes."

"Make it ten." Tim stormed off. Jackie leaned over me. "Thank you, dear," she whispered, in a voice as soft as her floral scent, and I went to work.

VISITING HOURS were almost up by the time I got to the hospital, But Tess was out of bed and standing by her window when I came in.

"Tess?" She didn't turn around. "It's me, Theda."

"I know." Something out in the gray cityscape must have been fascinating.

"Can we talk?"

She sighed, the robe that hung from her thin shoulders drooping with the effort. Turning to face me, I saw all the wear the drugs had wrought. "I guess I'm supposed to say 'thank you.' Or maybe, 'I'm sorry.'"

Either would've been nice, but I knew we were on sensitive turf here. "You don't need to, Tess. I'm not here about that." I pulled up a chair and sat, hoping she'd do the same. She leaned back against the windowsill.

"I know I should've let you know what was going on, Theda. I mean, I knew I was in over my head. But I never lied to you, Theda. I just never told you what was going on."

I thought about the conflicting stories, about how she'd put the discrepancies off on Bunny. She'd probably have told

Bunny that I was the one with the bad memory, if Bunny had reached her first. But that was irrelevant now.

"We're your friends, Tess. If you were in trouble, you could have come to us." She nodded, taking it in. "We love you. No matter what."

That seemed to get through to her and she finally slumped into the other chair, her hands over her face. "I know, Theda, it's just…" Her shoulders shook again, and I realized she was crying. I came over to her side and knelt, my arms around her till the sobs stopped.

"Here." I pulled some tissues from the night table box and she mopped her face.

"It's just that, I didn't think it was a problem. I just needed more energy, more time. And when everything started to go bad, it was too late. I needed the pills just to stay even."

"Is that what happened the night of your car crash?"

She nodded and reached for her water glass. "I felt like I was crashing and so I drove down to the South End, to my dealer, and scored some more." She took a drink. "I swallowed two pills dry while I was driving and I must have blacked out. But I must have taken my foot off the accelerator, because the car can't have been moving that fast. It was like I told you. When I came to, I had run into one of those concrete dividers. It didn't seem that serious, but I knew I couldn't go to a doctor, not with what was in my system. And I knew I couldn't call the cops. When I talked to Bunny, I panicked and I guess I forgot what I'd told her. By the time you called, I was calmer and I told you the truth." She smiled, her thin face lighting up a bit. "I guess that's why they say that the truth is better. It's easier to remember."

"Visiting hours are over, Miss." A male nurse in cheery pink scrubs stuck his head in. "And dinner's on its way."

I hugged Tess again. I could feel her shoulder blades through the robe. "What's next, kiddo?"

"Rehab." She looked straight at me. "At least the university has great health insurance. I'm going into a program as soon as this place gives me the all-clear. That'll be a few weeks. And then?" She shrugged, but she was still smiling.

"One day at a time, I guess." I didn't want to push, but my talk with Violet was still in my mind. "One thing, though. You don't have to say anything but just to keep in mind…"

She nodded, looking a little apprehensive.

"Would you maybe consider adopting a pet?" She laughed then, a startled exhalation of breath. "No, really. You don't have to commit yet. But, you see, Violet and I rescued a cat a while ago. It's going to need some care and loving to get back in shape. It's kind of battered. But I was thinking, maybe…."

"That we two could take care of each other?" I nodded. "I don't know, Theda. I don't even know if I'll have a job to go back to or be able to keep my apartment or anything. But it's a nice idea." She was thinking about it, I could tell. "A pet to take care of. Yeah, maybe that would be nice."

I left her then, as she climbed back into bed. Passing the attendant in the hallway, I saw he'd put a little flower on her tray. Where he got a flower in January, I had no idea. Someone else's bouquet, perhaps? But it made me smile, and I thought it would Tess, too.

THAT NIGHT, I WAS ON the phone, catching Bunny up on everything, when Bill came by. He was quite good on the crutches now, and although he still needed a cab seat to himself whenever he traveled, he seemed more his old self than I'd seen in ages.

"Dinner time!" I wound up with Bunny, who'd laughed her head off at the fashion spread story, and we agreed to meet at the hospital for a visit with Tess when she got out of the *Mail* tomorrow.

"Hey, I've got everything!" I rescued my plates, which Bill was balancing one handed, and let him bring the bottle opener to the table. He'd brought pizza and red wine, and I could smell the pepperoni. "Everything all right on the home front?"

"Pretty much." Musetta came over to sniff his hand and graciously receive some pets. "The little girl seems no worse for wear. Bunny's blooming and Tess is going to be okay, too, I think." I'd already told him about the rehab program, and my idea that fostering a cat might be good for her.

"And your hand?" I held it up. The scabbing was ugly, but it was also a sign of healing. "And your column?"

"Both more or less intact, thank you very much. In fact, I think things are pretty much back to normal."

"Good." He tore off slices for each of us and poured me a healthy glass of wine. "Because I have some news."

Uh oh, here it came. I took a bite, waiting. If he said anything about my naiveté, I'd have to agree. But if it was anything about my friends….

"I'm retiring." I nearly dropped my plate, and he raised his hand to silence me. "Listen, it makes sense. With my disability, I can get nearly the full pension and I'm going to cash out." He waited, but I'd learned my lesson. I drank some wine. "But I'm not going to just sit on the couch and watch sports." He was watching me closely now. I took another sip. "I'm buying into that old Irish bar behind the precinct. You know, that cop bar you hate? But I'm going to turn it around. Reed and I, we're going to make it into a jazz club."

He couldn't have timed it better. I'd almost swallowed before he finished and thus I only choked a little. My Bill? Running a club? And when had he gotten to know my handsome new neighbor anyway?

As I wiped my face and accepted some pats on the back, Bill explained. "It's all because of the New England Jazz Club. I've just been spending more and more time listening, and looking around online. There are just too few good clubs around, and virtually nothing booking the kind of music we listen to."

We. Oy. "But Bill, clubs are notoriously hard to run. The income is uncertain, the expenses are high. You've got staffing, liability and insurance issues. And if you add in booking music—"

"I know, Theda. I know. That's one of the reasons I'm going in with Reed. He's got the practical expertise, not to mention the connections. I've got the capital." I opened my mouth to protest. "And I'm not entirely crazy, babe. We're not going to charge a cover for the front room. It'll still be a cop hangout. Maybe more, since it'll be my place. That'll keep some income coming in. Hey, maybe it'll make the place safer, too."

"At least you won't have to worry about drugs, right?"

"Well, I'm sure we'll have plenty of other problems." He was smiling and looked so happy that I couldn't bring myself to mention all the other potential land mines. Like, for instance, that his girlfriend hated modern jazz.

"So, you'll come by sometimes, won't you?" He could read my mind. "I mean, on off nights, or after you're done with an assignment. At least we'll be on the same schedule, sort of."

"Of course, I will." Maybe I could get some other kinds of music in there on those off nights. I thought of Mitch. Maybe Tuesdays… "Congratulations, Bill. I know we'll make it work."

"We?"

I raised my glass. "You wouldn't think of entering clubland without me, would you?"

TWO MONTHS LATER, I still hadn't managed to get any rock music into the Last Stand, as Bill had renamed the old Irish bar. "Echoes of Custer," Reed had muttered, but the name had stuck. At least, thanks to his New Orleanian partner, Bill was booking some music I could listen to. And besides, it was pleasant to have another place to drop in when the night was done.

Tess was home by then. The university had kept her job for her, as well as paying her expenses. With meetings, she left by seven every night, and somehow her lab still seemed to manage to make its grant deadlines. She'd taken in Exene, finally, once the cat's side had healed, and under her care the skinny tabby had filled out to resemble a striped beach ball. Not that Tess would hear a word against her. "This kitty has saved my life," she'd say. "She keeps me going, each day, no matter how hard it gets."

For my own piece of mind, I tried not to get too involved in the trials of Paul Wexner and Ruth Hargebourt. But I'd testified to what I'd seen, and I was pretty sure how they'd turn out. No trace of Gail's blood ever showed up on Paul's car. Given the weather, that was not a surprise. But the drug charges would put him away for a long time; his bandmates, who had been smart enough to make deals, got lighter sentences. And after Ruth admitted to the poisoning, she grudgingly gave up the fire-bombing of the old building, as well.

The development progressed swiftly. Ten days after the explosion, Wilson and Crave filed all the papers—minus the request for a demolition permit—at the city hall annex. Everything was perfectly in order, everything notarized. And because the developer had some foresight, or because our neighborhood watchdogs had gotten to them, the set-aside for affordable housing was even bigger than what the law required. Patti was involved with sales, and said that the main building would include a well-equipped community center, too. The center, with its full-sized basketball court, made for good public relations, if nothing else, and the few protests were half hearted. Indoor basketball builds a lot of good will.

The old brick plant that had been a landmark for as long as I'd been in Cambridge was long gone by the time the developers broke ground, the frozen tread marks joined by countless others as the gray dirt mixed with brick dust and clay. Where the feral cats had disappeared to, I didn't know. I kept an eye out for that marmalade cat, but never saw her again. The kitten Musetta had rescued was coming along fine. She hissed at first, while Violet had her in the shelter, but she must have been young enough to get over her fear of humans. Last I heard,

Heather was fostering her, waiting for her friend to finish her last days in rehab. The young businesswoman had already domesticated the other feral kitten, a miniature marmalade, and I bet that the tiny tiger would soon be a contented lap cat, too.

Musetta, meanwhile, passed her check-up with flying colors. Besides losing a little weight, her confinement hadn't had any physical effect. Emotionally, it was subtle. Bill smiled when I told him, but I was convinced that she was more affectionate than ever. Even as the cold broke and the world outside began to thaw, my precious pet would lean against me, purring, whenever I sat down. I didn't mind that at all.